Kalorama Shakedown

A Harry Reese Mystery

The Harry Reese Mysteries

Always a Cold Deck

Humbug on the Hudson (short story)

Crossings

Kalorama Shakedown

Emmie Reese Mystery Short Stories

The Birth of M.E. Meegs

Hidden Booty

Psi no more...

For a glossary of period terms, biographies of the characters, and a complete chronology, please visit:

streetcarmysteries.com

Kalorama Shakedown

Robert Bruce Stewart

Street Car Mysteries

Florence, Mass.

First Print Edition, August 2013

Copyright © 2013 by Robert Bruce Stewart

All rights reserved. No part of this document or the related files may be reproduced or transmitted in any form, by any means (electronic, photocopying, recording, or otherwise) without the prior written permission of the publisher.

ISBN 978-1-938710-08-7

Street Car Mysteries

streetcarmysteries.com

*To the disenfranchised denizens of D.C.,
past and present*

1

Even before we left Brooklyn, I had an inkling we'd stumble on a corpse before the business was over. Not that I lay claim to powers of premonition. I was just drawing a logical inference based on the evidence before me. You see, not only had Emmie—my wife—insisted on coming along, the job itself was her idea. You might even say she anticipated it.

Now, I'd been investigating insurance claims for several years. All told, there must have been five dozen cases. But only a handful had involved a homicide. And all of those had transpired since I'd met Emmie the summer before last. I'd had plenty of cases since then that hadn't involved murder, but she'd taken little interest in those. She was downright blasé about my most recent case—a fire claim in Allentown. She said her time would be better spent shopping for draperies. Emmie had no more interest in shopping for draperies than I did. She simply had no enthusiasm for a case without the prospect of a body. Hence my inkling.

What neither of us knew then was that there'd already been a murder related to the case, three weeks before. It would be another week before we learned of it—and only after the same hand had claimed a second life. But I'm getting ahead of the story.

It was a cold December morning and we'd taken a crowded, stuffy car up Flatbush to the Fulton ferry docks. From there, we caught the boat that takes you right to the Pennsylvania's depot in Jersey City. Emmie went into the women's cabin and I made my way up to the bow. The ferry's cabins would be as crowded and stuffy as the street car, and the train promised more of the same, so I thought I'd fill up on fresh air. As it was, there was a rather brisk breeze blowing across the bay that morning, and by the time we boarded the train, my hunger for fresh air was well sated. We took our seats and Emmie immersed herself in a book, which was just as well since my face was still too frozen to allow for conversation.

We were heading to Washington, where I was to investigate a string of burglaries—all of which involved the loss of jewelry of some value. Beyond the size of the claims, there was nothing exceptional about any one case. But there did seem to be something of a pattern—as if they'd been performed by the same thief. Normally, my arrangement with insurers is that I receive a per diem and a bonus based on whatever I save them in claims. For instance, in Allentown, I convinced the insured to reduce his claim by the $3,800 he'd included for non-existent inventory, and thus avoid prosecution. The underwriter paid me ten percent of that amount, plus eight dollars a day. But this Washington case was different. My task was to find the culprit, and as much of the loot as possible. I was getting a flat $100, plus ten percent of whatever was recovered.

It was an unusual arrangement, one dreamed up by Emmie. Ostensibly, she was only coming along to visit a school chum, but that was complete nonsense. She had first taken note of these burglaries while reading the Washington newspapers at the library. *Why* was she reading the Washington newspapers at the library? Precisely the question I asked. Her answer was that she wanted to assure herself that Mr. Roosevelt had matters well in hand—this being not long after McKinley's untimely death in Buffalo. Utter prattle. National politics ranked immediately behind draperies in the roll of Emmie's concerns. She was up to something. My first thought was that it had something to do with the horse races at Bennings, the popular track just to the east of Washington. She had sworn off gambling that summer, but she'd made a similar assurance before. Then I found out the races at Bennings had ended the last week of November. That only increased my anxiety. Now I knew she was up to something, but had no idea what.

I was reading through the notes she had taken of the thefts when Emmie laid down her book. By then my jaw had regained a modicum of mobility and I took the opportunity to open conversation.

"You know, this seeming rash of burglaries could just be coincidence."

"Don't be silly, Harry. What are the odds of that many burglaries involving jewelry occurring in one city in a given six-week period?"

"Remote, perhaps. But given the size of the country, the odds of such a pattern occurring someplace at some time are decidedly short."

"But I wasn't reading the newspapers of every city. Just those of Washington."

"Yes, to keep up on Mr. Roosevelt," I smiled. "Tell me, who's to be the new Secretary of Agriculture?"

"Mr. Clement, of Ohio."

I doubted that was the case, but I'd unfortunately chosen as a test a question I wasn't myself prepared to answer.

"There is another possible explanation, Emmie."

"Explanation of what?"

"Explanation as to why these cases may be unrelated."

"And what is that?"

"Moral hazard."

"And what is moral hazard?"

"It's an aspect of human behavior insurers must take into account."

"What are you talking about?"

"Well, as an example, suppose a fellow has grown somewhat dependent on his wife. She prepares his dinner, cleans up after him, and, well, serves him in a variety of ways."

"In other words, she's allowed him to turn her into an *it*."

"An it?"

"A dolt. She should have listened to her friends and never married the man."

"Yes, well, in this case she didn't listen and he's become dependent on her. Now, suppose he sees a runaway street car headed for her. He'll pull her out of the way without a second thought."

"A true hero."

"Ah, your sarcasm is warranted. For he is no hero, simply a man looking out for his interests. Now, suppose he has a $2,000 policy on the old girl...."

"Are you suggesting this yap will allow his wife to be flattened by a street car for $2,000?"

"No, certainly not. This yap happens to be a pillar of his community," I assured her. "Nonetheless, the actuarial tables reveal that his reflexes will have slowed in proportion to the dollar amount of the policy. At $2,000 they will have slackened a bit, at $5,000 they're tortoise-like, and at $10,000, his feet are as lead. That's moral hazard. Simply put, people become less careful with things when they're insured against loss."

"Why couldn't you have just said that?"

"I thought the subject could use some color."

"So, what you're suggesting is that because the insurance companies have begun insuring against burglaries, the number of burglaries will increase."

"Precisely."

"But that doesn't mean there isn't a master jewel thief operating in Washington."

"Master jewel thief?"

"Well, she *has* evaded capture."

"She?"

"Or he, what does that matter?"

I should have been able to put two and two together right then, but we'd both become distracted by some people across the aisle having a game of bridge. They were playing for ten cents a point. I've alluded to Emmie's weakness for gambling, but may not have conveyed a true sense of her interest in the subject. It began with bets at horse races, but the unpredictability of the outcomes troubled her. In the meantime, she'd been taught some simple manipulations of playing cards. This led to the epiphany that cheating was a very effective way of shortening the odds. The culmination came that spring, when she ran a ladies' bridge academy out of our apartment. It was quite popular, for bridge was all the rage and Emmie had become something of a master of that game. Or, more accurately, she had become a master at gaming the game. And apparently the lady bridge players of Brooklyn were eager to learn this art. It was the money from that endeavor which paid for our abbreviated European tour that summer.

We had arrived in France expecting to stay some weeks, but left just a few days later when I took on a job finding some lost gold on a French steamship. It all came out fine in the end, but I wasn't sure that Emmie's enthusiasm for my taking the case wasn't tied to some wager that had gone against her. My suspicion was more or less confirmed when we arrived back in Brooklyn and she swore off gambling for good. And, as far as I knew, she had held to her pledge. Of course, I'd been going out of town quite a bit and there was little chance she'd spent the time knitting me socks. I could see her now measuring up the players in the game across the aisle. She smiled their way, but then turned back to me.

"What do you plan on doing when we arrive in Washington, Harry?"

"Send you on to the hotel while I pay a call on Detective Sergeant Lacy of the Metropolitan Police."

"We can send the bags on and I'll go with you."

"What about your school chum?"

"There's something I should prepare you for in that regard."

"There is no school chum, is there?"

"Oh, there most certainly is. And we'll be dining with her this evening. In fact, it's someone you know quite well."

"My God."

There was only one of Emmie's school chums I knew quite well and I wasn't particularly anxious to become reacquainted with her. That would be one Elizabeth Strout, though she had also used the alias Elizabeth Custis, and probably a few others besides. I was introduced to her while investigating a murder-for-insurance scheme, which, to her credit, she was not directly involved with. She had, however, been a principal of a divorce ring, and before that a sort of feminine barker for a bucket shop. In sum, not precisely the type of person you picture when your wife mentions a friend from her halcyon days at college. But the more immediate cause for concern was Emmie's comment of a little while earlier about a master jewel thief, whom she referred to as "she." I had no knowledge of Elizabeth's capacities in this regard, but I knew she was a young woman of myriad talents—and an extremely pliant moral compass.

"Has she confessed to you?" I asked.

"Confessed what? Elizabeth has taken a position as secretary to the Countess von Schnurrenberger. And the countess has gone to Washington to join her husband, who is with the German Embassy there."

"How did Elizabeth get a position as secretary to a German countess?"

"The countess was in Trouville when we were all there. We saw her at the hotel. Don't you remember?"

"Our time in France is a blur, but I certainly don't remember meeting any countesses."

"I didn't say we'd met her. Only that we'd seen her. Somehow, Elizabeth managed to be introduced to her, and then, one way or another, secured the position."

This part of the story had the sound of truth. Elizabeth was a champion at ingratiating herself. She had essentially ingratiated herself to France, crossing on the same yacht as Emmie and me, the *Spoils of the Sovereign*. It belonged to a man named Koestler who I had done some work for, solving that murder-for-insurance case. Emmie and I were invited on the cruise as thanks for our help in the matter. Elizabeth was working her way across. She had been hired by Koestler to keep an eye on his daughter, a girl easily led astray by men of dubious character. But there was a sort of side bet. If Elizabeth could maneuver the girl into a suitable marriage, she would be rewarded handsomely. She did, and she was. And apparently she wasted no time in finding her next appointment.

While pondering all this, I'd been flipping through Emmie's notebook. Suddenly, I noticed that the entry with the account of the initial burglary was dated September 24th, just three days after it occurred. I hope you see the significance of that fact. But in case you don't, ask yourself this: *How could she know there would be an unusual number of such thefts after only the first had occurred?* The subject demanded further investigation.

"Tell me, Emmie, when did Elizabeth arrive in Washington?"

"Oh, I'm not sure exactly."

"Sometime in September, perhaps?"

"Perhaps."

Suddenly, the inexplicable became somewhat more explicable. To summarize, three events occurred in September. First, the President was assassinated. Second, Elizabeth arrived in Washington. Third, Emmie began taking an interest in Washington newspapers. Emmie alleged that the first was the causation of the third. But, as I explained earlier, we can dismiss Number One as completely irrelevant. Quite obviously, it was Number Two that had led to Number Three. Welcome to Emmie-land, where learning the truth is like peeling an onion—there is always another layer. And in Emmie-land the onions can be decidedly thick. Since our first encounter, I'd say I'd been handed a good half bushel and gotten to the center of only a couple scallions. But setting the salad aside, we can safely deduce that Emmie had an expectation there would be a rash of burglaries in the nation's capital soon after the arrival of her school chum. Ergo, she had some knowledge of Elizabeth's plans in this regard. Or, at the very least, she anticipated some sort of relapse into habits her friend had exhibited previously. During lunch in the buffet car, I probed the matter further.

"Tell me, Emmie, were there many thefts among the students at Smith?"

"No more than average, I imagine. But I suppose there was some of your moral hazard at work."

"How so?"

"Well, if a girl knows her loving father will replace any loss gladly, she tends to become careless."

"Yes, and were they careless with things like jewelry? I expect some came to school with valuable trinkets in tow."

"I expect some did, but I don't recall seeing them."

When we returned to the coach, she picked up her book and said, without looking up, "You're barking up the wrong tree, Harry."

I could feel my eyes watering.

2

My appointment with Sergeant Lacy was for two o'clock, and it was just a few minutes before the hour when our train pulled in. But it was a short walk from the Pennsylvania depot on B Street to police headquarters on C Street, and if it hadn't been for the mishap with the peanut cart, we'd have been right on time. This being Emmie's first visit to Washington, I was pointing out the sights as I hurried her along. The Washington Monument necessitated a look back over the left shoulder, so it was easy to miss the peanut man to our right. The cart went over, and then I went over the cart—both making it through with only minor injury. Nonetheless, the vendor got a little heated. It was only by purchasing the several pounds of his wares that had spilled across the sidewalk that I was able to calm him.

Washington is a very different town from New York. Not as crowded, or as tall, and a complete lack of the intensity you feel while walking the streets of Manhattan. To some, this just made it dull. But it also made for a more genial town. Topple a peanut cart in New York and you're lucky to escape with your life. And that's not mere conjecture.

As we were crossing Pennsylvania Avenue—and admiring the Capitol to our right—I mentioned to Emmie that the sergeant might not be overjoyed with her attending our meeting.

"You can tell him I'm your stenographer, Harry. It will impress him."

"I wasn't aware you knew shorthand."

"I'm perfectly capable of giving the impression I know shorthand. Have you no imagination, Harry?"

I replied with a knowing grunt. Meaning: there is a difference between having an imagination and being mentally untethered. I wasn't sure she had interpreted the grunt correctly, so I went ahead and told her the rest out loud. She replied with a grunt of her own. Hers needed no explanation. By then we'd arrived at police headquarters. A doorman showed us to Detective Sergeant Lacy's office.

"You're late, Mr. Reese. Six minutes late." He'd actually taken out his watch to verify the extent of my lapse. Lacy was an older fellow, in his fifties probably, and not more than five foot six. He had a round head, covered in thin grey hair and accented by bushy grey sideburns. He wore an old suit that might have fit him in its younger days. And he didn't rise to greet me.

"My apologies," I told him. "But we come bearing gifts." I deposited the sack of peanuts on his desk. He opened it, peered in curiously, and then set it on the floor without comment. "This is Miss McGinnis, my stenographer."

"You travel with a stenographer?" He gave Emmie a skeptical appraisal, then turned back to me. "My, you are a big fish."

I'd never met a police detective like Sergeant Lacy. Given his looks and supercilious attitude, I was reminded of one of the detectives with whom Sherlock Holmes had to contend. But it soon became apparent he saw himself in a more prominent role. Eventually, he offered us chairs and I got down to business.

"As I said in my wire, I'm looking into a number of

burglaries that occurred here beginning in September."

"Which burglaries in particular?"

I read off the details of half a dozen.

"And what makes you think they are related?"

"Well, timing. And they all involved jewels of some value. But there are three where the circumstances seem especially similar, and I thought I'd concentrate on those."

"And what three would they be?"

"George Easterly, on the 21st of September. Senator William Merrill, on the 19th of October. And General Thomas Sachs on the 2nd of November. All occurred on Saturday evenings. All involved entry through second-story windows. And all made sizable insurance claims."

"You begin to interest me, Mr. Reese."

"Have you found some other connection among these?"

"Indeed I have." Then he sat back, placed his fingertips together, making an arch of his hands, and smiled.

I waited for the rest, but he obviously wanted me to solicit his wisdom. So I did. "What other connection did you find, Sergeant Lacy?"

He stood up and began circling the office. "All three men employed servants that resided in their homes."

"Surely, there's nothing unusual in that," Emmie said.

He was standing directly behind her now. "No, miss, there isn't. But all three were hired through the agency of one Julius Chappelle."

"Does he operate an employment service?" I asked.

"He does. Specializing in domestic service." His tone indicated he thought this a revelation. But if it was, it was a peculiarly opaque one.

"Had these three servants all been hired recently?" I asked.

"Not in the last year."

"So three men hired three servants through the same employment service sometime in the past. Is that so remarkable?" Emmie asked.

He had his hands on the back of her chair, and leaned down over her. "No more remarkable than a stenographer who doesn't take shorthand." He grabbed her notebook from her and carried it back to his desk. Then he sat down and tossed it to me. "There's nothing resembling shorthand there. Just some scribble, looks like a potato with whiskers."

I looked over the evidence, and he was correct. Emmie hadn't made the barest attempt at shorthand. Though she did show some promise as a caricaturist.

"She's new," I told him.

"And poorly trained," he added.

"Hardly trained at all," I admitted. "She was just released from the reformatory a few weeks ago. They do their best, of course, but...."

"Didn't seem to have done her much good."

"Too short a sentence," I smiled. A sharp jab from Emmie's boot suggested I'd had fun enough. "But getting back to the burglaries, are you suggesting these servants conspired with this man, Chappelle?"

"Perhaps. You see, I know the Chappelle family. Colored folk. This Julius's brother is in and out of here on a regular basis. Runs a policy operation. And I happen to know Julius himself is in frequent contact with his placements, even long after they've taken positions. Now, why might that be?"

"He's a conscientious businessman who wants to be

sure he maintains his clients' satisfaction?" I asked.

"Possibly. But unlikely."

"Is there any other reason to suspect the servants?"

"In the case of General Sachs, there is. His man, a Richard Cole, also colored, was home at the time of the burglary. He was in his room, just above that from which the jewels were taken."

"Was anyone else in the house at the time?"

"Only the cook. But she was down in her room in the basement. She says she didn't hear anything."

"What makes you suspect this Cole?"

"I should have added that the general has a dog, which roams freely about the house."

"Is the dog a suspect, too?"

"You think it's a joke, Mr. Reese. But shrewder minds than yours have reasoned out similar cases. The dog was in the house when the burglary occurred, and yet the cook heard nothing. Ipsolo facto."

"'Silver Blaze,'" Emmie interjected.

"Excellent, Miss...?"

"Miss McGinnis."

"I can see the reformatory did you some good. Yes, as Mr. Holmes himself reasoned, when the dog doesn't bark, we must ask ourselves why."

"Because the thief was well known to him," I added, hoping to move things along.

"Precisely."

"Have you turned up any of the jewels?"

"None from these three cases. We've checked the pawnshops and suspected fences. But no sign. They must have been sent on to be sold elsewhere. Further evidence, I believe, that there is an organizing force behind these crimes."

"But Cole hasn't admitted to anything?"

"No, not for the moment."

"Is there a chance I could talk to him?"

"He's been released. His lawyer should know where he is. Name is William Patterson, colored."

"William Patterson Colored?" I asked.

"I believe Sergeant Lacy intended to convey that he's a colored man, by the name of William Patterson," Emmie clarified.

"It's a good thing you did bring the young lady along, Mr. Reese. It seems you'd miss quite a lot without her help."

"Yes," I agreed. "There's little doubt about that."

"As it happens, I've made an appointment to visit General Sachs' household this afternoon. In order to make another search of Richard Cole's room. If you care to accompany me, I'll introduce you to the family."

"Yes, thank you," I said. Then I turned to Emmie. "Miss McGinnis, perhaps you would like to proceed to the hotel?"

"I wouldn't think of it," she reassured me. "There may be more literary allusions that need interpretation."

After filling his pockets with peanuts, Lacy led us out and we wove our way up to the Patent Office, on F Street. There we caught a Connecticut Avenue car. It soon filled up with homeward-bound shoppers and I made the mistake of giving up my seat to a woman with a small child. I spent the rest of the trip dodging parcels and trying to stay clear of swaying hat pins. I'm not normally one to criticize others' attire, but wouldn't any reasonable person conclude that a hat that requires the equivalent of a fencing foil to hold it in place might better be left at home on shopping days? Unfortunately, this was a time when women's millinery ran toward the complex. Flora and fauna were de rigueur. And I suppose if you want to attach an Oronoco souvenir stand to your head, it's going to involve some serious hardware. When we left the car, just below Dupont Circle, I noticed that both Emmie and the sergeant were eyeing my face.

"You cut your cheek, Harry. Let me have your handkerchief."

"How careless of me."

She wiped my face and handed the bloodied linen back to me.

"Come along, *Harry*," Lacy called over his shoulder.

We followed him to 19th Street, where he led us to a newly built—and somewhat imposing—home. He rang the bell and as we waited he took another look at my wound.

"You look like a man who's lost a duel. Doesn't he, miss?"

Emmie wisely left his question unanswered, turning away to avoid revealing her expression. Have you ever wondered why Holmes, despite being an able boxer, never popped the derisive police inspector in the jaw? I'm not an able boxer, but I did have a few inches and thirty years on the sergeant.

A moment later a pudgy young woman, a little older than Emmie, maybe twenty-five, answered the door. She introduced herself as Alice Sachs, and though she was minimally pleasant, it seemed obvious she wasn't all that happy to make our acquaintance. When I say she was pudgy, I don't mean excessively so. Just well fed. She was of medium height, with chestnut hair, and not noticeably unattractive.

We went in and she tapped on a door. It opened, she

spoke to someone inside and then led us further along to a parlor. Before I went in, I saw a woman wrapped in furs leave the room where we had first stopped. She looked over her shoulder at me—not a friendly look—and then exited the house. There was a fire going in the parlor and an old dog was sound asleep on a hearth rug. The general arrived a moment later. We exchanged greetings and when we'd all sat down, I explained why I was there and asked about the night of the burglary.

The general, a hefty widower of about sixty, told us he had been away from home at a dinner given by his business partner, another retired general named Leutz. He began to wax on about their experiences as young officers with Sherman's Army. Now, any man my age has been listening to accounts of the war—both real and imagined—for his entire life. I've already heard more about the fabled march to the sea than I care to know. Somewhere outside of Chattanooga, I cut him off by asking the nature of his business.

"Sachs & Leutz? We facilitate the acquisition of military equipment."

"I see." I didn't really. I've always thought money is a pretty adequate facilitator for the acquisition of just about anything. Having another finger in the pie isn't likely to quicken the process any. But I gathered that the work was profitable. "Your claim totaled $12,000, but I understand the bulk of it was one particular item."

"Yes, a brooch of my daughter's."

Alice looked up from the book she was reading to add, "A Boucheron brooch."

"And the jewelry was kept in a safe?" I asked.

"It's a simple thing, quite easily broken into. I have a replacement on order."

"May I see it?"

"Alice will show you. You don't mind, dear?"

"No, not at all," she said. But not convincingly. "Please come with me."

She led us upstairs to the library. Except for two windows and the doorway, every inch of wall was covered in shelves. A large table stood on one side of the room and on the other was a desk. She went over to this and opened a drawer and took out a little metal chest. It was just a money box, not even a well-made one, and had been pried open with a jimmy.

"As you can see," Lacy began, "done by an amateur. A professional would have easily picked the lock."

"Why not just carry it off under his coat?" I asked.

"Perhaps, because the thief—*being a resident of the house*—wasn't wearing a coat."

"Do you still suspect Richard?" Miss Sachs asked the sergeant.

"Yes I do, miss. Can you think of any other suspects?"

She made a noise which seemed to indicate derision for the question. "I'm certain Richard had nothing to do with it."

"But how can you be sure when you were away from home?"

"He's been with us for more than two years. He's had ample opportunity to steal anything he wished to."

"Would he have known the value of the brooch?" I asked.

"He knew it was valuable. I have no idea if his curiosity took him further than that."

"Your father isn't so sure he's innocent," Lacy pointed out. "Why dismiss him otherwise?"

"*I* didn't dismiss him."

"Was anything else taken?" I asked.

"No, just the jewelry."

"You were away the night of the burglary?"

"Yes, I'd gone to Boston. To visit a friend. Now, if you'll excuse me, I need to attend to something."

"All right, miss. We can show ourselves out. Is the cook downstairs?"

"Yes, she's in the kitchen. Good-bye, gentlemen, and miss." She left us and closed the door.

"What an unpleasant girl," Lacy said.

"Were the windows locked?" Emmie asked.

"No, they thought it unnecessary, and I'm in agreement. If you look, you'll see there's nothing really to climb up on. And a ladder would be rather obvious, with a street light so close by."

Emmie looked over one window and then the other. She was leaning out the second, to inspect the sill from outside, when she called to us. "Look, the wood has been chipped here. As if someone pried it up from outside."

I followed her over and sure enough, the wood was chipped as she said.

"I had noticed that, of course," the sergeant informed us. "But the exposed wood was damp and the rain had ended two hours before the crime had occurred. Ergo...."

"Ergo, it had been chipped already," I finished. "Brilliant, Detective Lacy."

"Why couldn't some water have dripped down after it had stopped raining?" Emmie asked.

"That might be possible," he conceded. Though his expression made it clear that Emmie had left his good graces.

We went up to the third floor, where Richard Cole had had a small room, but all that was there were some simple furnishings. Lacy made a cursory inspection.

"It's been cleaned, and I told them to leave it be," he complained.

"What is it you're looking for?"

"Just a clue. Any sort of clue. One can't anticipate these things, Mr. Reese."

Then we went down to the basement, where we found the cook washing vegetables. She was a small woman, about fifty, with just the vestiges of an accent I couldn't place. She told us about the night in question and added nothing significant to what Lacy had already told us. Both she and Richard Cole had been in the house that evening. After the meal she'd prepared for the two of them, she cleaned up and then went to her room, which was also in the basement. She assumed Cole was in his room, up on the third floor, but heard nothing.

"You see, Mr. Reese. She heard nothing."

"The dog," I asked, "does he often bark?"

"Oh, all the time," she said.

"I only ask because when we encountered him in the parlor he didn't seem to raise an eyelid."

"Oh, he's stone deaf."

"I see. So he *would* bark, provided he saw us approach."

"Might. But mostly it's the ghosts."

"You have ghosts?" I asked.

"He sees them. Scares me awful. He'll be sound asleep, then jump up all of a sudden and start barking."

We thanked her and went up and let ourselves out.

"Well, Sergeant," I said, "we have established one thing with certainty."

"And what is that, Mr. Reese?"

"The only thing that makes the dog bark reliably is spiritual visitations. Ergo, it wasn't the ghosts who committed the crime."

"Have your joke, Mr. Reese. Have your joke." Then he walked off.

3

It was after four when we started for the hotel. The cool air felt refreshing and so we decided to make our way on foot.

"Harry, you don't really believe that foolishness about the servant having stolen the jewels, do you?"

"Why shouldn't I?"

"The evidence of the window. And Miss Sachs was certain the man was innocent."

"A day doesn't go by where you don't read about the trusted employee who's been embezzling the funds for years."

"What about the mark on the window?"

"Contradicted by the mark on the metal box."

"How so? Couldn't the same tool have done both?"

"I'm sure it did."

"Now you're speaking in riddles."

Yes, and I was enjoying it. After all, Emmie nearly always spoke in riddles. One I remember clearly had occurred in August, not long after we returned from France. As I mentioned earlier, I'd been hired by an insurance company to find some gold that had been misplaced on the steamship *L'Aquitaine*. On our final day at sea, I did manage to locate the gold. Or most of it, anyway. I received $2,000 for my help, and it was that money which I used to set myself up in business. It was just after I'd rented a little desk room in Manhattan that Emmie told me she soon might have information on some noteworthy thefts somewhere south of New York. I was used to Emmie's cryptic pronouncements, but this was unusually Delphic even for her. I knew then she was setting the stage for something. And it was about that time she started reading the Washington papers. But it was only since we'd left Brooklyn that I had begun to learn what it was all about. The sky was darkening and then it started to drizzle. We ducked into Mrs. Knight's Oyster Saloon and Confectionary and ordered beverages.

"Would you care to reveal your line of inquiry, Emmie?"

"No, I have sound reasons for keeping my cards breasted. But surely you see it would be a mistake to focus on Elizabeth?"

"Yes, it's hard to picture her as a second-story man. If she wanted an old widower's jewels, I don't doubt she'd find it easy enough to arrange. But I never really suspected Elizabeth."

"You sounded on the train as if you did."

"Well, only because I suspected you of suspecting her."

"Oh, I may come to suspect her of such things sometime in the future, but I can't imagine she's progressed that far yet."

"Are you forgetting about her machinations with the divorce ring?"

"No. But I'm not speaking of any moral progress—or descent, if you like. I was referring to matters of craftsmanship."

Up until that point, I thought I'd been making some headway on my onion. Now a layer had regenerated. Before the night was over I'd have it peeled off again—but my eyes would be smarting once more. After her second milk punch, Emmie brought the matter up again.

"Harry, don't mention to Elizabeth anything about suspecting her. I'd like to keep things friendly."

"I thought you didn't suspect her."

"Let's not go through all that again. I'll simply tell her we've come to see the sights."

"All right. But if things become unfriendly, it's not likely to be my fault."

The Normandie, where we were staying, was on McPherson Square, just a few blocks from the White House. It was one of the finer hotels, and at five dollars a night, it should've been. Emmie had insisted on staying here, perhaps to impress her friend. We had ourselves dressed and ready by seven, but Elizabeth kept us waiting another half hour. And when she arrived, she wasn't feeling very apologetic about it.

Before we'd even gotten to the perfunctory hugs and how-wonderful-to-see-you-agains, she leaned right into Emmie and told her, "You're not going to meet her, Emmie. And that's the last we will say on the matter."

"Hello, Elizabeth," I said. "How lovely you're looking this evening."

And with Elizabeth there was no need to perjure oneself on this score. She was a striking blonde, a good five inches taller than Emmie, with a sense of fashion even I could appreciate. She looked like one of the girls in *Life*, or *Judge*, who cut men to the knees with their biting remarks. And she was no slouch when it came to the biting remarks either. When she wanted to be, she was amusingly witty. But when her mood had swung the other way, as it often did, it was best to give her a very wide berth.

"Hello, Harrison. I hope you can keep your wife out of trouble."

"*Harry,*" I pleaded.

"I'm sorry, Harry. I know you probably aren't involved in this. Why are you here, anyway?"

"Elizabeth, dear," Emmie cooed. "We've just come down to see the sights, and you, of course."

"Is that true, Harry?" She looked at me closely. "No, I can see it's not."

You know how some people can look you right in the eye and tell the most bald-faced lie without blinking? Well, I'm not one of those people. Interestingly, others usually mistake an inability to lie with integrity, so I suppose some good does come from it.

"Shall we go in to dinner?" I suggested. It took some effort to herd them into the dining room, but eventually we were seated.

"You know Emmie's come to meet my employer, don't you, Harry?" Elizabeth asked.

"The Countess von Such-and-such?"

"The Countess von Schnurrenberger. Yes."

"No, I didn't realize she took much interest in European aristocracy."

Elizabeth shot a look Emmie's way. "You mean he doesn't know?"

"Know what, dear?" she replied.

"All right then, I'll tell him." Elizabeth turned to me. "Harry, do you remember that little book you were working on when I stayed with you last spring?"

"*A Treatise on the Prevention and Detection of Fraud for the Underwriters of Burglary Insurance.* I have an extra copy with me if you'd like one."

"That's terribly thoughtful of you, but that's not why I bring it up. Do you remember bringing home one notably engaging chapter to share with Emmie and me?"

"Yes." This was a chapter that concerned Madame B____, a master jewel thief who operated throughout Europe. Or, rather, I should say *suspected* master jewel thief, as she'd never been convicted, or even come to trial. Suddenly, my *Allium cepa* was shedding layers like Salome on a hot day. Perhaps you remember from Chapter One of the present tome Emmie having referred to the culprit in our case with the very phrase "master jewel thief"? Well, take it from me, she did. And she also referred to the thief as "she." Which had led me to believe she suspected Elizabeth. However, what if it wasn't Elizabeth's arrival in Washington that had sparked Emmie's curiosity, but the arrival of the countess? This warranted probing.

"Am I to understand that the countess and Madame B____ are one and the same?" I addressed this to Elizabeth, but she just stared at Emmie, so I turned the question to her. "Emmie?"

"Oh, all right," Emmie relented. "Yes, they are one and the same. Mme. Veblynde, the captain's wife, told me so while we were on *L'Aquitaine*."

"And now you expect me to give you an introduction to the countess?" Elizabeth asked her.

"Well, you should prepare her for some sort of interview," Emmie answered. "You see, Harry is here to investigate a series of jewel thefts. All of which occurred after the arrival of the countess, and her entourage."

"And you think the countess is behind them?" Elizabeth addressed this question to me, but then answered it herself. "No, your scheming wife hadn't confided in you. How much were these jewels worth, Harry?"

"Individually, a few hundred to a couple thousand. Perhaps not of Madame B____'s usual standards...."

"At least *you* have some sense."

"...except for one brooch, valued at over $10,000."

"For God's sake. The woman is wealthy beyond our comprehension," Elizabeth informed us. "You should also know what happened to the last man who repeated the rumor that the count's new wife was a jewel thief. You see, the count is of the old school. This ill-mannered second secretary had to be sent back to Bucharest with a scar very similar to your own."

"Hat pin," I explained.

"And while we are revealing secrets, has Emmie ever confessed the truth about your little sojourn to France?"

"Which aspect particularly?"

"Its brevity."

"Elizabeth, don't go too far," Emmie warned her.

"Me go too far? That's rich, coming from you. Do you know why you were asked along on Koestler's yacht?"

"You told me you wanted us there as an example of a happy couple for the purposes of your match-making," Emmie said.

"Yes, that is what I told you. But the truth is I wanted Sally Koestler to see just how unencumbered a scheming wife might be in the right marriage. I'm sorry, Harry."

"That's quite all right, Elizabeth. I've tried to encumber her, but it just won't take."

"Why is it that no matter what absurd situation she creates for you, your only response is amusement?"

"I think they call it the survival instinct."

"Are you through, Elizabeth, dear?" Emmie asked her.

"Oh, I haven't gotten to the best part. Do you know

what happened to the money you brought to France, Harry?"

"It was all Emmie's money. And I have a pretty good idea."

"She lost the bulk of it to Koestler in a poker game, just two nights before we landed in Trouville. The little fool tried to cheat him, but he out-cheated her. Then, after we landed, she borrowed from me to try her luck in the casino. She lost, and was forced to sell me your ticket home simply to pay her debts."

"What you didn't tell me," Emmie countered, "was that you wanted our ticket on *La Savoie* so you could hound the countess into giving you a position."

"I didn't hound anyone!" Elizabeth had become heated. "And what *I* do is no concern of yours!"

The waiter had reached around her to remove a plate just as she spoke and her tone seemed to have shocked the old fellow. So I thought I'd ease his mind some.

"Isn't it nice when old friends get together?" I asked him.

He gave me a wary smile and retreated. During dessert, my two companions carried on a lively conversation in French. I caught a word here and there, but the gist of it was lost on me. Which no doubt was the intent.

Elizabeth's revelations didn't come as much of a shock. I had suspected something of the sort, just the details were fresh. But I was surprised to hear Emmie had been foolhardy enough to enter a game of chance with Koestler. You can be sure he's been fleecing people since he was in diapers. Of course, it was my own fault for agreeing to travel on Emmie's purse. Not that I have any qualms about spending her money. I have as much pride as the next fellow, but it doesn't get between me and a fine meal, or comfortable accommodations. No, that's not the problem. It's just that Emmie's associations with wealth tend toward the erratic. And the turns for the worse are generally the sharpest. One moment, you're anticipating a pleasant tour of Europe. The next, you find yourself broke in an expensive resort town. How we would have gotten back to Brooklyn if the job on *L'Aquitaine* hadn't turned up is best left unpondered. But it probably would have involved me shoveling coal in the bowels of some steamship while Emmie toiled in the boat's laundry.

When we'd finished and gone out to the lobby, I offered to hire a cab for Elizabeth.

"I believe I'd prefer to walk—it's only a few blocks back. But perhaps you'd give me an escort, Harry?"

"We'll both come," Emmie suggested.

"No, you stay here, Emmie," her friend insisted.

"All right. Well, good-night, dear."

They exchanged pecks and we went out to the street.

"How do you put up with her, Harry?"

"You dwell on the unpleasant side of it, Elizabeth."

"Oh? What is the pleasant side?"

"Well, life is never dull."

"Yes, I'm sure that's true. Now she's turning her hand to extortion. Your wife is a common blackmailer, Harry."

"You see? It's always something new. Just whom is she blackmailing?"

"Oh, never mind. Do you honestly suspect the countess? I mean, now that you know about...."

"It *is* a strange coincidence that these burglaries started just after you arrived."

"Yes, but the idea that she'd risk everything for some pieces of factory-made Tiffany...."

"Tiffany is unworthy?"

"Some of it, anyway. She says the cattiest things about the jewelry the women here wear."

"There is another possibility," I said.

"What do you mean?"

"Suppose some other party was aware of the countess's true identity. Someone inclined toward criminal behavior. They might make use of her past, hoping to throw suspicion on her."

"You aren't suggesting me, I hope."

"No, but I thought you might know who else is privy to the secret."

"Oh, I'm afraid that would include the entire diplomatic corps, and a good portion of the natives. It's not much of a secret at all."

"I thought the count was handy at squelching the rumor?"

"That poor Romanian was foolish enough to repeat what he'd heard at a reception the count was also attending."

We'd arrived at the German Embassy on Massachusetts Avenue. It was a big, grey stone building, having a kind of Gothic look about it. There was a lightning strike some distance away that heightened the effect.

"If you're so convinced that Madame B____ has retired to the staid life of a diplomat's wife, why'd you pursue the position as her secretary?"

"I wasn't aware of the extent of the transformation until I'd taken the job. She won't even speak of her past. Not the interesting part of it. Of course, it was never my intention to take up burglary, just to gain new experiences. But there's really little for me to do, except provide some diversion for the countess. And the count is continually making unwelcome advances in my direction. By the way, does Emmie know how to ride?"

"A horse? I've no idea, why?"

"I'm hoping for some fun tomorrow. Good-night, Harry."

Back at the hotel, I found Emmie taking a bath. I sat down beside her.

"So this was all about suspecting Madame B_____ was behind the burglaries?" I asked. "You were so sure she would take it up again when she arrived here?"

"I had no idea, but I was curious."

"Will you be disappointed if she turns out to be innocent?"

"Oh, I didn't come here to catch her." She revealed nothing more until she rose. I handed her a towel. "Harry, what do you know about riding? I mean riding properly."

"Little. But I'll barter what information I have for due consideration."

4

When we'd been seated for breakfast, Emmie asked what I'd be doing that morning.

"I thought I'd look up the other two victims, Senator Merrill and that Easterly fellow. Will you be accompanying me?"

"No, if you don't mind, I think I'll do some shopping."

"I don't mind. I suppose I can take my own notes. But it will be a blow to my prestige."

When we finished, I went off to telephone the senator's home. The maid told me he'd gone to his office at the Capitol and gave me instructions on finding it. After I hung up, I saw Emmie speaking to one of the desk clerks. Advancing stealthily, I distinctly heard her ask where she could hire a horse and purchase the proper attire of an equestrienne. I let him answer before joining her.

"Oh, there you are, Harry. I was just getting some directions. Shall we go out together?"

"Yes, I thought maybe I'd accompany you. Help carry packages."

"Don't you think you should attend to business? Look, there's Sergeant Lacy. Hiding behind that newspaper."

As we approached, Lacy gave up his blind and rose to greet us.

"Good morning, Mr. Reese. And Miss McGinnis."

"I'll leave you gentlemen to your work. See you at lunch, Harry." And she was off.

"I was passing by and thought I'd let you know I plan to interview Julius Chappelle this afternoon at his office. You may join me if you wish."

"The fellow who runs the employment agency?"

"Yes, that's the one. Care to come along?"

"I would, yes."

"I'll pick you up here about two. By the way, Mr. Reese, when I asked at the desk, I was told you were registered as man and wife."

"Well, you see...."

"Oh, it's no business of mine. I just want you to realize it's fruitless to hide things from me. I suspected you brought the girl along as something other than a stenographer when I saw the cheap ring she was wearing."

"Cheap ring?"

"Yes, plate, isn't it? Why does a man travel with a stenographer who doesn't know shorthand and place a two-dollar wedding band on her finger? To fool a hotel clerk, I said to myself."

"What if I told you she really was my wife?"

"Then I would ask myself, would a man prosperous enough to travel with a stenographer buy his wife a plate wedding band?" Smiling triumphantly, he went off.

The sergeant seemed to be pioneering a new branch of logic. But his assessment of the family jewels made me curious enough to remove my own ring and examine it. Although I couldn't decipher their meaning, I found the hieroglyphs on the back vaguely reassuring. The truth is that we bought the rings in something of a hurry on our wedding day. If my memory served, they cost more than two dollars, but it was Emmie who'd paid for them—with her winnings from the track.

It had been raining most of the night, but the sky

was clearing when I left the hotel and took a car up to Capitol Hill. At the senator's office, I found two young women typing away. One greeted me without looking up and advised me that the senator had left for a meeting of the committee he chaired. She suggested I had a good chance of catching him before it got under way if I hurried. Her directions seemed overly complex, but I soon learned it was just the opposite. Half an hour later, I found the Transportation Committee room. Except for a fellow sweeping the floor, it was empty.

"I was told the committee was meeting this morning."

"The committee's done met and adjourned. The man from the Pennsylvania's taken ill."

"I'm sorry to hear about the senator from Pennsylvania, but I...."

"Oh, he's not the senator from Pennsylvania. You might call him the senator from *the* Pennsylvania. You know, the railroad company. They don't like to meet less he's here. Else he gets angry with them."

"I see. I was hoping to find Senator Merrill," I told him.

"New Hampshire or Indiana?"

"Indiana."

"I think he might of said he wanted to get his hair cut. But that could of been New Hampshire."

He gave me directions to the Senate barber shop, where I found a half dozen men shaving a half dozen faces, but none of them belonging to Senator Merrill. A disapproving barber informed me the man from Indiana took his locks to an establishment a few blocks away on Pennsylvania Avenue, Southeast. Outside, I was trying to figure out where exactly Pennsylvania Avenue took up again when I heard someone calling my name. It was a fellow I'd been at high school with who'd gone off to work for the *Syracuse Herald*.

"I didn't know you were down here," I said.

"I'm the Washington bureau, for four years now."

I told him my story since we'd last met, and why I was in town. "Right now, I'm trying to find Senator Merrill's barber."

"New Hampshire or Indiana?"

"Indiana." I gave him the address.

"Ah, right down here."

He led me along yet another oblique avenue. This stretch was made up of low buildings—shops mostly—with a saloon or two on each block. It had a small-town feel. He told me about his adventures as a journalist, first in New York and then in Washington. As required in that profession, he'd become a determined cynic. At the barber's, there were two chairs. In the first a youngster was having a trim. In the other was an older gent with a towel over his face, and three fellows simultaneously chattering at him.

"That must be him. With the flies buzzing about."

Before he left, he invited me for a drink later. I accepted, and then went over to the fellow wearing the mask.

"Senator Merrill?" I asked.

He pulled down the towel. "No, Hutchinson."

"Pardon me, I was told I'd find Senator Merrill here."

"New Hampshire or Indiana?"

"Indiana."

"We'll be going into session shortly—he'll be busy until afternoon. What do you want to bother the man about?"

"It's an insurance matter."

"Insurance? That's my committee. What is it you need?"

"It's of a personal nature."

"Personal? All right. But remember to mention my name to your employer. Senator Hutchinson, the underwriter's friend in Washington. Don't forget, son."

Setting Senator Merrill aside, I went off to find George Easterly. He was a lawyer of some sort with an office on the third floor of a building not far from Capitol Hill. The elevator opened onto a large room with typewriters clanking and clerks rushing about. I was told Easterly was just finishing a meeting. A clerk took in my card and returned a minute later to lead me into a smaller, sunny office that had an uninterrupted view of the Capitol. The well-tanned fellow behind the desk greeted me with a smile that seemed only moderately amphibian. He was about forty, still trim, with neat brown hair, a small mustache, and a good tailor.

"What can I help you with, Mr. Reese?"

Before I could answer, a woman I'd not seen interjected.

"I should be going now, George."

I turned and nodded to the lady in question.

"Mr. Reese, this is Mrs. Spinks, a family friend," Easterly announced.

"How do you do, Mrs. Spinks."

There must have been something uncertain in my tone.

"Yes, it's Spinks, I'm afraid," she smiled. "An unfortunate name, but the late Mr. Spinks was a wonderful man. He owned half of Nevada."

"Idaho, I believe," Easterly corrected.

"Oh, was that it? Well, I'm sure George is right. I've never been west of Chicago."

"Cincinnati, I believe," Easterly countered.

"Now George is teasing me. I was in a show at the Chicago Fair back in '93. Did you attend the fair, Mr. Reese? Ours was a very memorable show."

"I did, yes."

"Do you remember Little Egypt, the dancer?"

"Yes, keenly."

"Well, I played the role of Little Memphis at a burlesque review a mile or two away. Perhaps you saw it?"

"Unfortunately, I was in the company of a puritanical aunt who had little appreciation for the finer arts. And she was footing the bill."

"Oh, how awful. And you would have been the perfect age for a show like ours."

"I'm sure I would have agreed. Did your show run long?"

"It did, but I was replaced halfway through by Little Schenectady. It was about that time that Mr. Spinks came along."

I suppose I could imagine Mrs. Spinks in a show back in '93, but it must have been near the end of her career. She was of an indeterminate age, more than forty certainly, and probably over fifty. Her henna-dyed hair was done up in an elaborate knot, topped with a sizable, yet tasteful, hat. She had an infectious laugh, and the amusement she took in her ignorance of the late Mr. Spinks' biography somehow came across as charming. She'd turned and was gathering up her things when Easterly repeated his question to me.

"It's about the insurance claim you made a couple months back. For some jewelry."

His first reaction was to glance over at Mrs. Spinks, but just briefly. "That was paid some time ago," he said.

"Yes, but it's not the claim per se that I'm investigating."

"Please sit down."

We both sat down, and I noticed Mrs. Spinks did the same on the couch beside us.

"There was something of a rash of claims this fall involving jewelry in Washington," I told him.

"I see. How many are we talking about?"

"Half a dozen since the end of September."

"But half a dozen thefts, in a city this size?"

"A half dozen claims. Most such losses aren't insured. Another troubling aspect is that none of the more valuable items have been recovered."

"Is that so unusual?" Mrs. Spinks asked.

"Well, taken together, it leads one to believe there's some connection between these cases. You see, the run-of-the-mill burglar isn't particularly cunning. He sees an opportunity and seizes it. Only then does he try to figure out how to get rid of the goods. Invariably, he sells to someone the police are well acquainted with. Here, we have someone stealing valuable items who also seems to know how to sell them without detection."

"I see," Easterly said. "So you think the same thief executed all of the burglaries?"

"Yes, or several of them anyway."

"Which several?" Mrs. Spinks asked. "You see, I know so many people here."

"Those of Mr. Easterly, a General Sachs, and Senator Merrill."

"New Hampshire or Indiana?" Easterly asked.

"Indiana."

"Have you spoken with them already?"

"I visited General Sachs' home yesterday, with Detective Lacy."

"Lacy," he said. "A good man."

"No doubt. I tried to see Senator Merrill this morning but had some difficulty finding him."

"I can help you with the senator," Mrs. Spinks announced. "He'll be coming to tea at my house this afternoon. I insist you join us."

"If you insist," I smiled back. Then I turned again to Easterly. "I understand you were out the evening of the theft?"

"Yes, my wife and I were at a reception at the British Embassy. When we returned, we noticed a draft coming from my den. I went in to close the window and noticed the safe open."

"The den is on the second floor?"

"Yes. But it would be an easy climb up the outside of the house."

"Were there any servants in the house?"

"Yes, the maid and the cook were both up on the third floor, and the governess was in my daughter's room with her. She sleeps there when we're out."

"But none of them heard anything?"

"No, all sound asleep."

"Did you hire any of your servants through the agency of a man named Chappelle?"

"I believe Lucy, the maid, came from Chappelle." There was another quick glance at Mrs. Spinks. "My wife would know better."

"Would you mind if I visit the house?"

"No, by all means. But could you make it tomorrow? My wife is out of town for the day."

"Certainly, I'll telephone in the morning," I said. "What sort of law do you practice, Mr. Easterly?"

"Law? Oh, I don't practice in the usual sense. You see, our business is more in the nature of facilitating the legislative process."

"What George means is he's a lobbyist," Mrs. Spinks clarified.

"Yes, I see. I imagine that's very lucrative."

"Oh, George, Mr. Reese disapproves." Mrs. Spinks seemed highly sensitive to my intonations. "You must repress that puritanical aunt's influence, Mr. Reese."

"I apologize if I sounded judgmental."

"You're forgiven. Isn't he, George?"

"Absolutely. I know the work strikes the average man as repugnant. But it's those same average men who send these fellows to Washington. Do you have any idea of the mentality we're dealing with?"

"Mentality doesn't enter into it at all," Mrs. Spinks added. And we shared her laugh.

"Exactly. The average first-term congressman arrives as an ego with shoes and a hat. You see, he's already an accomplished politician and the first thing the voter teaches the politician is that to have a strong opinion about anything is dangerous. So from the time he becomes an alderman, up through his years in the statehouse, he sheds his convictions one by one, until all that's left is...."

"An ego with hat and shoes?" I offered.

"Yes, just as you say. Now how can you run a government with people like that?"

"Auction off their convictions to the highest bidder?" I asked.

"I don't think you're convincing Mr. Reese, George."

"A short conversation with old Merrill ought to convince him."

"Of course, it wasn't the foolish voters who sent the senator," I pointed out.

"Indirectly, it was. They sent the fools to the statehouse who then sent us the bigger fool."

"You might want to guard your words, George. It could be very bad for business."

"Oh, Mr. Reese can be trusted." He said this as if I'd been placed in his pocket like a first-term congressman.

"Well, I should be going," I said. "Thank you for your help." I smiled as we shook hands. I figured it was either that or listen to another sermon.

"I'll go out with Mr. Reese, George."

When we reached the street she took my hand and told me I must make it to tea that afternoon. She gave me the address and then added, "Any time after two."

"A long tea?"

"It's more of a salon, but that sounds so pretentious. And don't judge George too harshly."

Then she caught a cab and was off. I took a car back to the hotel and went up to the room. About half an hour later Emmie arrived. I've always thought women in riding habits looked rather fetching. But Emmie's appearance that morning contradicted that notion. She was completely covered in mud, head to toe.

"How was the ride?"

"Oh, grand. It's nice to get out in the open air."

"It doesn't look like you spent much time off the ground. My riding lesson wasn't adequate?"

"Decidedly not, but the chief difficulty was the horse. Remind me to cancel my membership in the S.P.C.A."

"I didn't know you were a member of the S.P.C.A."

"Oh, yes, since I was a little girl."

"I would have thought you'd have built up some good will by now."

"Yes, so would I. Of course, Elizabeth should bear the brunt of the blame."

"Oh? How so?"

"Well, last night she agreed to help me gain an introduction to the countess."

"Was this after you blackmailed her?"

"Blackmailed her? What's she been saying about me? I only suggested that one expects one's friends to provide certain favors."

"And what favor did you provide her? Promise not to tell the countess about her criminal past?"

"No, certainly not. What do you take me for?"

I wisely set her question aside. "So Elizabeth did provide you an introduction?"

"She said the countess always goes riding in the morning, and suggested I could do the same. What she didn't tell me was that the countess is an avid cross-country horsewoman. Nor that she is as young as she is. Haven't you assumed she is an older woman?"

"No, not too old. Just how youthful is she?"

"Youthful enough. And when Elizabeth introduced me, she told the countess I was likewise an enthusiast. So she chose a particularly challenging path for us. How in the world are you supposed to persuade a horse to go up a muddy embankment?"

"I have no idea, but I imagine whatever you tried can be safely struck from the list. Did you at least get what you were after?"

"Oh, yes. The countess is dining with us this evening. I thought we could take her to the Shoreham."

"Isn't that the only hotel in town more expensive than this one?"

"She *is* a countess, Harry."

"Yes, of course. How do we address her?"

"I believe it's proper to use 'Your Ladyship.'"

"I can't see myself saying 'Your Ladyship' to anyone."

"Then try harder. This is important to me, Harry."

"Just why is it important to you, Emmie?"

"You'll find out in time."

I didn't doubt that. It was not knowing the manner of my finding out that caused me anxiety.

5

Elizabeth arrived just as Emmie finished dressing. We had luncheon sent up to the room and I told the two of them about my adventures of the morning.

"George Easterly?" Elizabeth asked. "Is he a tall man? I imagine about forty-five now."

"Yes, do you know him?"

"I used to know him, as a young girl. He was an associate of my father's."

"You lived in Washington?"

"No, that was in New York. Easterly had a position with Colonel Mann, the scandal-monger."

"Which scandal-monger was he?" I asked.

"The publisher of *Town Topics*. And still is, I believe."

"What's *Town Topics*?" Emmie asked.

"Oh, they print all sorts of gossip about the 400. 'The Astors' second parlor-maid seems to have left town rather abruptly, just as young master Astor has been shipped off to Europe....' That sort of thing."

"I've never seen it," Emmie complained.

"It doesn't have much of a circulation. That's not how the colonel makes his money."

"How *does* he make his money?" I asked.

"Blackmail, of course."

"So if the Astors had just paid, the piece would have been omitted," Emmie said. "Isn't that a little dangerous?"

"Oh, it's never that blatant. Instead, the colonel's

representative calls Mr. Astor and asks if he'd like to subscribe to a special edition of some silly directory of the noted families. The morocco-bound volume being just five-hundred-and-seventy-five dollars. Mr. Astor knows the meaning behind the offer. He accepts, and the piece on his heir is redacted. Now the story reads that he was merely inebriated at a social event."

"Sounds rather ingenious," Emmie said.

"I pray for you, Harry."

"What role did Easterly play?" I asked.

"I believe he was the representative. But this was eight or nine years ago, and I was just a child."

"A mere ingénue," Emmie added.

"So, Easterly has reformed."

"Oh, I doubt that," Elizabeth said. "More likely advanced to a safer position. My father was of the opinion that the colonel's enterprise was decidedly precarious."

"Yes, Easterly struck me as a man who knows how to look after himself," I said. "What are you doing this afternoon, Emmie?"

"Elizabeth is showing me the sights," Emmie answered. "And you?"

Before I could answer, there was a knock on the door. Lacy had arrived. I said good-bye to the ladies and went out with him. He led us down K Street to Julius Chappelle's employment agency.

"Have you come up with something new on Chappelle?" I asked.

"No, but I like to keep these people sweating. Once they've sweated enough, they begin to talk."

"I'm still not sure why you suspect the man. Has he ever been tied to a crime?"

"As I mentioned, his brother, one Samuel Chappelle,

runs a policy operation. And there's a rumor that Julius himself has taken up with a white woman."

"Is that unlawful?"

"It's something to hide, certainly."

Chappelle's agency was located in a neat brick townhouse. A young woman at a desk in the outer office stopped us to ask our business. Or rather, she tried to stop us. Lacy barged right past her and into an inner office. I didn't like being party to a police raid, so I hung back in the other room. I could hear Lacy bellowing, then he stuck his head out and summoned me.

"Come along, Reese. Come along."

Chappelle was a man at least in his late fifties. He was tall, over six feet, and had a stocky build. His hair was a salt-and-pepper grey and his face clean-shaven. He was dressed impeccably and had an air about him that made it hard to picture him sweating. Lacy introduced me and told him about my investigation. Chappelle offered me his hand.

"Anything I can do to help, Mr. Reese."

"Mr. Reese will be working with me," Lacy warned him. "And you can be sure we'll get to the bottom of these thefts. Whoever is behind them will rue the day, you have my word on that."

"And which day might that be, Sergeant?" Chappelle asked him.

"Which day? Why the very day he was born."

"Well put, Sergeant. I believe the citizenry of our fair city rests easier knowing you are on the case."

"Yes, well..., as well they should," Lacy agreed. Then he turned to me. "See what you can get out of him." With that, he left us.

"I apologize for the entrance," I told Chappelle. "I was

under the misapprehension we had an appointment."

"That's quite all right. The man's a cretin, but he's not as bad as some. Please, take a chair, Mr. Reese."

We sat down and then I asked him what he could tell me about Richard Cole.

"I sent him to General Sachs in the spring of 1899. Before that, he worked for a congressman who, regrettably, lost re-election. He's been working these types of jobs for ten, fifteen years. No complaints before now. And he seemed satisfied with how the general and his daughter treated him. Not richly compensated, but a little above the norm."

"So not much reason to steal the family jewels?"

"None whatsoever. Until that fool arrested him, Richard Cole had a flawless record."

"Have you spoken with him since the theft?"

"I have, briefly. He insists he saw and heard nothing."

"Would you know where he is now?"

"His lawyer would. A man named William Patterson."

"Sergeant Lacy mentioned the name. Where do I find him?"

He gave me the lawyer's address, then added, "He's a hard man to get hold of. I would suggest going to his office first thing in the morning, before court begins."

"Yes, I'll do that."

"Do you suspect Cole?"

"No, not really. I'm operating on the assumption there's one person, or group of people, behind several different thefts."

"Yes, that's Sergeant Lacy's theory as well. He seems to think that person is me."

47

"He mentioned that. He told me he'd determined the servants in two other cases had also been placed through your agency."

"Yes, with Mr. Easterly and with Senator Merrill. He thinks that significant."

"He also mentioned that you maintain contact with your charges after they've been placed. You seemed to confirm that with what you said about Cole's attitude toward the Sachses."

"It's merely a professional interest. If General Sachs is satisfied, he will recommend the agency to a friend. It takes little time or effort to stay in touch."

"Yes, I see."

"Let me jot a note to Patterson, as an introduction."

He did so and handed it to me. We shook hands again and I left him. It was almost three by then, which seemed like a good time to drop in on Mrs. Spinks' salon. She had given me vague directions to an address above Dupont Circle, so I headed up Connecticut Avenue to find it.

If it had just been a matter of the Sachses' theft, I would have guessed it was done by someone inside the house. Lacy may have been a complete fool and still been right about that. But then what was the connection to the other thefts? Simple coincidence? That seemed unlikely. If the others, Easterly's and Merrill's, had the look of inside jobs, I might find myself suspecting Chappelle, too.

When I realized I was lost, I stopped a fellow and asked if he knew Phelps Place. He told me it was down in Georgetown. A second fellow overheard us and came over to correct him.

"No, no. LeDroit Park. Other direction entirely."

"That's Pomeroy Street," a third fellow told the second.

Then a fourth man stopped and seemingly put the matter to rest.

"Young man, I work in the District Assessor's Office, and I can say with certainty that there is no Phelps Place."

Meanwhile, the second fellow had come to blows with the third. Apparently, this was a town where feelings toward street nomenclature ran high. Their scuffle had attracted a small crowd of spectators, including a street cleaner. It was he who informed me that Phelps Place was just a hundred yards to the west of where we were standing.

This was typical of the time. Like Brooklyn, or Buffalo, or any of a dozen other cities, Washington was in a building boom. Streets were laid out, countryside subdivided, and houses—grand or modest—were going up everywhere. In this part of Washington, they were at the grand end of the spectrum. Not Fifth Avenue grand—more like the comfortable grand you find on certain blocks in Brooklyn.

As yet, Phelps Place held only a few houses and they were just getting around to laying the curbing. To the west you could see the remnants of the what-had-been—sparsely spaced wood-frame houses, an old orchard, then further on, forest. Mrs. Spinks' home was easily spotted with a half dozen carriages parked in front. My knock was answered by an English butler.

I'm not normally one to give a lot of thought to furnishings, but no one entering Mrs. Spinks' house could avoid the topic. It was about three steps beyond opulent, just this side of outlandish. The entry hall was made up like a room in an Ottoman palace. There were brass lamps hanging down from the ceiling, Oriental tapestries draping the walls, and the chairs all held tasseled cushions. Every piece of furniture incorporated some complex inlay, and in place of a mantel, there was an elaborate brass hood above the fireplace. And this was just the entrance hall.

From there, I was led into a large room that likely was intended as a dining room. On entering, one needed to adjust to a decidedly Western sensibility. There were two life-size portraits, one obviously of Mrs. Spinks and the other, I presumed, of her late husband, which flanked a large stone fireplace that might have been looted from one of Charlemagne's castles. There was no table, and just a smattering of chairs around the fringes of the room. At the far end, drinks were being dispensed at a short bar. Above, a huge chandelier hung from an elaborately painted ceiling. And a matrix of carved woodwork surrounded the windows and doors.

But the most incongruous feature was the large framed slate that dominated one wall. There was a young woman standing on a stool before it and she was writing out a list of words and names: New Orleans (3rd), Woodtrice, Prince Blazes, Judge Steadman, Swordsman, Banish, and Helen Paxton. I assumed this must be some parlor game the elite of Washington partake in. There were about a dozen others in the room, mostly men but a few women too. Mrs. Spinks was speaking with some gentlemen and seemed not to notice our entrance. Eventually, the butler cleared his throat and announced me.

"Oh, Mr. Reese, there you are. I was worried you wouldn't come."

The room, and the whole house, had the subdued

lighting which best suited Mrs. Spinks. She looked ten or fifteen years younger than when I'd met her in Easterly's office. She introduced me to the others in the group: a congressman, whose name I missed, a Dr. Gillette, and a young Englishman named Cox. Then she drifted off with the congressman.

"What do you think of Washington?" I asked Cox. "I don't suppose it compares well to London."

"Oh, it has its attractions. And you become used to the privations. But now I've been assigned to the embassy in Bangkok. I'm not altogether sure what to expect there."

"Mrs. Spinks' billiard room might give you a taste," the doctor interjected. He seemed the odd man out—on the short side, maybe thirty-five, with thick eyeglasses and a hesitant manner—while everyone else in the room was of the imposing, confident type you expect to find running the affairs of a country. "Are you a sportsman, Mr. Reese?" he asked.

"Not avidly." I noticed that all eyes were on the large slate. The young woman had written numbers beside each listing. Odds. Suddenly, all was clear. What she had compiled was a list of the entries for the third race at New Orleans. Mrs. Spinks was running a poolroom.

There was nothing terribly shocking in this. There were poolrooms catering to every social class. All one needed was a telegraph line that carried the race results, and a pool of willing dupes. And both were readily available. At that very moment, in cities all over the country, suckers would be assembled in poolrooms betting on the races in New Orleans. Few of them had ever been to New Orleans, or had any clear notion that the track actually existed, but that didn't matter. They might as well be betting on a camel race in Timbuktu. Give them colorful names and convincing odds, and they'd put their last dollar on Sultan's Delight in the fourth at six to one. Once the race had concluded, everyone relaxed again, and Mrs. Spinks returned with an older fellow on her arm.

"Mr. Reese, here is Senator Merrill." As we shook hands, she whispered in my ear, "I found him asleep in another room. You have to speak clearly. He's getting on." Then she added in a normal voice, "Senator Merrill is chairman of the Commerce Committee."

"Commerce?" he asked. "No, dear, I feel certain it's Transportation."

"Oh, yes. I'm sure you're right," she conceded before excusing herself.

Merrill looked to be close to eighty. He was a tall, reasonably fit man, and outside of the loss of hearing, he seemed lively enough. It was easy to imagine him as a handsome fellow a few years back. But age had taken its toll and his face wore an expression like that of a baby fighting a losing battle to stay awake—the eyelids fixed at half-mast. The conversation was slow going, on account of his hearing, and in order to preserve the modicum of narrative flow my chronicle has had up to now, I'll summarize. On the night of the burglary, the senator and his wife had gone to the White House for dinner. The jewelry was kept in a wooden box in a drawer of his wife's dressing table in her second-story room. When they arrived home, the drawer was open and the jewelry gone. A window pane had been broken, which is presumably how the thief gained entry. The maid and the cook were in their rooms on the third floor and heard nothing.

"And it was your wife's finest jewelry that was taken?" I asked. Several times.

"Oh, yes. Yes it was. All the good stuff."

Soon after, he was led off by a representative of an express company and I found myself chatting with Cox. During the lull between the last race at New Orleans and the first coming from California, he recommended we visit the billiard room to test the doctor's idea that it would prepare him for his trip to Siam. But I could have used something to prepare me for the trip to the billiard room. We went back out to the entry hall and then into a large parlor. Here a group of women seated in outsized chairs was having tea. They were surrounded by potted palms and lamps with tasseled silk shades. On the floor, the pelts of a leopard and a polar bear had been laid to rest. The immense head of a moose was mounted above the mantel. And further up, from sconces near the ceiling, a pair of owls was preparing to swoop down on some prey they may have spotted among the garlands of dried foliage that were draped about freely.

We nodded to the inhabitants and then passed along a hallway to our destination. The billiard room's walls were covered with delicately painted landscapes involving cranes and peacocks and flowers. And above the mantel was an odd-looking suit of armor and a set of swords. But Cox said it was all wrong for Siam. "Japonais," he pronounced.

"What do you make of this place?" I asked him.

"You mean, what's it all about? I think that's rather obvious."

"Our hostess is running a high-class betting parlor?"

"No, no. Not at all. That's just the bait."

"Bait for what?" I asked.

"Look at the guest list. Suppose you wanted to keep abreast of all the goings-on in town, and then nudge them in advantageous directions. The easiest way is to charm the powerful. There's nothing more to it. I've no doubt Mrs. Spinks runs a respectable establishment."

"No doubt at all?"

He smiled. "You mean the gambling? She doesn't make a penny off of it. That's the chief attraction. No crooked odds at Mrs. Spinks'."

"That's the second way she distinguishes her place from the average poolroom."

"And the first?" he asked.

"She has a pool table."

I had taken a liking to Cox, and not simply because he laughed at my jokes. But the camaraderie lasted only until our final game. I was setting up a shot when my stick just touched the cue ball. And I mean *just* touched. Barely perceptible. But he insisted it counted as a shot. I had to plumb the depths of my composure to keep from wrapping my stick around his neck.

When I left him, I missed a turn and ended up in the kitchen. A maid led me back via a different route, passing through the telegraph station in the butler's pantry and then into the former dining room where the races were posted. The crowd had enlarged some and it took a little maneuvering to make my way to the front of the house. Mrs. Spinks was near the door and I told her I needed to be on my way.

"We're open every afternoon," she said. "You must come again."

"Yes, I certainly hope to. By the way, you haven't been the victim of a burglary, have you?"

"Oh, no. Not here."

I don't suppose I was surprised to have learned that Mrs. Spinks was in the same business as Easterly. Her

Mrs. Malaprop act was as overdone as her decorating. What I couldn't figure out was why she had taken such an interest in my investigation back at Easterly's office.

6

It was after five and I was late for my rendezvous with the fellow from the *Syracuse Herald*. I wasn't entirely sure why I was meeting him at all—I couldn't even remember his name. And as near as I could recollect, he hadn't been particularly friendly with me in school. Still, I couldn't see what harm could come of it.

I found him, as arranged, in the barroom of the Cochran Hotel. He was with some other members of the vast Washington press corps: the *Des Moines Leader,* the *Pittsburg Daily News*, and the *Chicago Evening Post*. They were a convivial bunch and before I'd even sat down, the *Daily News* had ordered me a drink.

"Harry here is looking for a master jewel thief," the *Herald* scoffed.

"That so?" the *Evening Post* inquired. "You know any master jewel thieves, Joe?"

"No," the *Leader* replied. "In this town, all we have is common horse thieves."

They shared a much larger laugh than the joke deserved and I began to suspect the boys hadn't spent the day at their typewriters.

"Any luck with Merrill?" the *Herald* asked.

"That wasn't him at the barber's, but I met up with him at Mrs. Spinks' salon later."

"You were invited to one of her doings?" the *Daily News* asked. "Aren't you the swell."

"I met her at a fellow named Easterly's office. He was one of the victims of the master jewel thief."

"Easterly a victim? Your master thief better have checked for his wallet before he left the house."

"Who does Easterly work for, exactly?" I asked.

"Whoever paid him last," the *Leader* said. "Right now, the railroads."

"There's a move to regulate freight rates," the *Herald* explained. "The railroads are content to keep things just the way they are. Of course, the farmers feel different, and they have a lot of votes in the Senate."

"Like Senator Merrill of Indiana?" I asked.

"Yeah, he's one of the linchpins. Chairman of the Transportation Committee."

"So if the railroads can convince him to vote against it, they're safe?"

"Oh, old Merrill can't vote against it," the *Evening Post* explained. "Not if he ever wants to go back home to Indiana. But he can pigeonhole it."

"A committee chairman is like a ward boss," the *Herald* added. "He rules his fiefdom with an iron fist. He chooses what they vote on, when they vote on it, and what amendments get through. He can stretch out the debate for a year, until no one remembers what it's about. Or he can amend the bill until it's so different from how it began that the people who were for it are now against it. He'll kill it, but not by voting against it. And only after the railroads have paid."

"You paint a dark portrait of the senator," I told them.

"Oh, Merrill's one of the better," the *Daily News* said. "We've got the Honorable Clark of Montana back in the Senate. You remember him?"

"The Copper King?"

"That's right. He's been buying his way into the Senate for ages now. Only, a couple years back he got a little too obvious about it. The Senate took the high ground. Refused to seat him. So, he went back to Montana for a short rest. Then the same state legislature he'd bribed a few months before took another vote, and guess who won?"

"Clark?"

"Sure, but now it was all on the up and up, so they let him take his seat."

After the third or fourth round, I glanced at the time and realized I'd need to hurry back to the hotel to change for dinner. In the brief time before I'd returned my watch to my vest pocket, all four of my companions had slapped me on the back and taken their leave. Then the barman presented me with the bill. The size of it removed any doubt: the boys had spent their afternoon anticipating my arrival.

Back at the Normandie, Emmie had already begun the most elaborate dressing ritual she'd ever performed. The chambermaid she'd roped into helping her was allowed to leave and I was pressed into service. Under normal circumstances, Emmie isn't one of those women who need an age to prepare themselves for public viewing. Give her an hour and she'd be ready to grab a quick meal at a lunch counter.

"How did your inquiries go?" she asked. "Did you learn anything noteworthy?"

"No, not really. But what was it that fellow said? 'Laws are like sausages—it's best not to see how they are made'?"

"Something like that."

"Well, it might be best if we ask Mary to strike sausage from the breakfast menu when we get back."

When she had finished, she asked me for a verdict. This step in the process has always struck me as peculiar, because Emmie is so disparaging of my taste in women. If I comment that Miss Applegate was looking particularly well last evening, she'll explain that what I mistake for beauty is mere subterfuge and vulgar contrivance. Unfortunately, the chief difference between Miss Applegate and Emmie is that the former has mastered the arts of subterfuge and contrivance. With Emmie, effort is rarely rewarded. She looks her best as the Lord made her and the more she fumbles with it the more she veers from her objective.

"Well?" She was still waiting for my verdict.

Any man in that position is naturally reluctant to open his mouth. Like Paris, whatever his judgment he has about a two-thirds chance of making the wrong choice, and when he does, all hell will break loose. In this case, I was saved by a timely knock on the door.

It was a woman, not yet thirty, about Emmie's size, with bright red hair and freckles. She wore a simple suit and a hat just large enough to be worthy of the name. A green ribbon, like a schoolgirl might wear, streamed down from the hat. She was English, but she spoke so excitedly I understood barely a word. Then Emmie came over and introduced me to the Countess von Schnurrenberger.

"I am sorry, my dear," she said. "I wanted to stop you before you came down. I have a much better idea than dining at the Shoreham. That place is no fun at all. And the food's nothing to speak of."

"Of course," Emmie told her. "Whatever you recommend."

"There is a place I have always wanted to go to, but

it's so difficult for me to get out and do as I'd like. Have you heard of Mr. Harvey's Oyster Saloon?"

"No. But it sounds delightful," Emmie said without much enthusiasm.

"I've been there," I told her. "On a previous visit. It's a cut above the average oyster saloon."

"Is it?" she asked. "I hope not too far above."

The only thing the least bit aristocratic about the countess was the way she dismissed me, telling me I could wait in the barroom downstairs and that she and Emmie would be down presently. Until then, her manner had reminded me of a shop girl. She had the same ease with conversation, making constant use of her wide mouth and bright blue eyes to express what words couldn't convey quickly enough. Though she was not outstandingly attractive, it seemed unlikely she'd ever had trouble being noticed. Emmie was right—it was difficult to reconcile the image this young woman presented with that of Madame B____, master jewel thief, or, for that matter, of a German countess.

It was about half an hour before they finally came down. The time had been spent re-dressing Emmie and now she, too, was in casual attire. They were chattering away like sisters. Sinister portents. For now, just an amorphous grey cloud on the horizon. But I had a well-founded fear it would take on a darker and more substantial shape in time.

The three of us wedged ourselves into a cab and were whisked down to Pennsylvania Avenue. Harvey's was a huge place that mainly catered to tourists and those who wanted to say they'd been to an oyster saloon without having to rub shoulders with the clientele of an actual oyster saloon. A moment after we'd been seated the countess rose and walked out of the restaurant. Emmie and I looked at each other, then followed.

"Mr. Reese, I would like to go to a real oyster saloon. Is that too much to ask?"

"Certainly not—they're a dime a dozen in this town."

We wandered down toward the big market and found a place on Louisiana Avenue that the countess took a fancy to—Mr. Rudd's. The barman pointed to a table and we carefully made our way between spilling beer and flying spittle—an issue of the latter just missing the countess's right shoe. When we were seated, she looked down at the three or four inches of sawdust and God knows what else that covered the floor.

"Why do Americans spit so, Mr. Reese?"

"Harry, please," I said. "Some are chewing tobacco, but mostly for the sport of it."

"How thoroughly disgusting."

"I suppose that's another reason."

"Do you think they'll serve the oysters on the half-shell?" the countess asked me.

"They'll serve them however you ask, but I'd strongly suggest well-fried, or thoroughly steamed."

"You're afraid they may not be as fresh as they might be?"

"I fear so, yes."

We ordered a few dozen and I asked the countess where she was originally from.

"Shropshire. I miss it terribly. Well, I shouldn't say that. It's a too-quiet place. What I mean is that I miss being a child there."

"Were you on a farm?" Emmie asked.

"My father was a sort of free-lance swineherd. An expert at raising fat pigs."

"I always thought pigs came fat," Emmie said.

"Oh, these pigs were very, very fat. Medal winners." Then she turned to me. "I understand you are here as a private investigator, Harry."

"Yes, of a sort. Just checking into some insurance claims. Very routine stuff." I thought it best to avoid the topic of jewelry entirely. One false word and the count would be giving me a wound to match the one from the day before.

"Claims on what precisely?"

"Oh, a variety of things."

"But principally?"

"Well, the largest amounts were for jewelry."

After the slightest of twitches, she smiled again. But it was a different sort of smile. Something in her manner had changed. The frivolity vanished.

"I find it curious that any claims on jewelry here could amount to much at all. From what I've seen, it's all third-rate. From New York."

"There were several pieces of custom Tiffany work," I said.

"Yes, some quite respectable, I'm sure. But nothing notable."

"A Boucheron brooch."

"The only so-called Boucheron I've seen was an obvious fake. Do you insure fakes?"

"No, not intentionally. I don't suppose you remember who was wearing this fake Boucheron?"

"No, I know very few people here. A woman, certainly young. When I complimented her for finding such a serviceable replica, she was quite offended."

"Would you recognize her?"

"Her, perhaps. The brooch certainly."

Emmie, who'd been uncharacteristically quiet, finally entered the conversation. "Do you know a great deal about jewelry?"

"Yes, my dear, I do," the countess said. Her words were accompanied by an expression that would freeze a charging bull. But then she warmed up again. "You must come to dinner at the embassy tomorrow evening and I'll show you some pieces from my collection. Then you will understand something about jewelry."

"That would be wonderful," Emmie said.

"Tell me, Emmie. Why did you accompany your husband to Washington?"

"To see Elizabeth, partly."

"Yes, dear Elizabeth. And yet she didn't join us."

"I invited her, of course. But she said she had a prior engagement."

"She has had many such engagements recently. It's made her a somewhat unreliable companion. And one craves diversion here. It's a rather dull town. And living at the embassy...."

"But there must be dinners, receptions...."

"Yes, dreary receptions where everyone is on their guard and careful not to say anything that could offend a soul. The most entertaining spot here was the race course. But now it's closed for the season."

"Did you go out to Bennings often?"

"Oh, every afternoon. It's too bad there's nothing similar now. No casino. Oh, well."

"Emmie's had some adventures at the track."

"Has she? I hope they ended well."

"If you ever come up to Brooklyn, we could take you to some places," Emmie suggested.

"Is there a casino in Brooklyn?"

"Of a sort," Emmie told her. "And ladies-only poolrooms."

"So Brooklyn is considered a resort town?"

"We like to think of it that way. Don't we, Harry?"

"Oh, yes. The Monaco of Long Island."

Then, rather abruptly, the countess turned the topic of conversation to our love life. She wasn't content with the details of our ostensible courtship. She probed ever deeper, then made references to a book translated from the Sanskrit and privately published by Sir Richard Burton, the fellow who brought us the *Arabian Nights*. The countess said she had a copy of this "sacred text" and would lend it to us. Then she gave us a taste of the contents. Suffice it to say the swan position did not involve ballet. I would share the conversation in its entirety, but she was a master of euphemism, and I failed to make an adequate record. I was more than a little embarrassed. And Emmie, who could be very forward on most subjects, turned fifty shades of red. I rather doubted the countess cared what went on in our bedroom. She simply wanted to let us know who was the superior force at the table. I, for one, needed no further convincing.

"Harry, didn't we pass a theatre on the way here?" The countess's mood had changed yet again.

"The Bijou. A burlesque house, I believe."

"Sounds delightful. Take us there."

I never would have expected that entertaining royalty would be so inexpensive. Three tickets set me back seventy-five cents. Before we took our seats, Emmie excused herself and we waited for her in the lobby.

"Why did Emmie really accompany you, Harry? Is she meant to spy on me?"

"No, certainly not."

"But you do admit she came here to see me?"

"Yes. At least I think so. But I'm only rarely able to divine what's going on in her head."

"I suppose life would be rather monotonous if you could."

"Yes, I suppose. But I wouldn't mind a little monotony from time to time."

"Be careful what you ask for. One evening at the German Embassy and that thought will be wiped from your mind," she smiled. "I just wanted to make sure she posed no danger...."

"Well, being in Emmie's vicinity always seems to yield a certain amount of danger, but usually for yours truly."

"As well it should be."

The Bijou billed itself as the Weber & Fields of Washington. That was about as true as my calling Brooklyn the Monaco of Long Island. The one saving grace was that it attracted a high-spirited crowd. The catcalls from the gallery, and the rejoinders from the stage, made the countess nostalgic for the music halls of London. We stayed until the bitter end and then went off in another cab. When we arrived at the embassy, I took the countess to the door.

"Good-night, Harry," she said. "By the way, did you know you're being followed?"

"Followed?"

"Yes. I assume it's you he's following. He's a rather ordinary-looking man. About your size. Wearing a charcoal grey suit. He has dark hair, a narrow mustache, and tends to hold one hand in the other when he's standing still. I saw him outside your hotel when I first arrived and again outside the restaurant. But I don't see him now."

"I'll keep an eye out, thank you."

"When you get back to your hotel, take Emmie up to your room and then make some excuse to go back down. Take a look outside and I wager you'll see him on guard, making sure you're in for the night. Well, I'll see you tomorrow."

She went in and when we got to the Normandie, I did just as she instructed. It took some looking, but I finally did see the fellow on the south side of the square. I made as if to pick up something I'd dropped earlier and went up to our room.

7

It was obvious that our encounter with the countess had thrown Emmie off balance. She said hardly a word that night. But by the next morning, she'd recovered her equilibrium.

"I don't suppose there's any question the woman we've met is Madame B_____."

"I didn't realize you had any doubts about that," I told her.

"Only when I first met her. Last night was a different matter. I haven't been so intimidated since my first-year Greek class."

"She certainly knows how to control a situation. But does that go hand in hand with being a jewel thief?"

"It goes hand in hand with being quick-witted. And she seems to be going to some effort to convince us she isn't involved—inviting us to dinner at the embassy."

"Maybe she's just trying to be helpful. And to satisfy your curiosity. Is it mere curiosity that brought you here, Emmie?"

"No, not mere curiosity."

We had breakfast sent up to the room and read the morning paper as we ate.

"Look at this, Harry." Her finger pointed to a small story about a burglary. Among the items missing were said to be jewels "of some value."

"Are you suggesting the countess went out after we brought her home?"

"No, I'm not." She looked at me meaningfully.

"You think Elizabeth has progressed further than you first suspected?"

"It would explain why she pursued the countess in the first place. And why she's been absenting herself with increasing frequency."

"Don't you think the countess would have put a stop to it pretty quickly?"

"Perhaps," she said. "What explanation do you have for all the evenings out?"

"If I were to guess, I'd say Elizabeth is developing some new scheme. Say, seducing under-secretaries at all the embassies and using them to steal secrets she peddles to others."

I could see that the outlandishness of my scenario appealed to Emmie.

"Do you really think that, Harry?"

"It's more likely than Elizabeth climbing up drainpipes to break into bedrooms."

"Perhaps. What are you doing this morning?"

"I'm going to see Richard Cole's lawyer and find out where Cole's staying."

"Do you honestly believe he stole the general's jewelry?"

"Maybe. Or maybe he knows who did. I have to do something with my time."

I left her dressing. When I reached the street I looked high and low, but saw nothing of the fellow who clasped his hands. Then I hopped on a car heading back towards the Capitol. I found William Patterson's office on D Street, the small anteroom filled with people. They were all colored and most seemed of the laboring class. I sent in my note from Chappelle via the office boy and ten minutes later I was called in. Patterson was a man of less than average height, but stood ramrod straight in an effort to elongate himself. He was clean-shaven, and only about thirty-five or forty. But he had a haggard look, with dark bags under his eyes. It reminded me of Abe Lincoln, only more so.

"Forgive the wait, Mr. Reese. It's a full docket today. Sit down, please." He motioned to a chair and then sat down himself. "Mr. Chappelle tells me you're looking into the case involving Richard Cole. Who exactly do you represent?"

"The insurers. There's been a series of burglaries here recently, a number involving valuable jewelry."

"Wouldn't that be indicative of a common actor in the crimes?"

"Yes, something like that."

"I can assure you, Richard Cole stole nothing. And if you met the man you'd know at once it's ridiculous to think he's responsible for a string of burglaries."

"That's one reason I'd like to meet him. To see for myself."

"Any other reason?"

"He might have heard or seen something."

"He insists he neither heard or saw anything when the crime occurred."

"Assuming the crime occurred as it is alleged to have."

There was a long pause before he replied. "I wonder if we are thinking along the same lines."

"I imagine we are. Did Cole ever say anything in that regard?"

"He wouldn't dare. Who would take the word of a colored servant over that of his white employer? And what would it gain him but unemployment?"

"Yes, I suppose that's true enough. It's puzzling that Lacy never seems to have thought along these lines."

"It's my experience that most police detectives are lazy hooligans. They have difficulty actually solving a crime, so they push and shove, threaten and beat, and when results are demanded they arrest the nearest colored man. Richard Cole is a perfect example. Now he has lost his home, his job, and the chance of living respectably. He has no money to move elsewhere. What will he do? He will survive. He will survive by doing odd jobs of ever-decreasing legality. Then Lacy and Company will say, 'Look at this shiftless negro. We were right about him all along.' That room out there is full of Richard Coles living at some point along that continuum. Are things so different in New York?"

"Well, the cops are hooligans, but they're never very lazy about it. And I don't suppose there are enough colored men about to pin all the crimes on them. But the general picture is the same. Of course, it's probably the same in London, or Moscow, too."

He laughed a bit. "All right, Mr. Reese. I'll have Joseph take you to Cole." Then he called in the office boy.

"If you'll just give me the address, I'm sure I could find it myself."

"No, that's not very likely." He turned to Joseph, a boy of about thirteen. "Do you know Cabbage Alley?"

"No, sir."

"Do you know Selig's grocery, on Delaware Avenue?
"Yes."

"Just beside it is Cabbage Alley. Take Mr. Reese to Mrs. Lawrence's house there. He is to speak with Mr. Cole. Make sure you tell them you came from me. And then you hurry back here."

"Yes, sir."

I thanked Patterson and then Joseph and I walked the half mile or so up Delaware Avenue to a little above G Street. Just as Patterson had said, an alley led off from beside the grocer's. On one side, it looked like an alley you'd see anywhere, with a row of stables belonging to the houses that faced the street. But across from these were several low houses that had all seen better days. Most were wooden, and leaned so much in one direction or another that nothing seemed to be holding them up beyond faith. A couple others were made of brick, but it had to be the sloppiest masonry work I'd ever seen. About what I'd expect if I were to set about building such a house.

Joseph made inquiries and we were directed to the home of Mrs. Lawrence. A small child let us in. The inside was neat, but shabby. And the house was full of steam. Mrs. Lawrence was a laundress. Joseph told her why we were there and that Patterson had sent us. But that didn't seem to lessen her suspicion of me. She told him Cole was no longer there. He asked where he'd gone and her answer was incomprehensible to me, and apparently to Joseph. He asked again and she elaborated. He led me out of the house.

"She says he's gone to another sister's house. There wasn't room enough here. She said that sister's name is Mrs. Wright and she lives in Twine Alley."

"Twine, like a piece of string?"

"I think that's what she said. She said you take the car to Georgetown, the one that goes down P Street, and get off at the new market, before you get to the bridge. It's right near there."

"I don't suppose you could accompany me?"

"No, sir. I'd better get back."

"Do you think she was telling the truth?"

"Can't say, sir. But if he was staying there, he'll be gone now."

I jotted down the instructions and read them back to him just to be sure. Then I gave him two bits and he was off. Senator Merrill's place was a little further east of where I was standing, just up Maryland Avenue, so I thought I'd stop by there before going off in the other direction.

The senator's home held down the corner of a row of brick townhouses, all very respectable. The kind you'd see in Park Slope. A maid led me into a parlor and I waited there for some time before the mistress of the house arrived. Mrs. Merrill was much younger than the senator, just over forty, and a good deal more attractive. The one thing they had in common was a kind of drowsy look about them. But while he was merely a tired old man, she was a handsome woman with a languid air. She drooped down on a divan as if just the act of introducing ourselves had exhausted her. It was a well-practiced pose, but one better suited to a girl half her age. A Persian cat jumped up in her lap and, seeing them together, you'd think the cat had been chosen for its resemblance to Mrs. Merrill. She—Mrs. Merrill, not the cat—had a headful of brunette hair that was allowed to flow about her face. It took a moment before I realized she was the woman I'd seen leaving the Sachses' home on the first day of our visit in Washington. It had been a brief look in a dim hallway, but there was no mistaking the face.

"I don't know what I can tell you, Mr. Reese. We were out for the evening, and when we came home, we found we'd been burglarized."

"Yes, the window was broken, I understand. Was there much glass about?"

"Glass? Yes, I suppose so. Helen cleaned it up."

"Around what time did you arrive home?"

"Oh, past midnight."

"Who else lives in the house?"

"Helen, the housemaid, and the cook, Sarah. Jacob lives above the stable."

"And they were all here that evening?"

"Helen was away for the day. Her mother was ill. Sarah was here. Jacob dropped us off at the White House and picked us up there. What he did in the meantime I can't say. We knew it would run late."

"So Sarah was the only one in the house."

"Evidently."

"Might I speak to her?"

"Yes, I suppose that would be all right."

But instead of having the maid take me to Sarah, Mrs. Merrill brushed the cat aside and rose to her feet. She led me down to the kitchen, where the colored cook was making a pie.

"Sarah, Mr. Reese would like you to tell him what happened the night of the robbery. You remember."

"Yes, ma'am," Sarah answered carefully.

"You were in your room?" I asked.

"Yes, sir. Up at the top of the house." She looked at me while speaking, but then shot a glance at her employer.

"And you didn't hear anything?"

"No, I'm a good sleeper. Never hear anything."

"Not even the window breaking?"

"No, sir. I never heard the window breaking."

It was clear Sarah would say nothing while in the

presence of Mrs. Merrill, and it was just as clear I wouldn't be left alone with her. So I thanked her, and asked to see the room in question.

"To what end, Mr. Reese?"

"To get an idea of how the burglar got in. I'm trying to tie this with some other burglaries."

"I see. Of course."

It was a large bedroom, with a circular turret that formed the corner of the house. The window which had been broken was just above the entrance. It would have been an easy climb for an experienced second-story man. The jewels had been in a box on Mrs. Merrill's dressing table.

"The senator said all your most valuable pieces were taken."

"Yes, that's correct."

"What were you wearing that evening?"

"That evening?"

"Yes. I imagine a White House dinner must be a bit of an occasion."

"You forget that the city was still in mourning, over the death of the President. It was a small affair. I wore some items of my mother's. Simple pieces."

"Yes, of course."

Then she called the maid, who led me to the door.

"Helen, do you remember sweeping up the glass the night of the burglary?"

She paused. "No, sir. I'd gone to my mother's."

"Oh, yes. I'm sorry. Mrs. Merrill mentioned you'd gone to Baltimore," I lied.

"Yes, that's right."

"I don't suppose Jacob is about?"

"No, he's not, I'm afraid."

I thanked her and left. You meet a lot of deceitful people investigating insurance claims, and most of them aren't half as good at lying as they think they are. But that had to be the poorest group of liars I'd ever encountered. Obviously, the Merrill family was having money problems of some kind and turned to their friendly insurance company for a timely disbursement. I'd already been suspecting something of the sort with General Sachs and his daughter. But if both were cases of fraud, it was difficult to imagine a connection between the crimes, unless someone was decidedly indiscreet. I wouldn't have thought it was something you brag about to your friends.

I went up to the other end of the block and circled back down the alley. I found a middle-aged colored fellow watching another colored fellow hoist bales of hay up into a loft. I assumed the man on the ground doing the watching was the senior partner and so addressed him.

"Jacob?"

"That depends."

"Depends on what?"

"What it is you want this Jacob for."

"I'm investigating a burglary...."

"He's Jacob," he said, pointing to the man in the loft.

I hailed the fellow, took out a silver dollar, and made as if to toss it to him. The first man grabbed it from my hand.

"I'm Jacob," he said. "What burglary?"

"Here at the Merrills', back in September."

"He's Jacob."

I smiled and took out another dollar. Once again the first fellow grabbed it.

"We was at the White House that night."

"You dropped them off there, and picked them up, but what about in between?"

"There's a story there, all right. But it's a three-dollar story."

It was an arresting tale, involving a game of craps, several bottles of whiskey, two knives, and a French coachman's trip to the hospital. But the crux of it was that Jacob spent the evening carousing with his fellow drivers and had no information about what happened back at the house.

Now I was more interested in speaking with Richard Cole than ever. It wasn't that I thought he'd stolen the jewelry, but just the opposite. If there had been no burglary, there had to be some other reason for his dismissal. And since he'd already lost his job, he'd have little to gain by lying for his former employer. I got on the proper car to Georgetown and found the West End Market on P Street. It was small for a public market, but since the neighborhood was still half vacant lots, that wasn't too surprising. I asked several people about Twine Alley before I found a postman who was able to point me in the right direction.

The chief difference between Twine Alley and Cabbage Alley was that the homes here had been built recently. But they didn't look much better for their apparent youth. It was as if they'd been built pre-dilapidated, just to speed the squalor along. I couldn't find anyone about at first, but eventually roused an older fellow who insisted he knew neither Cole or Mrs. Wright. He suggested I come by that afternoon, as his grandson might have some better intelligence.

8

A little while later, when Emmie and I were seated in the Normandie's dining room, I asked how she'd spent her morning. She told me she'd gone to see Elizabeth.

"Did she confess?"

"I never saw her."

"She was out?"

"She was in, but I was told she wasn't feeling well and would not be receiving visitors."

"Maybe she twisted an ankle escaping from last night's raid."

"I don't seriously suspect Elizabeth."

"But just the same, you're curious to know where she spent the evening."

"Curious, certainly. Yesterday morning she was determined to orchestrate my encounter with the countess, but then showed not the remotest interest in having dinner with us."

"Maybe she realized the countess could handle you quite ably on her own."

"Yes, perhaps," Emmie agreed. "What did you learn this morning? Did you speak with Richard Cole?"

"No, only his lawyer. Then I visited Mrs. Amanda Merrill, the senator's wife."

"And how did you find her?"

"Looking quite well, I'd say. But I'd seen her before."

"Where?"

"That first afternoon, when we visited General Sachs. She had been meeting with him when we arrived. I saw her briefly as she slipped out of the house."

"You didn't mention it."

"I had no idea who she was at the time."

"Did you learn anything concerning her burglary?"

"I learned there was no burglary."

"Seriously?"

"Yes. But don't look so disappointed. Fraud is my bread and butter."

"But it's so... prosaic."

"Well, maybe I can ginger it up for you. The general's case is also fraud."

"Are you saying that because the countess told you she'd seen a fake Boucheron brooch?"

"Partly," I said.

"Couldn't that have just been someone else?"

"Sure. But there's also the clumsy way they set up the supposed burglary. The thief looked nowhere but the metal box containing the jewels. So we can assume he knew where these were kept. Then he stands there banging it open with a metal bar when he could have just picked it up and made his exit."

"That's what you meant when you said the mark on the window was contradicted by the marks on the box?"

"Yes. If it was a real burglary, there was no reason to pry open the box there. Lacy was probably right, the mark on the window had been made before that night. But so were the marks on the metal box."

"What will we be doing this afternoon?"

"We? I was planning on visiting the Easterly household. Would you like to accompany me?"

"I've nothing better to do."

"Will you be coming in the guise of stenographer, or paramour?"

"Paramour?"

"That's what Sergeant Lacy thinks you are. 'Why does a man travel with a stenographer who knows no shorthand?' he asked himself. And then there's the fact you're wearing a plate ring."

"What a pernicious little man. In fact, it's not plate."

"What about mine?"

"Oh, yes, yours is. But I didn't think you'd care. After all, it's been over a year and you hadn't noticed."

She was right, of course, I didn't really care about the ring. But it did make me wonder what else I hadn't noticed.

Easterly lived a ways out, still in Washington, but north of the city proper. We took a car up to Columbia Road, and there caught another that ran across Rock Creek gorge and then up the extension of Connecticut Avenue. We passed a scattering of houses and after about a mile we arrived at the entrance to Cleveland Park, a suburban subdivision. After two or three blocks of increasingly showy homes, we arrived at the Easterlys'. It was a handsome Queen Anne. Not the showiest of the bunch, but the one that best achieved a balance between aesthetic appeal and ostentation. There were broad stairs leading to wide porches, and above, a healthy number of turrets and gables. And all colorfully painted. A maid greeted us at the door. She said she expected her mistress back shortly and led us to a parlor to await her arrival.

The room was obviously used only formally, which frustrated Emmie terribly because she so enjoyed snooping. She went about looking under and behind things, but there was nothing the least bit personal. Until a little person entered the room. A girl, of about five or six. She'd come in silently, unnoticed by Emmie, who had just opened the drawer of a small table.

"What are you doing?" the girl squealed.

This sent Emmie skyward. I developed an immediate fondness for the child and we shared a smile at her handiwork.

"Oh, I was just looking for some paper," Emmie replied. Then she compounded her predicament by speaking to the child in a patronizing tone: "And what's your name?"

It always amazes me that people make this mistake with children. How can anyone forget that childhood was one endless series of schemes. You wanted something but were dependent on someone else to get it. And it was difficult to imagine Emmie being anything but the adroitest of schemers. I'd wager she had complete control of her parents by age four. But to return to the present, our hostess wasn't done with Emmie yet.

"My name is Sesbania," she announced.

"Is that really your name?" Emmie asked.

"Of course it's my name!" she shouted.

"I'm so sorry," Emmie said, dropping into a chair.

"That's all right, I forgive you. Who are you?"

"We're sort of detectives," I told her. "We've come to investigate your burglary. Do you remember it?"

"I remember it very clearly. But no one else seems to. The police haven't done a thing. What are your names?"

"I'm Mr. Reese. Harry, if you like. And this is my wife, Emmie."

"While we're alone, I'll call you Harry and Emmie. But when Mother comes home, I'll use Mr. and Mrs. Reese. Otherwise she'll get all corrective."

"Very judicious," I told her. "You are wise beyond your years."

"Yes, I know that," Sesbania agreed. Emmie was still looking a little shocked, so she went over to offer comfort. "Don't worry about my name. I know it's uncommon. Mother named me for a flower she remembers from when she was a little girl."

"What color flower?" Emmie asked tentatively.

"It must have been magical, because every time Mother tells me about it, it's a different color. Father says it has thorns, but I think he's just teasing me. Mother is a South American beauty, Father says."

"Oh? How did they meet?"

"Father says he won her in a card game in the Argentine. Do you think that's true?"

Emmie, unsure if it was just a rhetorical question, stammered, "Well, I...."

"It might be true," I said. "Foreign ways are not like ours."

"I think it may be allegorical," Emmie suggested.

"Like a fairy tale?" Sesbania asked.

"Yes, just like that."

"Do you ever think you are living in a fairy tale?" she asked Emmie.

"Oh, yes. Quite often. In the same way I imagine people in fairy tales think they are living in the real world."

"That would explain why some people don't realize they are in a fairy tale."

Clearly, they'd reached a sort of philosophical understanding. Now Sesbania turned her sharp little eyes on me. "How about you?"

"Yes, how about you, Harry?" Emmie joined in.

"Well, living with Emmie is either a fairy tale or a nightmare, I'm not always sure which."

"Is she a witch?"

"I couldn't say with certainty," I said. "What are the distinguishing characteristics?"

"Does she have powers? I mean, can she make things happen?"

"Oh, yes. She can make things happen."

Then she turned back to Emmie. "North, South, East, or West?"

"North."

"Are you sure?"

"Because I don't look old? That's because in civilized countries, I must hide myself."

"Do you know the Witch of the South?"

"Oh, yes. We're very close."

"Good. We may need her." Then she pointed my way. "But what is he?"

"Winkie, I'm afraid."

"Oh." She looked disappointedly at me, then turned back to Emmie. "Did you free him?"

"Yes. But I often wonder why I bothered."

There was a noise at the door and Sesbania went off to greet her mother. Their voices were so similar it almost sounded as if the girl was talking to herself. Then she led her mother into the room and Emmie and I rose to greet her. Mrs. Easterly was a dark-haired woman of about thirty-five. She was short, with an ample bosom that seemed all out of proportion. By no means a beauty, she had an expressive manner you couldn't help but find engaging. In that sense she seemed much more childlike than her daughter. I hadn't really formed an image of Easterly's wife, but if I had, this would not have been it.

"This is Mr. and Mrs. Reese, Mother. I've been entertaining them. They've come about our burglary."

"Oh, yes, George said to expect you. It slipped my mind, I'm very sorry."

"That's quite all right. We've been having a lovely time."

"Yes?" she enthused. Then she looked down at her daughter. "Did you sing them a song, dear?"

"No, Mother. We were discussing literature."

Her mother laughed and gave her a little hug and then led us into the living room, the center of which was taken up by a huge Christmas tree. It was a sunny day and light from several large windows set the elaborate decorations sparkling. We all sat down and Mrs. Easterly had coffee and chocolate brought in.

"Do you remember the night of the burglary, Mrs. Easterly?" I asked.

"Yes, we went to a reception at the French Embassy."

"Mr. Easterly thought it was the British Embassy."

"Oh, who can remember? But he's probably right."

"When did you get home?"

"Oh, after the last car. We had a carriage."

"And who was in the house?"

"I was," Sesbania volunteered.

"Did you hear anything suspicious?"

"Perhaps."

"What did it sound like?"

"Wings flapping."

"Hmmm. Do you think we could see the room where the burglary took place, Mrs. Easterly?"

"Oh, yes. Of course."

The four of us went upstairs to a den, with Sesbania leading the way.

"That window had been open," Mrs. Easterly told us. "And the safe was open."

"Where is the safe?"

"Oh, would you like to see it?" She walked over and revealed a small wall safe behind a painting.

I looked it over and then asked if she knew the combination.

"Yes, do you want to see inside?"

"Yes, if it would be all right."

I stepped back where I couldn't watch too closely and she dialed it open.

"There's nothing in it now, just some papers of George's." She set these on a desk beside her and just then the maid arrived.

"Excuse me, Madam. Mrs. Gregory is here."

"Oh! I forgot the dressmaker. I must go see her." She turned to Sesbania. "You take care of Mr. and Mrs. Reese. I'll be back soon."

The papers she had set aside were bonds, with a goodly number of coupons remaining.

"Well?" Sesbania asked. Clearly she was expectant of some results.

"What sort of wings?" Emmie asked.

"Winged monkeys, of course."

"Yes, I feared so," Emmie said.

"Were these pieces of paper in the safe the night of the burglary?" I asked.

"No, it was empty."

"Was anything else taken?"

"No, just the jewelry. Although, since that night I haven't been able to find one of my dolls."

"I hope not a dear one," Emmie sympathized.

"Not terribly dear." Then she turned back to me. "Aren't you going to ask about clues?"

"Were there any clues of note?" I asked dutifully.

"Monkey droppings, for instance, things like that?"

"Father said I should look for monkey droppings, too. There is only one clue. Would you like me to show it to you?"

"If it wouldn't be too much trouble."

She led us to her own room—a little child's palace—reached under the bed, and pulled out a carved wooden box. She looked about inside it for a while and then pulled her hand out.

"Here it is!"

She seemed to be holding nothing at all. Emmie sat down on the bed and Sesbania delicately handed the phantasm to her.

"It's a red hair," Emmie said. "And very long."

"Yes," the girl agreed. "And no one here has hair that color."

"This could be very important," Emmie told her.

"I thought perhaps it belongs to Glinda."

"But she wouldn't take your things."

"No, but she may have come to protect us from the winged monkeys."

"Yes, she would certainly do that," Emmie agreed. "You had better keep this here. And guard it carefully."

I'd grown somewhat used to my periodic visits to Emmie-land. But I still found it unnerving when we ran into some other member of her tribe. Emmie's newfound compatriot led us downstairs to rejoin her mother. Mrs. Easterly modeled her new dress for us and then took me to speak with the three servants who'd been in the house that evening. They'd heard and seen nothing. Then Sesbania mentioned Molly.

"Who's Molly?"

"She's my governess. She's taking a nap and I'm not

allowed to wake her until four o'clock. When I was little, I was the one who took a nap, but now she takes the nap. Isn't that curious?"

"Frankly, no," I said. We thanked the ladies and were about to go out when the girl tugged at Emmie's hand.

"You're forgetting!"

Emmie thought for a moment and then leaned down and kissed Sesbania on the forehead. Then the girl turned to her mother.

"Did it leave a mark?"

"Oh, yes, I see it very clearly," she confirmed.

We took our leave and went off to await the car back into town.

"What an idyllic life that child leads," Emmie said. "I hope it won't be too much of a shock when she needs to go off into the world."

"A shock for her, or the world?" I asked. "What was all that about flying monkeys and directionally-bound witches?"

"How could you be unaware of *The Wonderful Wizard of Oz*?"

"I'm aware of the phenomenon, I just haven't gotten around to reading it. I didn't realize you enjoyed children's books, Emmie."

"If you think I'm going to accept criticism of this sort from a man who thinks an evening at Weber & Fields is the acme of culture, you are grossly mistaken."

"I apologize for maligning your taste," I said. "Did that hair look familiar?"

"I was just humoring the child," Emmie said.

"A long red hair. Perhaps Madame B_____ is up to her old tricks after all?"

"Don't play horse with me, Harry. And don't gloat."

"You mean you suspect it's another case of fraud?"

"How could a burglar know the combination of their safe?"

"I have a feeling anyone knowing the family would have a pretty easy time guessing the combination."

"Why do you say that?" she asked.

"Mrs. Easterly had no trouble remembering it, yet she had three lapses of memory during our brief time with her. Five will get you ten, the combination is the month, day, and year of that little dear's birth. Or something equally transparent. Maybe Lacy's right about the servants."

"You don't believe that," she said. "What about those securities?"

"You noticed the bonds?"

"I recognized them as securities of some sort. Why would you put something valuable in a safe you believe someone has broken into without trouble?"

"Indeed. The most curious thing is the similarities among the three cases. They all tell much the same story, but no one has put any effort into making the stories convincing."

9

When the car reached Dupont Circle, I told Emmie I wanted to visit Twine Alley and she decided to accompany me. It was late afternoon and the sun was just beginning to set over Georgetown. We made our way to the alley and then to the home of the old man I'd met earlier. He remembered me and asked us to come in, then motioned us to the only two chairs in the room.

"Has your grandson arrived home?" I asked.

"No, but I expect he'll be here shortly."

He offered us coffee and we accepted. While he went into a back room to prepare it, we surveyed the room's meager accoutrements. He came back, set cups before us, lit a kerosene lamp, and sat down on one of the two beds. The coffee did bear a resemblance to what we knew as coffee, but there seemed to be much else going on in it.

"This is quite good," Emmie told him. "What do you put in it?"

"Roasted dandelion, mostly." Then he went on to give her the details of the recipe, which seemed mainly to involve various weeds easily found in city lots.

It was then that the door swung open and a young fellow, maybe fifteen or sixteen, ran in. The abruptness of it caused Emmie to drop her cup. It fell to the floor and shattered. The boy looked us over for a moment, uttered a brief greeting, then moved a bed, lifted a floorboard, and stuffed something in the cavity below. Then he replaced the board and bed. In the meantime, Emmie was picking up the pieces of the cup.

"I'm so sorry," she said.

"That's all right," the boy told her. "There's another."

His grandfather dutifully went off and filled another cup and presented it to Emmie.

"Your grandfather thought you might be able to tell me where I can find Richard Cole," I began. "I was told he was staying in the alley here with his sister, a woman named Mrs. Wright."

"Mrs. Wright?" He looked at the old man, who shook his head. "There's no Mrs. Wright around here."

Just then the door flew open for a second time. And for a second time Emmie's cup went crashing to the floor. The new arrival was a cop. He scanned the room, then looked hard at me. He pointed at the boy and asked, "How long's he been here?"

"Oh, since we came. An hour or more." I looked to Emmie for confirmation.

"Yes, at least an hour," she said.

"What are you two doing here?"

"Spreading the Gospel," she told him and waved a little book she'd taken out of her bag.

He seemed somewhat skeptical, but left just the same. I got up and shut the door he had neglected to.

"Thank you," the boy said.

"It was the least we could do, what with my wife destroying your tableware." I thought I'd make use of the good will we'd engendered and asked again about Mrs. Wright. He confirmed she wasn't living in the alley and he'd never heard of her. "And you don't know of a Richard Cole?"

"No—who told you he was here?"

"A Mrs. Lawrence, his sister."

He looked over at his grandfather, who again shook his head.

"I guess Mrs. Lawrence don't want you to find this Richard Cole," the boy said. "Why are you looking for him?"

"There was a burglary at the house where he worked. He was accused of it and lost his job. I'm sure he's innocent, but I think perhaps he can tell me who did do it."

"Why do you care?"

"I represent the insurance company. You see, some valuable jewelry went missing and the insurer paid the man who owned the jewelry a lot of money."

"So if you can find it, they get their money back?"

"Yes, then they give me a part of it."

"If I can find this man...."

"Richard Cole's the name. Say five dollars?"

"Ten?"

We shook hands and I told him all I knew about Cole.

"Where are you staying?"

"The Normandie."

"I'll come by there. About the same time tomorrow."

Before we left, Emmie took out several dollars and gave them to the old man for the china she'd demolished.

"But ten more if I find Richard Cole?" the boy asked.

"Yes, of course," I assured him.

Outside, it was already getting dark and the electric street lights were coming on. We hurried back to the hotel to change for dinner at the German Embassy. This time, there was no question Emmie would be pulling out the stops. That didn't bother me, but she had also arranged to rent a complete white-tie outfit for me. Had it fit, it would only have been uncomfortable.

We arrived a few minutes late and were told the

others had already been seated, but our entrance seemed hardly noticed. There were a dozen separate conversations going on along the long table. Most in French. I was seated between Elizabeth and the countess, and Emmie was opposite me, between the count and a younger German. The count appeared to be about fifty-five, a suave-looking fellow with a crooked nose. We'd missed the oysters, but were just in time for the turtle soup and hock. Then came a little pastry filled with chicken and capers and what-not. The fish was a giant sturgeon that was paraded around the table for us to admire. Next was rare roast beef, served with champagne.

The food was all excellent, but the conversation wasn't quite as enjoyable as it might have been. The countess was giving most of her attention to some fellow on her other side, or to Emmie, who was having a wonderful time with the count and the other fellow. And Elizabeth seemed to be in a funk. I'd encountered her icy moods before and I can tell you that when combined with her acerbity, they could be a little daunting. But this seemed to be something a little more nuanced. When I asked her if she'd enjoyed her day, she gave me a look that combined equal parts contempt and despair. I'd call it melancholia if I thought Elizabeth were capable of that emotion.

So, with no other recourse available, I just pretended to be in on other people's conversations, nodding in their direction and making little laughs when it seemed appropriate. But the fare made up for the lack of entertainment. A salmi of pheasant came after the beef, and I think we'd moved on to Burgundy by then. Then there were some cheeses, and finally a mousse served with Tokay. I don't know if this was a typical dinner at the embassy, but if it wasn't for the collar reducing my esophagus to the circumference of a straw, I could get used to it rather easily.

When the meal was over, the countess summoned Emmie and me to her apartment. Elizabeth came up with us, but almost immediately excused herself and went off to her room.

"What's the matter with her?" Emmie asked the countess.

"It's either the curse, or she is in love. Which is a curse in itself."

"Elizabeth in love?" I said.

"What would be so odd about that, Harry?" the countess asked.

"It is difficult to imagine," Emmie agreed. "But I suppose it can happen to anyone."

"Yes, my dear," the countess said. "Look what happened to you."

Both looking my way, they shared a laugh. I try not to take these things to heart, but it seems the more good-natured you are about other people's slights, the more it looks to them as if you have a bull's-eye on your forehead.

The countess had Emmie sit at her dressing table and carefully laid out a square of black velvet before her.

"Now, my dears, you will learn something about jewelry." She went over to a wall that was made of recessed panels, then opened a half-hidden cupboard with a key. She removed a small box and set it on the table.

"These are by old Monsieur Felize," she said as she carefully set two gold earrings and a matching pendant on the velvet. They each held a teardrop pearl and a tiny green stone. The gold work itself was a delicate leaf pattern. The total amount of gold would be less than half of a ten-dollar gold coin.

"What are the stones?" Emmie asked.

"Chrysoprase."

"Are they valuable?" I asked.

"Not particularly. The freshwater pearls are of the first order, but even they aren't prohibitive. The value is derived from the workmanship." She put these away and took out a small box containing a bracelet. "This was made by the younger M. Felize, when the Japanese style was all the rage."

"Cloisonné," Emmie said.

"Yes, and look how fine the work is." While Emmie was still admiring it, she went back to the cabinet and took out another box. This held a brooch that depicted a young girl's head backed by flower petals. All surrounded by a gold stem shaped into a heart, with a diamond and pearl suspended below.

"Is she carved from ivory?" Emmie asked.

"Yes. This is by Henri Lever. You might think it a little too sweet, but it has great sentimental value to me." This she fastened to her dress. The next box contained a brooch of a peacock, with the tail feathers forming an elaborate filigreed background. They were gold, and dotted with small gems.

"This is by M. Lalique."

"It's beautiful. Is it carved?"

"Layered enamel. Look at the subtle gradations. It's exquisite."

"Has it been appraised?" I asked.

"You are such an American, Harry. You think the value of jewelry is the weight of the gems multiplied by some figure you take from a table."

"But surely there is a relation?"

"Yes, but it isn't as simple as you made it out in your little book."

"My book?"

"Yes, I read your work on burglary insurance."

"I'm flattered."

"Oh, don't be. You pointed to the Tiffany yellow diamond as the pinnacle of the jeweler's art."

"Well, in addition to being large it was expertly cut."

"Yes, and what have they now? A curiosity. What woman would wear that lump? Only the crassest."

"Of course, insurance is a crass business," I said. "Sentiment and artistic merit aren't covered unless they're backed up by an appraisal. You see, there needs to be an insurable interest."

"Insurable interest?" the countess asked.

"Yes." It was clear I'd need to explain the subject. "Suppose a fellow wants to take out a five-thousand-dollar policy on his wife...."

"Harry," Emmie interjected. "This had better not involve the death of another wife."

"Okay, it works just as well the other way. Say this fellow has a ten-thousand-dollar policy on his head. Now, suppose he's been out of work for six months, and then loses his last twenty dollars in a poolroom. The wife, having learned her tables at school, calculates that he's worth a lot more to her dead than he is alive. This is excess coverage—the value of the husband dead less the value of him alive. And we know that a wife's propensity to poison her husband is directly related to this excess coverage, plus or minus the net disagreeableness of his habits."

"How do we know that?" the countess asked.

"Oh, we have the statistics, trust me," I assured her. "And this is why the insurance company insists on restricting the coverage to the dollar amount of the loss: so the husband is never worth more dead than alive. Or the jewelry worth more after it's gone missing."

"I suppose that makes some sense," she allowed. "Is your life insured, Harry?"

"No, I figure Emmie can fend for herself, and there's no point putting temptation where it shouldn't be."

"Yes, no doubt that's wise."

"Tell me, why are you showing us these?" I asked. "To convince us you've no need for valuable jewelry?"

"To show you what type of jewelry I value."

"But you don't think I suspected you of burglarizing houses here?"

"Had the thought not crossed your mind?"

"Briefly, but it quickly went on its way."

"And you, my dear?" she asked Emmie.

"Me? No, certainly not," she lied.

"But you did come to meet me?"

"Yes," she confessed.

"To see my jewels?"

"No, but I have enjoyed it very much."

"Then why?"

"Could we discuss it tomorrow?" she asked, then glanced at me.

"I see. All right, we will discuss it tomorrow. There is something else I want to show you. It's Boucheron, like the girl's brooch you're looking for." This time she went to another panel, unlocked it, and pulled out a wide, curved box that she placed before Emmie. "Open it." Emmie did so.

"Oh, my."

It was a whole set of jewelry—the countess referred to it as a parure. It included a necklace, earrings, a bracelet, a brooch, and even a tiara. All intricately worked and covered in small diamonds. A lot of diamonds. I wasn't foolish enough to ask about the value, but even measured crassly by the pound, this set had to amount to something notable. The countess removed the necklace Emmie was wearing and put this one on her. It took a bit of doing because there were about a half dozen separate clasps. It had several bands that wrapped around the neck and tentacle-like things that reached down the bodice. Then she invited Emmie to put on the earrings, and the bracelet. Emmie was reaching for the tiara when the countess stopped her. She let Emmie admire herself for a bit longer, and then announced the show was over. While the countess was stowing the jewelry away, Emmie told us she'd like to go say good-night to Elizabeth.

"You'll find her on the third floor, with the servants." The countess then gave her more specific directions and she left us.

"Last evening, Harry, Emmie mentioned ladies-only poolrooms. Do you think they exist here?"

"I imagine they have them here, why?"

"As I told you, life here is so very dull. How would I locate such a place?"

"That's a difficult question, especially for a stranger." Then I remembered Mrs. Spinks' had a smattering of female guests. "However, I do happen to know a place, mostly men, but very first-class."

"A poolroom? I mean, one can wager there?"

"Oh, yes. And at reasonable odds."

"Will you take me to this place?"

"I'd be glad to. But there are some society types

there, senators and what-not. They may recognize you."

"Yes, but I'll recognize them as well."

"That's true. I just wouldn't want to do anything to upset the count."

"Forget the count."

"If you think it will be all right," I said, rubbing my partially healed cheek. "But don't mention it to the wife. No sense tempting the gods."

We'd just finished making arrangements when Emmie returned. While saying good-bye, she caught sight of the countess's copy of *The Wonderful Wizard of Oz*. She nudged me to make sure I saw it too.

"There's a little boy here whose father feels he's too old for it. He comes here and I read it with him. He calls me Glinda, on account of my red hair."

She gave us her leave to go and a servant escorted us out of the embassy. We walked back to the hotel.

"Odd she didn't bring up her battle with the flying monkeys over at the Easterlys'," I said.

"You see, Harry? Everyone but you knows about the Wizard of Oz."

As we went into the hotel, I glanced about. Sure enough, the same fellow was standing in the same place, clasping his hands in the same way.

10

The next morning, Emmie donned her now restored riding outfit and we went down to breakfast.

"I admire your willingness to get back in the saddle," I told her.

"It's the only sure way of meeting with the countess. At least it hasn't rained in a couple days."

"Yes, the ground will be nice and hard," I said.

"I plan on finding a friendlier horse. What will you be doing?"

"I think I'll try Richard Cole's lawyer again. Maybe he has another address."

"You don't trust the fellow from Twine Alley to make good?"

"Oh, he will if he can. But what if Cole's out of town?"

"Why aren't you searching for the jewelry? If you find that, you've proven the fraud."

"People committing fraud rarely allow insurance investigators to search their homes for the evidence."

"Yes, I suppose you're right. Well, happy hunting."

I took a car back to Patterson's office and found it once again full of supplicants. I sent my card in and was summoned a short while later. Patterson was behind the desk, looking a little less grim than the day before. Across from him was a tall man with a neat little mustache.

"This is Mr. Chappelle, Mr. Reese. He has a hearing today." We shook hands and then all sat down.

"I'm sorry to intrude on you, but I wasn't able to locate Cole at the address you gave me."

"Yes, Joseph told me. He also told me he didn't think the woman was telling the truth about the address she gave you."

"He was right about that," I said. " I thought you might know of another relative, maybe outside Washington?"

"No, he assured me I could find him at his sister's. But he was never formally charged, and isn't obligated to stay in contact. I wonder if Mr. Chappelle—I mean Julius Chappelle—might have another address. Perhaps from when Cole first came to him."

"You know my brother then, Mr. Reese?" Chappelle interjected. "I'm Sam. Julius may have mentioned me." Then he gave me a broad smile.

"No, but I believe Sergeant Lacy did." Except for being just as tall, Sam Chappelle didn't look much like his brother. He had to be at least twenty years younger, and where Julius had the look of a comfortable, well-fed businessman, Sam had the aspect of an athlete.

"Oh, yes. Sergeant Lacy and I have been acquainted for some time. A true servant of the people."

"You speak more generously of him than he did of you."

"He can afford to make enemies—he has the club. Whereas I must live by my wits."

"Is it a good living?" I asked.

He laughed, as did Patterson. "Well, not as good as my brother's perhaps, but better than Mr. Patterson's."

"I always thought lawyers did pretty well for themselves."

"Normally. But you see, Mr. Patterson is a credit to his race."

"And that doesn't pay as well?"

"No, indeed not. It may be good for the soul, but not the stomach. Am I not correct, Brother Patterson?"

"You are all too correct, Brother Chappelle."

"Of course, he might gain himself a place in the Pantheon of Negro Men of Note. But the image the sculptor strikes, if he is honest, will be one of an emaciated, exhausted soul. We all applaud the credit to his race, but no one among us—not even the negro shopkeeper—is willing to extend him the credit he needs to live. He is, alas, a poor risk."

"As our new President learned just a little while back," Patterson said.

"Mr. Roosevelt?" I asked.

"Oh, yes," Chappelle answered. "Surely you heard of Mr. Booker T. Washington's visit to the White House?"

"Yes, I read that that ruffled some feathers down south."

"Ruffled some feathers? Mr. Roosevelt lost himself a million votes. Simply because he invited the supreme credit to his race over for a modest meal. You see, Mr. Roosevelt didn't realize what a poor risk his guest was. But he'll not make the mistake a second time. And you can be sure that message is understood all up and down the line. Indeed, the market for credits to their race has soured. Brother Patterson must content himself with a periodic laudatory profile in *The Colored American*, and the intermittent gratitude of the paupers you saw waiting outside. Is it enough, Brother Patterson?"

"No, decidedly not, Brother Chappelle. But you left off the fees from bandits like yourself. It's you who keep food on my table."

"You see, Mr. Reese," Chappelle explained, "I must earn enough for my own keep, and also for that of the credit to his race. It's my sole wish that I might thereby absorb some of his divine goodness."

"Most unlikely, Brother Chappelle."

"Alas, I wish in vain." They shared another laugh. "But I've kept you from your quest for this man, Mr. Reese. Cole, was it?"

"Yes, Richard Cole. Lacy suspects him of having something to do with a burglary."

"Then that is reason enough to think him innocent."

"Yes, but there's more to it. You see, I'm fairly certain there was no burglary, just insurance fraud."

"And you represent the insurer?"

"Yes. I'm hoping Cole might know something about it. He lived in the house."

"What makes you think he would confide in you if he does?"

"Well, he's already lost his job. He has to be feeling a little wronged."

"And you think for the sake of revenge, he'll reveal the truth?"

"Yes, that and ten dollars."

"You are paying too high, Mr. Reese. But you can console yourself that you are making a contribution to Brother Patterson."

"How so?"

"You give this Cole his pieces of silver, he spends them playing policy with me, and I remit them to Brother Patterson for services rendered. But I have delayed you both. I should be going on my way. Until this afternoon, Brother Patterson. Mr. Reese."

"I should be going, too," I said.

We walked out together. "You know, there was a little more to Lacy's theory," I told him.

"And what was that?"

"I'm actually looking into three different burglaries which all occurred within a few weeks of each other. Lacy mentioned that some of the servants in each of the houses were supplied by your brother's agency."

"All from his stable," he laughed. "You can take my word, my brother is not using his minions for stealing the belongings of their employers."

"Why do you refer to them as his minions?"

"Oh, pay no attention. A poor choice of words."

"Would you rank your brother as a credit to his race?"

"No. My brother charts his own course. He is an enigma, even to me."

"But like you, he lives by his wits?"

"Yes, even more so. Julius is a shrewd man. He doesn't need to hire Mr. Patterson to keep himself out of jail. Good day, Mr. Reese."

"Good day, Mr. Chappelle."

I took his friendly advice and caught a car over to Julius Chappelle's agency. I was told he was interviewing an applicant, but it wasn't long until he was free and I was led into his office.

"I'm having some trouble locating Richard Cole," I said. "Mr. Patterson gave me an address, but Cole seems to have moved on. He thought you might have an earlier address, from when he first came to you."

He went out and came back with Cole's file and read it over. "When he came here originally, this was some years back, he was staying with a brother. But he never left an address. He simply called back until I found him a position."

"How did you check up on him without an address?"

"People with credentials don't apply for positions paying ten dollars a month. Most of those I place have come up from the South with little but the clothes on their back. If they are hired, they will have the privilege to work sixteen hours a day, seven days a week, with every other Sunday off. After a few years, when they have some credentials, they can take a better job paying fourteen dollars a month, with Sundays and every other Thursday evening off. But there they have reached the top. It isn't an attractive proposition to someone who isn't hungry. There is always more demand than supply."

"I don't suppose you put that in your newspaper advertisements," I said.

He chuckled. "No, I say as little as possible."

"Is it a good business?"

"It's profitable. But if you're looking to buy it, Mr. Reese, I'm afraid you're too late. I have a buyer."

"Moving on to something else?"

"Yes."

"Do you have Cole's brother's name there?"

"Yes, Albert. Albert Cole."

"Thank you. Speaking of brothers, I met yours a little earlier."

"Samuel? Oh, at Mr. Patterson's, no doubt."

"Yes. He's quite the philosopher."

"A very amusing conversationalist. Regrettably, the police department attracts men with little appreciation for the wag."

"When I mentioned Cole, he referred to him as one of your stable."

"Did he?"

"Yes, and he referred to your placements as your minions. What did he mean by that?"

"You'd have to ask him. Samuel is loquacious to a fault."

Once it was clear he wouldn't be revealing anything further, I went back to the hotel to meet Emmie for lunch.

"How did it go this morning?" I asked. "Did you satisfy the countess?"

"I told her why I came, if that's what you mean."

"Can I know?"

"It's not important that you know. What did you learn this morning? Did you find Richard Cole?"

"No, hopefully our friend from Twine Alley will find something."

"What will you be doing this afternoon?"

I had little enthusiasm for taking Emmie along to Mrs. Spinks', so I lied. "I thought I'd check in with Lacy."

"What on earth for?"

"To see if there have been any other developments, like that burglary the night before last. What will you be doing?"

"I'm performing a service for the countess."

"What sort of service?"

"A confidential one."

After lunch, Emmie departed and I stopped at the desk to look at their city directory. There was no Albert Cole listed.

"Harry, I forgot you were staying here." It was my old classmate, the fellow from the *Syracuse Herald*. "How about a drink? It'll be on me."

I had a half hour until I needed to meet the countess, so I went into the barroom with him. Out of the ether, two of his comrades appeared—the *Boston Globe* and the *Denver Rocky Mountain News*. We talked some about baseball and what-not, but these fellows didn't let much distract them from the work at hand. I'd been to college, so I knew something about drinking. But these boys were of a different class. In ten minutes, we'd been through about four rounds. Or rather, they had. I was still on my first. I wasn't sure what a cocktail cost at the Normandie, only that it wasn't going to be cheap. The *Herald* had called the check for himself, but I wasn't going to take chances. I kept to the side nearest the exit and was ready to make a dash for the lobby at the least provocation. I was damned if I was going to be roped into filling the bottomless hollow leg of the fourth estate.

After about the fifth round, I saw the *Rocky Mountain News* make what looked like a furtive move toward the door. I took it as my cue. Unfortunately, in leaping back from the bar I tripped over an old fellow and knocked him to the floor. I had no choice but to stop and help him up. I was sure the fellows had taken the opportunity to evaporate, but there they were, standing firm. The *Herald* even invited the old fellow to the bar.

"Make way for the congressman," the *Globe* shouted.

"I'm not a congressman."

"Harry, you decked the chairman of the House Committee on Benevolent Appropriations!" the *Rocky Mountain News* told me.

"No, I'm the new Collector of Customs for Duluth."

"A drink for the Collector of Boodle for Duluth!"

I began to relax a little. Partly from the liquor, but principally because the boys had found themselves a new sucker. Still, I didn't take any chances. When it was time, I said not a word and was out the door and on the street in five seconds flat.

11

At the embassy, I asked for the countess and then waited at the door. In no time she came down and we got into a carriage. That first evening she'd been dressed like a shop girl, and the next both her manner and her gown were decidedly formal. Today she was somewhere in between, in a fashionable dress with the little Boucheron tiara atop a mound of red hair. She was like a chameleon, but with freckles and a title.

"Emmie mentioned you sent her on an errand," I said.

"I thought that would be the best way to ensure she wouldn't know about our outing. I sent her to Baltimore. To deliver a package. Do you think there's a Holland Street in Baltimore?"

"I'm not sure, I've only been there once or twice. Why?"

"I told Emmie to deliver the package to a Frenchman living at 1524 Holland Street and await his reply."

"But you're unsure of the address? She can look the name up in the directory."

"I suppose she could, had I given her a name."

"You forgot to give her the man's name?"

"What man?"

"The Frenchman who may, or may not, live on Holland Street."

"Oh, I don't know anyone living in Baltimore. Is it a nice city?"

"I doubt many of its inhabitants would describe it

that way, but it has a certain charm—provided you like grimy industrial towns."

"And you do?"

"Well, perhaps *like* is too strong a word. But I feel a kind of nostalgic comfort when I visit them," I confided. "So Emmie's mission is a futile one. I wish I could watch."

"You two seem to be playing some sort of game all the time."

"Isn't that what marriage is all about?"

"Not my marriages."

"How many have you had?"

"Just the two. Monsieur B_____ and the count."

"Whatever became of M. B_____?"

"He died. Shortly after we were married."

"I'm sorry," I said.

"Are you really? Whatever for?"

"Just politeness. What was in the package you gave Emmie?"

"A paradox."

"That seems fitting. What form did it take?"

"I gave her strict instructions that under no circumstances should she open it."

"That was a mistake. There's some chance she'll obey your injunction on the way to Baltimore, but when she finds there's no Frenchman at 1524 Holland Street, the wrapper will be off before you can say Jack Robinson."

"Of course. That's the essence of the plan. Inside is a piece of jewelry and a note. The note is addressed to the Frenchman, no name of course, simply Monsieur. In addition to telling him that his involvement in the burglaries has gone undetected, it asks him to give the brooch to

Emmie as a reward for following my instructions."

"That's ingenious," I said. "And it sounds foolproof. When I try this sort of thing on her, it usually ricochets back at me."

"I assume she'll try to wrap it back up, but I used a colorful paper and an overabundance of glue, so there's little chance she can do that without it being obvious."

"Oh, even if it could be done, Emmie would never resort to anything so simple. She'll have an hour on the train coming back to think up an explanation. Give Emmie's fecund imagination an hour and the results are unfathomable."

"Will it be entertaining?"

"Undoubtedly, assuming you don't mind giving up the brooch."

"Oh, I genuinely meant it as a gift. Do you remember the Lalique peacock she admired so last night?"

"Yes, a very generous gift."

"Not quite that generous. It was a second, more modest Lalique. This one a cameo on a rose background. It conflicted with my hair. What is the name of our host?"

"Hostess. Mrs. Spinks. She runs some sort of influence-peddling operation and uses the race results as a lure. I meant to ask, how shall I introduce you?"

"As the Countess von Schnurrenberger. You can leave off the 'und Kesselheim'—everyone does."

"You aren't afraid of compromising your position by visiting a betting parlor?"

"I assume discretion is assured."

"Yes, of course. I would just hate for some rumor to get back to the count. If you were seen escorted by me...."

"Why do keep bringing up the count? Are you afraid of him?"

"Well, Elizabeth made it sound as if he had a bit of a temper."

"I will take care of the count."

Later, I'd learn just how true that was. But in the present, we arrived at Mrs. Spinks' and the coachman helped the countess down. It was then that I realized he was the man I'd seen outside our hotel the previous two nights—the man the countess had warned me about. I suppose she could tell from my expression that I recognized him.

"Mr. Reese, this is Thomas. Thomas, if I'm not out in ten minutes I'll remain here until five. You can come back then."

"Ja, Frau Gräfin."

"I am sorry about the subterfuge, Harry."

"You sent him to spy on me?"

"Only to make it look to you as if he were. I felt you might be a threat to me, and I wanted to give you some comparable unease. Did it work?"

"Not really. Thomas doesn't look threatening enough. Besides, since I met Emmie, a sense of unease is my constant companion."

The English butler took our things and then led us into the large room where the races were posted. He announced us to Mrs. Spinks.

"Mr. Reese, how lovely to see you again. I'm honored, Frau Gräfin. Or do you prefer 'My Ladyship'?"

"'My Lady' will do. It's kind of you to welcome me into your home, uninvited." Then she saw the blackboard and deciphered its meaning immediately. "Are we late?"

"The first race at New Orleans just finished, but there are five more, and then there's Oakland." She summoned the young woman who handed out the racing sheets. Then the countess and Mrs. Spinks conferred on the various entries. This part of the proceedings always struck me as a silly formality. Anyone with the least amount of sense knew the results were determined the evening before in some Storyville bordello. If you didn't happen to be a party to the saturnalia, you might as well resort to blind guesswork.

"Here you are again, Mr. Reese." It was Dr. Gillette, whom I'd met on my previous visit. "How are your investigations proceeding?"

"So-so."

"No breakthroughs in identifying the culprit?" He'd removed his eyeglasses and was polishing them with a handkerchief.

"Not yet, but there's a chance something will come through this evening."

"I wish you luck. I suppose that means your visits to the scenes of the crimes yielded some clues?"

"Yes, some clues. And I learned my wife is a witch." There was loud laughter off my stern. It was Easterly.

"He means my daughter. She told me about your visit. It was kind of your wife to humor her."

"I'm not altogether sure who was humoring whom. They seem to have the same taste in literature."

"Did Sesbania show you the red hair? She's convinced that's the key." He was smiling, but I had the impression there was some intent in his bringing it up.

"Red hair?" the doctor asked.

"Yes, she found it in the den."

"Could it be the thief's?" the doctor inquired.

"Oh, I'm sure it was just some visitor of my wife's."

"Does she take her visitors to the den?" the doctor asked.

"No, not generally."

The two of them were a study in contrasts. The doctor—short, and with his thin hair parted in the middle—looked as awkward as he came across in conversation. Easterly—tall, handsome, and carefully groomed—had all the poise and easy manner his appearance promised.

The countess approached us and I introduced the men. The doctor couldn't keep himself from surveying her hair, then gave me a knowing look.

"Have we met before, Mr. Easterly?" she asked. "At the Russian Embassy?"

"No, but I was in France a year ago. I think we might have crossed paths then, though we were never introduced. At the casino in Boulogne, perhaps?"

"Yes, that must be it." Then they lapsed into French and strolled away.

"You'd never guess she was a countess to look at her," the doctor said. "Isn't her accent English?"

"Shropshire."

"You know, there are rumors about her. Nonsense probably, but it did seem curious, her arriving with you."

"Oh, that's easy to explain," I said. "Her secretary and my wife were friends in school."

Of course, that didn't explain it at all and the doctor looked suitably puzzled. But I'd tired of his company and excused myself, making my way back to the billiard room. I was roundly beaten by a congressman, an admiral, and finally some fellow who'd come by to make a delivery. Just as I was readying to leave, Easterly entered the room. We played a game and made small talk about New York, his beautiful home, etc. Then I thought I'd have some fun.

"I heard there's some legislation proposed to finally regulate railroad rates," I said.

"Proposed. But completely unnecessary. And dangerous."

"Dangerous?" I asked.

"Yes. You see, people don't understand the immense investment required to build and maintain a railroad. Do you know how many moving parts there are in the average steam locomotive?"

"A good many, I imagine."

"Or the lifespan of a railroad tie?"

"Not long?"

"No, not long at all. There's always some trestle that needs to be rebuilt, or rolling stock that needs to be replaced. What the shipper doesn't appreciate is that 62% of railroad revenue goes toward investment."

"As high as that?"

He smiled. "Well, perhaps it's 26%. But the point is the same. It's not simply a matter of paying the engineer and buying some coal."

"I'm surprised you feel so strongly about the issue," I said. "But I suppose when it's a matter of principle, one has no choice but to take a stand."

He laughed. "Well, I do have a number of railroads as clients. Nonetheless...."

Thankfully, even he couldn't keep it up and it died there. It's no surprise that most men doing his kind of work come across as unctuous and devoid of character. But somehow Easterly rose above it. Or at least he could turn it off and laugh at himself. It was about then that General Sachs entered the room. Easterly asked if he'd like to join us in a game, but it was obvious the general's girth would make playing pool difficult. He seemed not to remember me, or maybe was just surprised to see me at Mrs. Spinks'. It became apparent he had something he wanted to say to Easterly. It also became apparent he wasn't going to say it in front of me, so I left them and went off to see how the countess was entertaining herself. I found her watching the race results and surrounded by admirers. Even sleepy Senator Merrill was standing in attendance. Mrs. Spinks had been left alone, but she didn't seem to mind.

"I must thank you again for bringing the countess, Mr. Reese."

"The customers enjoying her visit?"

"Customers, Mr. Reese?"

"Just a figure of speech."

"And how is your work going?"

"I'm making progress. I should have it wrapped up soon."

"Really? Not too soon, I hope."

"What do you mean, 'too soon'?"

"I just meant we'd be deprived of your company."

She almost managed to say that as if she meant it. It was then that Easterly and the general entered the room. The general wasn't looking himself. His face was flushed and he seemed a bit agitated. I've always felt that older fat men shouldn't let themselves get agitated, as they have a tendency to look ridiculous. And here was living proof. He strode toward us and Mrs. Spinks excused herself to join him. Then the three of them left the room through the door to the butler's pantry. Curious, I sauntered around to the parlor and the hallway beyond, which I knew to be an alternate route to the kitchen. From there I hoped I might creep into position to hear their conversation. But by the time I'd made it around there wasn't much of it left.

The general had become even more flustered. He

made some indistinct accusation and then clearly mentioned the name Chappelle. Mrs. Spinks answered, "How dare you!" This was punctuated with a slap. Then she said, "Get that ass out of here," the last line sounding more like Little Memphis, the burlesque showgirl, than Mrs. Spinks of Phelps Place. I hurried back the way I'd come and arrived in the racing room just as Mrs. Spinks herself appeared. In the intervening moments, she'd regained her composure and was looking as sprightly as ever. I saw no more of Easterly or the general that afternoon.

There was no reason to be surprised that the general attended Mrs. Spinks' functions, given his business as an arms merchant. And the fact that he traveled in the same social circles might provide the connection between the three burglaries. Suppose Easterly, trying to curry favor with the senator, shared with him his success at insurance fraud. Then the senator made an indiscreet comment before the general. No, that was a little hard to swallow. Still, it seemed as if it was seeing me that had discomfited the general and precipitated the conference. Did that mean Mrs. Spinks was involved? And what could the general be accusing Chappelle of? Perhaps Chappelle found out about the fraud through his minions and was blackmailing them. That didn't seem too likely, either. It might be profitable in the short term, but it would certainly be bad for his business in the longer term.

The races were just getting under way in Oakland when I took leave of the countess and Mrs. Spinks. I wanted to make sure I was back at the Normandie when, or if, my informant arrived. I entered the hotel and saw the *Herald*, *Globe*, and *Rocky Mountain News* leaving the barroom. I ducked behind a pillar. Then a rather sickening thought came to me and a brief chat with the bartender confirmed my fears: the damn hyenas had charged my room.

I went upstairs and at about 5:30 there was a knock. It was my friend from Twine Alley.

"Come in," I said. "I take it you met with success?"

"I found him all right."

Then there was an awkward pause until I handed him his ten dollars.

"Do you know Jefferson Street? In Georgetown?"

"No, but I can find it."

"Go down past the canal, the fifth house down on the right side. It's a boarding-house. Richard Cole's been staying there, with his brother."

"Albert?"

"You knew the name?"

"Not until today. Did you see Richard?"

"No, but he spent last night there and the girl expected he'd be back tonight."

I thanked him, and then he left. At about six Emmie came in. She went immediately into the bath and I joined her.

"Did you accomplish your task?"

"For the countess? Yes, of course."

"What did it involve?"

"Oh, it was simple, really. Did you learn anything today?"

"Remember that fellow we met yesterday? Whose china you annihilated?"

"The one you hired to find Richard Cole?"

"Yes. He stopped by and told me about a house in Georgetown. I thought I'd go by after dinner. Will you be accompanying me?"

"I'm exhausted. I think I'll stay here."

"Suit yourself." I went into the other room and called down to have dinner sent up to us. Then I searched the things Emmie had left behind on her way to the bath. There was no trace of the countess's package, or the brooch.

12

Emmie was just emerging from her bath when dinner arrived. She put on her kimono and sat down. The chances were slim she honestly intended to spend the evening in the room reading. And left to her own devices, there was no telling what sort of mischief she could get herself into. I needed to convince her to join me. And having been made privy to the countess's scheme, I was in just the position to do it.

"I don't suppose you could divulge the nature of the task the countess assigned you?"

"That would be indiscreet."

"Nothing involving the burglaries, I hope? Fencing jewelry, etc.?"

"No, of course not." She looked placid enough, but I thought I detected a glimmer of concern.

"Are you sure you won't accompany me to Georgetown? Cole may have something telling to tell."

"Telling to tell?"

"Well, the primitive part of my brain liked it and before the more advanced portions could take a stand, it had too much momentum for the lips to stop it."

"I hope next time they'll put up more of a struggle."

"Yes. But getting back to Cole, he may be able to reveal something interesting. Of course, that's assuming I can find the man he's staying with. I didn't get an exact address. Just that he's a Frenchman on Jefferson Street."

"A Frenchman?"

"Yes, name of... what was it... St. Julien."

"St. Julien?"

"That's what he said."

There was a pause. I could see her brain working. "Was this Frenchman in Georgetown the same man the countess thought was in Baltimore?" she was thinking to herself. The veil of fatigue lifted. I had her.

"Perhaps I should go, Harry. You might need a translator."

"Oh, I'm sure we could muddle along. The fellow has to have picked up some of the language if he's living here."

"But just in case."

"Yes, maybe you're right. Better to be prepared."

She left the table and began dressing. I savor the occasions when I can give Emmie something to puzzle over. I suppose it's their rarity that makes them prized. She deals out conundrums like they're ten cents a dozen, but mine come dearer. Unfortunately, they also tend to be a good deal briefer. The waiter had arrived to take the plates. He'd just picked up the empty wine bottle when Emmie turned for her hat. Her eyes caught the label and then she shot a look at me. St. Julien had seemed like a very reasonable French name. She wavered. She began to set her things down.

"Did I mention the canal?" I asked.

"Canal?"

"Yes, the Frenchman lives just down from the canal."

"Is there honestly a canal?"

I asked the waiter to confirm the fact.

"Oh, yes. There's a canal in Georgetown. And this time of year, it doesn't smell nearly as bad."

His words carried an authenticity that Emmie

couldn't resist. She picked up her things and we left the hotel.

Those unacquainted with the history of my association with her might well be wondering why the mere mention of a canal would be enough to persuade Emmie to join me that evening. To a person of normal sensibilities, a canal is nothing more than a sponge for endless public subsidies and a convenient place to dispose of detritus. But to Emmie, it's a nexus of diabolical intrigues. Canals had featured in several of the cases she'd been involved in, and always with a body floating in among the table scraps. That might not seem like a very romantic image, but by now you must have realized that Emmie's weltanschauung is not the weltanschauung of a healthy mind.

It was dark when we caught a Georgetown car. This one ran up the far western end of Pennsylvania Avenue, crossed a bridge, and then merged onto M Street, Georgetown's main stem. We got off at Jefferson Street and followed it south. A block along we came to a bridge that crossed over the canal. And this was the real thing—not one of those block-long industrial canals. There was an actual lock, and a little farther on, an actual canal boat. I was relieved. If we'd come up sans both canal and Frenchman, Emmie was likely to become difficult.

But while I was content with the mere existence of the canal, Emmie insisted it bore further investigation. We walked along the tow path about two or three blocks in each direction. When she was satisfied there were no floating bodies, we continued on to the house on Jefferson Street. A middle-aged colored woman answered the door and asked us in.

"I'm looking for Richard Cole," I said.

"Oh, we ain't seen him since morning."

"Is his brother Albert in?"

She called upstairs and a moment later a middle-aged fellow came ambling down. At first, Albert denied that Richard had been staying with him at all. Then when I told him I knew differently, he amended his testimony. Apparently, Richard had been warned someone was looking for him and had made other living arrangements.

"Why won't you leave him alone?" he asked.

"He has nothing to be afraid of," Emmie said.

"I just wanted to ask him some questions. Who is he avoiding? The police?"

"No, he just does what he's told. You'd better go now."

"Told by whom?"

"I don't know anything about it. You'd better go."

We did as he asked.

"I don't understand, Harry. If he hasn't done anything wrong, why is he avoiding you so assiduously?"

"He doesn't know who I am. And maybe he *has* done something wrong. Or knows who has and is afraid of him."

"The general?"

"Perhaps. But there's also Julius Chappelle, the fellow who runs the employment agency. Remember, he placed Cole at the general's home, and also a servant at Senator Merrill's, and another at the Easterlys'. Lacy suspects he might be behind the burglaries."

"But we know there weren't any burglaries."

"Yes, but Chappelle definitely has something going on. I think he makes use of these servants he's placed, though for what I can't say."

"Then maybe it was Chappelle who told him to stay away?" she asked.

"Yes, maybe."

We had once again reached the bridge over the canal. That's when we saw it. Well, him, more properly. There was a man struggling to climb out of the water below. He was in the well of the lock. The gates were open and so the water was low. There was a good eight feet of stone wall above him.

"I wonder how he was killed?" Emmie asked.

"He's definitely alive. See the splashing?"

"Perhaps the water is just sloshing the body about."

"If that's the case, it's doing it in an Irish brogue. I'll look for a rope or something."

"Were you pushed in?" Emmie yelled down to the man. "If so, by whom?"

"Hand me something, woman!"

"There's no reason to take that attitude. You need to cooperate if you want our help."

The fellow directed an epithet her way that left little doubt he was still mortal. By then I'd found a length of rope and sent it down to him. I maneuvered him to the lock gates, where there'd be something for him to hold onto. Throughout this, he and Emmie were carrying on a lively dialogue, she trying to interrogate him as to the circumstances of his spill, and he venting his spleen in the colorful manner one would expect of a fellow who lived along a waterfront. One of his final remarks really went beyond the pale and I hesitated before finally pulling him from the water. Then I noticed Emmie standing with a board raised up over her head. Whether she actually intended to dispatch the fellow, I can't say. But that was the conclusion reached by the policeman who had just arrived at the scene. He wrestled the weapon from her and asked for an explanation. I told him we had happened upon the fellow and endeavored to render assistance.

"He did, but she was going to let me drown!"

"I merely asked if you were pushed in, and if so, by whom."

"What'd that matter?" the policeman inquired.

"If he had been pushed in, and *did* drown, it would be murder. Surely, as an officer of the law, you can appreciate the need to know the culprit's name?"

And had this officer of the law been of the same variety as Sergeant Lacy, no doubt he would have concurred with Emmie's reasoning. Regrettably, he was the prosaic sort of cop who finds the sight of a woman preparing to put a drowning man to permanent rest by whacking him on the head with a plank indicative of something amiss.

By then the fellow I'd fished out of the water was turning a little blue. His bath had been a chilling one. All that had kept him from freezing was the warm glow of the drunk he'd no doubt enjoyed earlier and his enmity for Emmie. Now, both were fading. I suggested we find a fire to set him before and the officer helped me get him to a watchman's shanty at the nearby gasworks. After some hot coffee, he looked as if he just might survive. Thinking it would be best to extricate ourselves from the cozy setting before he recovered his voice, I explained to the cop that Emmie was a temperance organizer, and her enthusiasm for the cause made her prone to uncontrollable bouts of violence. That didn't elicit the response I had hoped for, so I gave him five dollars.

"What about him?" he asked, nodding at the fellow thawing.

"What about him? I fished *him* out of the canal."

"Yes, but your wife insulted him."

Emmie started to respond, but I quieted her. We were in the hands of the Hibernian brotherhood. I gave the fellow a dollar and we went out, followed closely by the watchman, who seemed to be of the opinion he deserved something for rental of the shanty. I gave him two bits.

"I don't suppose you know a Richard Cole? He was staying with his brother, Albert, at a boarding-house just down Jefferson Street, below the canal. But he disappeared this morning."

"A short man?"

"I never saw him."

"I can find him, but it has to be worth my while."

"A dollar?"

He glanced over his shoulder at the shanty with the cop inside.

"All right, five dollars. Can you find him tonight?"

"I can't leave here. Come back tomorrow. I'm on at six."

"Tomorrow evening at six. I'll see you then."

"But who do I say wants to see him?"

"The name's not important. Just tell him I'll bring him the money he's due."

We walked up to M Street and waited for a car.

"What money is due Richard Cole, Harry?"

"I'm conjecturing that if he was told to make himself scarce, he probably expects some compensation for it. Speaking of compensation, you owe me six dollars, Emmie."

"Why do I owe you six dollars?"

"For bribing the cop and paying off your victim. The shanty rental is on me."

"I can't believe you're being so petty, Harry."

A car stopped and we boarded. "I still don't understand why Richard Cole would need to hide out," Emmie said.

"Well, at first I thought the general let him be accused just to deflect suspicion. Then maybe he paid Cole to stay away to keep Lacy thinking along that line. But maybe there's something more to it than that."

"Such as?"

"What if Cole knew the general staged the burglary? And what if he told Chappelle?"

"You think Chappelle is blackmailing the general?"

"I wouldn't have guessed it of him, but then something happened this afternoon."

"What happened?"

"I was at a sort of... literary salon. Run by an associate of Easterly's. They invite the powerful to come by and be feted, flattered, and what-not, all in the service of influence peddling. I'd met Senator Merrill there, a couple days ago."

"And what happened today?"

"I saw the general in conference with Easterly, and his associate."

"So they all know each other? What was said at the conference?"

"I didn't catch much of it. But I did hear the general mention the name Chappelle, in a rather unpleasant tone. And then Mrs. Spinks slapped him."

"Who is Mrs. Spinks?"

"Easterly's associate. The hostess of the salon," I explained. "I don't know if she slapped him because of what he said, or simply to shut him up. But I think it was the former, because she then ordered Easterly to get him out of her house."

"She was annoyed?"

"Yes, decidedly."

"He did strike me as a fool, and I suppose this confirms it."

"How so?" I asked.

"If you find yourself in a murder mystery, with the readership anxiously awaiting a corpse, it's profoundly unwise to go about annoying people to the point of violence."

"Sound reasoning, Emmie. Actuarially, his life expectancy has depreciated to mere days. Of course, no one is completely safe."

"Excepting Sesbania."

"Yes, excepting her, of course."

"But if Chappelle isn't blackmailing the general, what is his connection?"

"I believe it was seeing me that first upset the general, and the conference appeared to be an outgrowth of that. So maybe the general just surmised that Chappelle told me there hadn't been a burglary."

"Did he?"

"No, but I wouldn't be surprised if he does know the truth of it. Of course, it could be the Chappelle the general mentioned wasn't Julius, the owner of the agency, but his brother Sam."

"Who's he?"

"He runs a policy operation."

"Wasn't it Lacy who told us that?"

"Yes, but Sam Chappelle himself confirmed it. And I suspect he has his fingers in other assorted ventures."

"But if there never were any burglaries, why involve a man like that?"

"I can't say. I still have to figure out how they're

connected. But at least now I'm sure they are connected."

When we'd gotten up to our room, Emmie announced she had some news.

"News about what?"

"Elizabeth. The countess was right. Elizabeth is in love."

"Did she tell you that?"

"She couldn't bring herself to use the word. But that's the gist of it."

"Are you sure it isn't a ruse?"

I'm not overly suspicious by nature, but we were talking about a woman who had seduced men simply to be able to testify as a co-respondent at the divorce proceedings brought on by their scheming wives. And who, in an earlier episode, had steered her friends toward a fraudulent bucket-shop for a percentage of the take. And while attending college had sold her classmates phony translations of the classics. More recently, she spent her summer manipulating two naïve fools into an ill-starred marriage in order to satisfy the bride's rich father, her employer. And in each case, we can rest assured that she had a good time doing it.

"Oh, I believe it's real love," Emmie said.

"And it's the unfamiliar feeling that's been making her ill?"

"No, something more typical."

"Her love is unrequited?"

"No. It's requited. But they're being forced to separate."

"His parents learned Elizabeth's habits and have forbidden the match?"

"No. He's an Englishman. By the name of Cox. He'd been assigned to their embassy here. But...."

"But now he's been sent to Siam. Bangkok."

"Yes, he left yesterday. But how on earth did you know that?"

"I played billiards with him, at Mrs. Spinks'."

"You played billiards at this literary salon?"

"Yes, in between discussing Balzac and that other fellow."

"What other fellow?"

"Oh, what does that matter? The important thing to note is that Cox is a thoroughly bad character."

"How could you come to that conclusion from discussing Balzac and playing billiards with him?"

"You can tell a lot about a fellow by playing billiards with him. In this case, it was revealed that he's a nitpicker of the most contemptible sort. We were in the midst of a friendly game when my cue just brushed up against the ball. He insisted it counted as a stroke."

"What is he like otherwise? Is he good-looking? He must be to have Elizabeth swooning."

"I suppose he's what you would call handsome, in a prim sort of way."

"Tall?"

"Yes, fairly tall."

"And a pleasing physique, I imagine."

"Yes, yes. He was in all ways attractive. Even his little mustache," I reluctantly conceded. "But nonetheless a prescriptive prig."

"He sounds not unlike Elizabeth. She enjoys playing the pedant herself."

"What a pleasant time they'll have at the breakfast table."

13

On leaving the dining room after breakfast, we found Sergeant Lacy waiting for us.

"Hello, Sergeant," Emmie said. "How delightful to see you again."

"And yourself, miss. Or is it missus?"

"I have trouble keeping track myself. He's very fickle," she said. "To what do we owe the pleasure?"

"I just came by to consult with Mr. Reese. But you're welcome to join us."

"No, I've some typing to see to. Good day, Sergeant. Until luncheon, Mr. Reese."

Lacy watched her go to the elevator.

"A most agreeable girl, Mr. Reese."

"Oh, yes. Very accommodating."

"I've heard you're looking for Richard Cole."

"Yes. He's no longer at the address his lawyer had. I don't suppose you have any ideas?"

"That lawyer assured me he would keep track of him," he said. "My own suspicions are beginning to move elsewhere. But if he has nothing to do with the crime, why is he hiding?"

"Perhaps he isn't hiding, but just having difficulty finding a place to live. After all, you did cause him to lose his job. How did you know I was looking for him?"

"The walls have ears, Mr. Reese. The walls have ears."

"And you are in communication with these walls?"

"Oh, yes. Yes, indeed. I see things even when I'm not about."

"Hear things."

"How's that?"

"These associates of yours—the walls—have ears, and through them, presumably, you hear things. Or do the walls have eyes as well?"

"You do have a way of making a muddle of things."

"I've had that complaint before. What about that burglary the other night? The newspaper said the thieves took some jewelry."

"Little things. Nothing like those you're focusing on."

"You mentioned your suspicions are moving elsewhere. Do you have a new suspect?"

"No. No one saw anything. No one knows anything. But I'll tell you what's curious."

Then he paused, waiting for my prompt. "What is curious, Sergeant?"

"You have three people: Easterly, Merrill, and Sachs. All powerful men, and all claim they were robbed of very valuable items. And not a peep."

"You were expecting peeps?"

"What I mean is, usually powerful people like that tend to become disagreeable when they feel the police aren't performing their duty. Very disagreeable."

"But this time, not a peep," I said. "You begin to interest me, Sergeant. I think we're working along the same lines."

"Then you think it's insurance fraud?" he asked.

"It's beginning to look that way, yes."

"Well then, I believe I'll have to leave the matter in your hands."

"There are no laws forbidding fraud in the District of Columbia?"

"Yes, there are, of course. But suppose I pursued that line? I go swear out warrants, search their homes, and then fail to discover anything conclusive. I'd find myself working the night shift at the penitentiary. And when I came home in the morning, Mrs. Lacy would spend the daytime hours making me miserable over the loss in pay."

"Hmmm. We wouldn't want that to happen. Of course, I don't remember Mr. Holmes ever allowing himself to be intimidated by powerful men."

"Mr. Holmes's pay wasn't dependent on a congressional appropriation."

"That's true. I don't remember any mention of congressional appropriations."

"I'll give you any help I can, but it must be soda vochey."

"Because the walls have ears...."

"Exactly. Well, good luck to you, Mr. Reese."

And he was off.

I didn't find Lacy's change of mind particularly reassuring. Somehow, I was more comfortable when we were on different tracks. But there was something to his reasoning. Did the conspirators count on the police being too intimidated to act? It would explain why they put so little effort into feigning the crimes. But why there was a conspiracy at all remained a mystery. I hoped a visit to Julius Chappelle might yield some intelligence. At his office, I was told he was in with a prospective client. The girl went back to her typing, but when she paused I took the opportunity to pose a question.

"Has Mr. Easterly been by recently?" I asked.

"Why, no." Then she got a puzzled look on her face. "Why do you ask?"

"I saw him yesterday and he mentioned Mr. Chappelle."

She nodded and went back to her typing. About ten minutes later, Chappelle showed a matronly woman out of his office.

"Please remember, Mr. Chappelle, not more than twelve dollars. And make sure the girl speaks proper English," she said. "I can't be educating field hands."

"Absolutely not, Mrs. Remington." He walked her out and came back a few seconds later. "Mr. Reese, please come in."

I did and we took our seats.

"I see what you're up against," I said.

"Mrs. Remington? She came in expecting to pay ten dollars. A minor victory."

"How are you compensated?"

"I receive the equivalent of two months' wages. But only at the successful conclusion of the first month."

"So you need to place quite a few people to make any real money?"

"Yes, but it's a comfortable living."

"Yet you're giving it up? You mentioned during my last visit that you were selling the business."

"Quite right," he confirmed. "But why this interest in my affairs, Mr. Reese?"

"I'm going to put my cards on the table, Mr. Chappelle. As I told you earlier, I've been investigating the burglaries at the homes of Easterly, Merrill, and Sachs. And you confirmed you had placed servants at all three of their homes."

"Yes, but there's nothing odd in that."

"Well, perhaps not. But there is something odd about these burglaries. Or rather, alleged burglaries."

"Why do you say 'alleged burglaries'?"

"Because I'm sure these were all fraudulent claims."

"Isn't that fairly common?"

"Very common. But what isn't at all common is finding a group of people who've each made a fraudulent claim confer about it."

"And what makes you think these three have conferred about it?"

"The supposed crimes are nearly identical, as if they were cribbed from the same source. And I've seen them speaking to one another."

"This isn't as large a town as New York, Mr. Reese. Prominent people here all know one another."

"Maybe. But I have some reason to believe their conference had some relation to the frauds."

"May I offer a conjecture?" he asked.

"Please do."

"Suppose someone like Mr. Easterly, a sharp fellow, came up with the idea first. He receives his payment and, through some indiscretion, Senator Merrill hears of it. Have you met Mrs. Easterly?"

"Yes, a nice woman."

"A lovely woman. The salt of the earth. But one finds it easy to imagine her letting something slip."

"Yes, but that would have occurred to Easterly. Why would he even tell her? And it would be easy enough to keep it from her."

"All right. Then suppose Easterly wishes to gain favor with a powerful senator. That's his business, after all. He lets him in on it for purely venal reasons."

"That sounds a lot more likely. And then?"

"Then? Well, somehow Sachs hears of it. Maybe Merrill and he socialize together."

"Oh, they do. Easterly as well."

"Then that explains it."

"I came up with a similar explanation. But the more I think about it, the more absurd it strikes me. Easterly's plenty venal, but he isn't an idiot. And what motivation would the senator have to reveal a secret like that? No, I think there's something more to it," I said. "It's interesting you came up with the proper order that the claims were submitted."

"Mere conjecture."

"Did I mention where I saw these men socializing?"

"No, I don't believe so."

"At Mrs. Spinks' salon. You recognize the name?"

"Oh, yes. I know of Mrs. Spinks' salon."

"Have you placed people in her household?"

"I have, yes."

"Well, perhaps you can explain why Mrs. Spinks took it upon herself to slap the general's face when he mentioned your name?"

"No, I'm afraid I can't." He tried to suppress a chuckle, but failed. "You saw this? Where?"

"At her house. But I didn't exactly see it. They were having a private conference. With Easterly."

"What fools." He shook his head and looked over his shoes. Then he rose to his feet. "Well, Mr. Reese. I have some business to attend to. Perhaps another time?"

"Yes. Another time."

In getting up, I knocked a hat off a stand. I reached down and picked it up. It was a sort of helmet, made out of gold brocade.

"A present for a child," he told me.

I walked back to the hotel. Chappelle obviously knew what was going on, but I didn't see much chance of persuading him to share that knowledge with me. His comment about Mrs. Easterly had given me an idea. Maybe *she* was the weak link. Given the right prompting, she might inadvertently provide the clue I needed. I telephoned the house, but was told she would be out all morning.

Of course that left Sesbania—unguarded. I stopped by a bookstore in order to purchase the proper guidebook for an excursion to the Land of Oz, and during the long car ride acquainted myself with the strange habits of the various peoples of the Wizard's domain. They weren't much stranger than what I'd encountered in the Eastern District of Brooklyn. But at least in New York the apes were earthbound, and the trees relatively docile.

The Easterlys' governess wasn't prepared to allow me to see the girl. But while I was wheedling her, Sesbania overheard us and intervened. Appreciating that she'd been outmaneuvered by a superior force, the governess—apparently a student of Clausewitz—ceded the field.

"Hello, Harry."

"Hello, Sesbania. I come as messenger from the Witch of the North."

"Why didn't she come herself?"

"Oh, she has other business to attend to," I said. This didn't seem to satisfy her, so I added some detail. "The Munchkins have gone on strike."

"What does that mean?"

"Well, they refuse to go back to work until... until improvements have been made in their working conditions."

"Munchkins don't work."

"Don't they?" Little parasites. "Well, that's just it.

Their lives lack structure. And they resent the paternalistic nature of the system."

"What on earth does that mean?"

"I'm not altogether sure. I'm just repeating what I was told. The point is, the Witch of the North needed to attend to matters Munchkin this morning."

"Oh." She still wasn't completely satisfied, but I'd worn her down. "What was her message?"

"Her message?" She was going to want something good and my brain wasn't cooperating.

"You forgot, you silly Winkie!" She offered me some help. "Was it about the red hair?"

"Yes, that's it, the red hair. That's it precisely." Inspiration struck. "She's made contact with Glinda, the Witch of the South."

"*Really?*"

It's rare I manage to excite a female in this way and I relished the moment. Granted, this one was just six years old. But one has to take one's conquests as they come.

"Oh, yes," I confirmed. "I met her myself. Charming lady."

"Did you meet the Quadlings?"

"Yes, I met them, too. German speakers."

"Will I be able to meet Glinda?"

"Oh, yes. But first we need to solve the riddle."

"What riddle?"

"Who took your mother's jewelry."

"The winged monkeys! I told you."

"Glinda suggests that's not the case. And as you know, she was here."

"Because I have her hair."

"Exactly. And she has generously said you may keep

that. But she wonders if you know a lady named Mrs. Spinks?"

"Oh, yes. She comes to see us often."

"Does she bring any friends when she does?"

"Sometimes."

"Do you remember their names?"

"Well, last time there was a general. And a French man, whose name I don't remember."

"Did you hear what they were talking about?"

"No, it sounded very boring. But I do remember the place."

"The place?"

"Yes, Kalorama. Father said it's like Oz, only nearer. Do you know it?"

"No. But what did they say about this Kalorama?"

"I *don't* know! I told you it was very boring."

"Yes, you did," I said. "Was Mr. Chappelle there?"

"No, not that day."

"But you do know him?"

"Of course I know him! He's the lion."

"The Cowardly Lion?"

"Only he's not really cowardly."

"No, a malignant rumor. How about the Scarecrow?"

"Mr. Grieber, of course."

"Who is Mr. Grieber?"

"The postman. And Mr. Clapp is the Tin Woodman. He delivers the milk."

"Of course. It slipped my mind for a moment. Well, thank you for the help, Sesbania. But we should keep our meeting a secret."

"Why?"

"Well, Glinda would prefer it."

"When will I meet her?"

"Soon. Very soon."

"Don't forget."

"Oh, no. I won't forget."

Then she went off to torment the governess and I returned to the hotel. At the desk I was given a hand-delivered letter from the countess. She informed me that I would be escorting her to Mrs. Spinks' again that afternoon. Then I went up to the room, where I found Emmie attending to her toilette. Elizabeth was there as well, slouched down in a chair, one finger playing lazily with a blonde tress that had slipped out of place. And evidently she was in an amiable mood.

"Hello, Harry," she said.

That might not sound particularly friendly, but with Elizabeth, that was as good as you are likely to get. And when it wasn't immediately followed by some sarcastic morsel of mockery, I thought perhaps she was doing impersonations.

"Hello, Elizabeth. Feeling better?"

"Yes, thank you."

I was certain that if I raised the subject of her love life, the good mood would evaporate. So I kept to other matters.

"Do you have any idea where Kalorama is?"

"No. It's Greek, you know."

"It had that ring to it, that's why I thought I'd consult you."

"For God's sake, don't jolly me, Harry."

"I'm serious."

"It's rather simple. *Kalos* is beautiful. *Horama* is sight. A place offering a beautiful sight. Emmie could have told you that."

"Oh, Harry knows *kalos*. He wrote me a poem using 'callipygian.'"

"Harry writes poetry?"

"One poem," I clarified. Embarrassing moments were always a little more embarrassing when shared with Elizabeth.

"What did you rhyme with 'callipygian'? The only thing that comes to mind is 'pigeon.'"

"The penultimate line concluded with 'callipygian lass,'" Emmie told her. "You can guess the end."

"Oh, very well done, Harry."

"Thank you, Elizabeth. That's high praise."

"Well, don't get a swelled head over it. Where is this Kalorama supposed to be located?"

"I'm not altogether sure, but I suspect somewhere near here."

"Maybe a resort of some type," Emmie offered. "Does this have something to do with the case?"

"I believe it might. But all I have is the word, and that it was something discussed by Mrs. Spinks, Easterly, the general, and some other fellows. It could be there's no connection at all."

"What will you be doing this afternoon?" Emmie asked.

"Oh, this and that. Has the countess given you another task?"

"No. She gave us tickets for a matinee: *Mistress Nell*."

"What task did the countess give you, Emmie?" Elizabeth asked.

"Harry's making a jest of some sort."

It always struck me as odd that their friendship seemed to involve such large doses of deceit and the sort of manipulative behavior one doesn't usually expect of one's friends.

Emmie had risen and was standing near the bed, looking down. When I entered the room, I had tried to hide my reading material by covering it with my coat. But one corner stuck out. And that was enough to trigger Emmie's recognition. She pulled out *The Wonderful Wizard of Oz*, and of course Elizabeth had to come over and see what had intrigued her.

"You went to see Sesbania without me," Emmie cried.

"I needed to move forward. Besides, you were occupied with suppressing a revolt among the Munchkins. I hope you weren't too brutal about it."

"What did you tell her?"

"I more or less promised her an audience with Glinda. Just how game do you think the countess is?"

"What are you two talking about?" Elizabeth asked.

"If I were to stop and explain, we'd miss the show."

14

While Emmie and Elizabeth rushed off to their matinee, I made my way back to the embassy to pick up the countess. We boarded the carriage and I could tell at once she was perturbed by something.

"Did you collude with your wife last night, Harry?"

"If that's another euphemism, I'm not familiar with it."

"I mean, did you reveal to her what I told you yesterday?"

"About the trip to Baltimore? No, certainly not. I made an allusion to a Frenchman, but only in aid of confusing our common antagonist."

"Apparently it didn't work. Then she never mentioned her outing?"

"No, but it was pretty unlikely she would."

"Or the brooch?"

"No, not the brooch either. She didn't return the package?"

"The damn girl beat me, Harry."

"I know the feeling. What did she tell you?"

"She came by this morning and thanked me for the brooch. I said, 'Did you meet the Frenchman?' 'Oh, yes, I found him,' she said. 'But you had the street name wrong—he lives on Hollins Street.'"

"Did the imaginary Frenchman send a reply?"

"Yes, that was all too easy. Miss Slyboots told me he said, 'Tell Madame, merci.' That was all."

"You have my sympathy, but I warned you. I think

your big mistake was to give her too much time to think about it."

"Well, I won't make that mistake a second time."

"Going for a return bout?"

"Most assuredly," she said. "By the way, remember that Boucheron brooch I mentioned?"

"The fake?"

"Yes. I saw the girl last evening and she was wearing it again. I made a point of getting her name this time. Sachs. Alice Sachs."

"That's the one. I suppose they could have had the fake made as a replacement."

"Oh, this was no fake. I admired it closely."

"Are you sure?" She gave me a withering look in lieu of a reply. After a suitable amount of withering, I tried again. "So the same girl who wore the replica previously was wearing the real brooch last night. Was her father there?"

"I don't remember seeing him. She came with a younger man. I believe I saw him at Mrs. Spinks' yesterday, but I don't remember his name."

"That sure was brazen of her. The alleged theft was in all the newspapers."

"Alleged theft—it was fraud then?"

"Yes, there seems little question. Both that one and the other two I'm investigating. And they're all linked somehow. And somehow Mrs. Spinks is connected as well."

"Really?"

"Are you surprised?"

"Not shocked, I suppose. But I wouldn't have thought she was involved in something so sordid."

"Oh, I doubt she's mixed up in the fraud. I think the

insurance claims were made to raise cash to finance a deal of some sort. She might be another party to that deal. By the way, does Kalorama mean anything to you?"

"It was an estate of some sort. If you go up Massachusetts Avenue, a little past Dupont Circle, you come to another circle, but with only a few houses on it. Just beyond that was some sort of estate called Kalorama."

"How do you know about it?"

"The count pointed it out to me. It's where we go riding. Emmie can show you."

"She didn't know the name. Neither did Elizabeth."

"There's nothing there really to see now."

As we left the carriage I stopped her.

"There's something else I should mention. Do you remember meeting Easterly yesterday?"

"Yes, I do."

"His little girl is expecting a visit from Glinda."

"Is she?"

"Yes. I just thought I'd mention it in case you run into her. She found a red hair and she's convinced it belongs to Glinda."

"I hadn't intended to make a career of the role."

"No, of course not. I just thought you might run into her on some occasion or other."

Inside, there were already a fair number of guests milling about. I didn't see anyone I knew except Mrs. Spinks, who was her usual graceful self. My presence might have worried the general the day before, but it wasn't enough to throw her off her game. While she was explaining the rules of the house to some newcomer, the countess pulled me aside.

"Let's see what's upstairs, Harry."

"Upstairs?"

"Yes, come along."

I couldn't fathom what she had in mind. The first stop was a large bedroom, with hulking, carved mahogany furniture and a matching mantel over the fireplace. The wallpaper featured little cherubs running about a dark maroon landscape with the odd columned ruin here and there. The ceiling held a tasteful depiction of a bacchanal—even the satyr was well-mannered—surrounded by a gold cornice of intricately molded plaster. But the finishing touch was the china basin at the side of the bed. It took me a moment to figure out what purpose it served, as it displayed workmanship rarely found in a spittoon.

"What an odd room," the countess said.

"I've seen this sort of thing before. Gilded Age Baroque. This is more restrained than some I've encountered."

I noticed she was jotting notes on a piece of paper.

"Decorating ideas for the embassy?" I asked.

She laughed. "Can you imagine? No, this is for my own purposes."

We went to a second bedroom, which was the opposite of the first. Much smaller, but bright and cheery, with a simple four-poster bed. It could have been in the house of a prosperous farmer.

"What do you think of Mrs. Spinks' establishment, Harry?"

"Well, I could imagine getting used to any one room, but moving about the place is a little disorienting. It's like living in someone else's opium dream."

"Do you partake of opium, Harry?"

"No, I was speaking broadly."

"Perhaps you should try it," she suggested. "But I

wasn't addressing the house. I meant her business."

"You realize the gambling isn't where she makes her money?"

"Oh, yes. She explained the outline of her enterprise yesterday."

"That was very forthcoming of her."

"We had a long chat after you left. But it all seems so uncertain. I just can't imagine this type of operation back home."

"Of course, in England, the poor man can't vote."

"I don't see what that has to do with it."

"It just makes things much simpler. You see, in this country, we give the poor man his vote. But the rich and powerful aren't any fonder of the idea than they are back in England. So now they have to go to the bother of taking it away from him again. Of course, they have to be clever about it. They let the poor man have a say in who gets sent to Washington, but then corrupt the fellow the moment he gets off the train. A good number come pre-corrupted. I suppose you could end corruption tomorrow if you just took the vote away from everyone but the rich. But that would put a lot of people out of work."

"Such as Mrs. Spinks?"

"Yes, but I wouldn't be concerned about that. An American's right to vote for the rich man's lackey of his choice is sacrosanct. There will be Mrs. Spinkses in Washington long after we're dead and buried."

"That's reassuring."

"Is it? Not the word I would use. But I suppose a country is nothing without its traditions."

It was at that moment that Mrs. Spinks came upon us. Rather than being offended at the invasion of her privacy, she seemed to welcome it, leading us into her own bedchamber. The furnishings here weren't what you would call tasteful, but they were at least less jarring than some other parts of the house. She began describing everything in detail and the countess would now and then make a note or two. I excused myself and wandered about on my own. I came to a study and was looking about in a vague sort of way when I heard Mrs. Spinks at the door.

"Can I help you find something, Mr. Reese?"

"No, just admiring the desk here. Walnut, isn't it?"

"English walnut, the butler says. But let's go down and enjoy the afternoon's entertainment."

As we descended, I posed a question.

"There's something I wanted to ask you. What do you know about Kalorama?"

"Kalorama? It was the home of some rich man. Built almost a century ago. It was a very large piece of property. I believe this whole area is carved from it. But that was years back. The house burned down long ago. Why do you ask?"

"Oh, no reason."

I was hoping to give her a jolt, but either I was too obvious about it or she just wasn't easily jolted. We went into the large room where the races were listed and I was handed my card. I put five dollars on The Giver at twelve to one. I could never bring myself to bet on the favorite. But The Giver wasn't in a giving mood that day and I quickly lost interest in the horses. Dr. Gillette arrived and I cut a path to him.

"How are things going, Mr. Reese?"

"I've located one of the more valuable items."

"You have?" He contorted his face into something I suspect was meant to be a smile, but it would be charitable to call it that. It was the sort of smile you might come up with when a visiting relative suggests extending her visit.

"Well, I believe I have. Have you had any trouble with burglars? Seems to be an epidemic here."

"Fortunately, no," he said. "Not that I have anything particularly valuable. And no jewelry—I'm a bachelor."

"I've known a few bachelors with some pretty fancy jewelry."

"Not my taste."

I was about to spring Kalorama on him when he excused himself rather clumsily and went off to another room. It was clear I wouldn't be learning anything further at Mrs. Spinks' that afternoon. Another avenue of pursuit was in order and I had something in mind. I went off to take leave of the countess and our hostess and found them both in the entrance hall, discussing the brass work. After I said good-bye to Mrs. Spinks, the countess announced she would accompany me out as she was in need of some air. When I closed the door behind us, she turned to me.

"I neglected to tell you earlier, Harry. I found out what Emmie's purpose was in coming here."

"Did she tell you?"

"Yes."

"I suppose there's a chance she isn't misleading you. What did she say?"

"She wishes to write my biography."

"Well, that does have the ring of truth to it. She aspires to be a writer."

"What has she written?"

"Not a lot. She's easily distracted."

"Yes, I thought as much. Good."

I had the distinct feeling that whatever the countess felt was good about it wouldn't be my idea of good. But she refused to elaborate. She was already at the door when she called after me.

"Oh, there's something else I forgot to mention. Plan on coming to the embassy tomorrow evening. You and Emmie both. There's a fancy-dress ball. I'll send some costumes around to the hotel for you."

"Sounds entertaining," I said. "Might I ask why you're taking such a keen interest in Mrs. Spinks' furnishings?"

"Just a lark. Probably nothing will come of it."

Then I went off to see Julius Chappelle. The erstwhile Cowardly Lion was in, but the girl returned with the news that he was unavailable.

"Tell him if he won't see me, I'll send in the winged monkeys."

She stared at me for a moment, but then delivered my message. Presently, I was led in and Chappelle greeted me with a big smile.

"The truth has been revealed," he said. "Was it the golden cap?"

"I only learned of its meaning after consulting the sacred text. So you're a friend of the Easterly family?"

"It's a diverting household."

"Yes, decidedly. But how did you become acquainted?"

"I could tell you it was purely through my business. I supplied their cook."

"You could tell me that, but I wouldn't be very likely to believe it."

"No, I imagine it's too late for that," he agreed. "If I do confide in you, and you agree it has nothing to do with the matter that is your primary concern, can I depend on your discretion?"

"Discretion is an essential part of my business."

"Yes, of course," he said. "I assume by now you have a pretty clear understanding of the nature of Easterly's business?"

"He told me himself. Much the same as Mrs. Spinks', I gather."

"Yes, exactly. And, much the same as many others' here."

"Including yourself?"

"Yes, including myself."

"Are the three of you partners?"

"Nothing so formal. But our businesses complement one another."

"What exactly is your business?"

"Mostly, just as it seems. I place domestic help."

"And the rest of it? You have your people spy on the people they serve?"

"I don't need to encourage anyone to spy. That's a servant's prerogative, and one of their few entertainments. But I do suggest things they might pay particular attention to. Say, conversations on amendments to the tariff schedules."

"And these people, fresh up from the fields as you said, are capable of comprehending tariff schedules?"

"Perhaps not. But don't underestimate the capabilities of someone from the fields. They are masters of deception, by necessity. And most are literate, or partly so. After a few years, they begin to pick things up."

"Was Richard Cole in this group?"

"Yes, he was."

"Is that why he lost his job? He was found out?"

"Perhaps. I had thought it was simply the result of Lacy casting doubt on him. He became a convenient scapegoat. But from what you related this morning, about General Sachs mentioning my name, I feel it may be he found out Cole was looking over his shoulder."

"But why is he so hard to locate?"

"Frankly, I don't know."

"You honestly have no idea where he is?"

"No, I honestly don't. But that doesn't mean I'm willing to help you find him."

"I'd be surprised if you were. What can you tell me about Kalorama?"

"I'm not a party to that."

"But Easterly and Mrs. Spinks are."

"You need to discuss that with them. I give you my word, I have nothing to do with it. Or with any burglaries, or alleged burglaries."

"How can I be sure that's true?"

"You can't be sure. But you have my word."

I made to leave, but before he opened the door I stopped him.

"Whatever your relationship with the others, I assume you have their ears."

"Is there a message?"

"Just that I won't be leaving town until I get to the bottom of this."

"And if the claims are withdrawn, and the money returned? Will that satisfy you?"

"It might satisfy the insurers. But it would leave me out in the cold, unless I can explain how I brought about the withdrawal of the claims. And to do that, I'll need to expose the fraud."

"I see. What is needed is a resolution that will satisfy

all parties. I'll deliver your message and advise that they avail themselves of your offer to negotiate."

We shook hands and I left him. I hadn't realized I'd offered to negotiate, but I couldn't see any harm in it.

15

Emmie was in the room reading when I arrived back at the hotel.

"How did you find *Mistress Nell*?" I asked.

"Oh, fine. But for a play about a courtesan it left too much to the imagination."

"You found your imagination wanting?"

"Hardly that. Have you learned anything about Kalorama?"

"Kalorama is, or was, a large estate. To the northwest of Dupont Circle."

"That's where we went riding."

"The countess mentioned that. She said there isn't much to see of the estate now."

"But what does it have to do with the insurance claims?"

"I think these men were trying to raise money in order to speculate on real estate in the area of this Kalorama."

"Have you confronted them?"

"Not directly. I don't really have anything to confront them with. I need to get some specifics, dates and lot numbers. Once I can show a chain of events, I think they'll become agreeable about withdrawing the claims."

"And you can get your ten percent?"

"Yes, I hope so."

"If you can get all three to return the money, it would be more than $2,000, wouldn't it?"

"Yes, but let's not go spending it yet. To get them to

cooperate, I'll need to make sure the insurers go along with it too."

"They always seem to."

"Yes, but they aren't going to like the idea of people forming syndicates to defraud them. These fellows were using them as banks, and being pretty obvious about it. They might want to make an example of someone."

"Do we have time to eat supper here?"

"Why not?"

"The man in Georgetown said six o'clock."

"He said he'd be there from six o'clock. There's no reason to appear too eager. Does this mean you're coming with me?"

"I'm certainly not going to wait here."

"All right, but tonight we steer clear of the canal."

"That was hardly my fault."

"If you hadn't been there, the evening would have been decidedly more tranquil."

"You wouldn't even have noticed that man in the canal. He would have drowned."

"I wouldn't have known he existed, and been the better for it. These things happen, Emmie. Every night of the year a certain number of drunks are going to stumble into a certain number of canals. It's been happening since the flood. Besides, if that cop hadn't arrived, you would have bludgeoned him to death anyway."

"I only wanted to put the fear of God into him."

"Well, let's not save any souls this evening."

"All right, Harry. You made your point. There's nothing gained by harping on it," she said. "Of course, if we hadn't encountered the drunk in the canal, we wouldn't have met the watchman who is going to find us Richard Cole."

"The watchman who *might* find us Richard Cole. I'm beginning to wonder if Richard Cole exists at all."

When we went down to dinner, I asked Emmie about Elizabeth's change of mood.

"She says she's making plans, but was unwilling to reveal anything further."

"Plans to follow this Cox fellow to Bangkok?"

"I thought about that, but I can't see how even Elizabeth could arrange that."

"Koestler must have given her a tidy sum for marrying off his daughter."

"She spent most of that in France. Elizabeth enjoys shopping," she said. "No, I don't think she has fortune enough to travel halfway across the world and set up a household in a strange land."

"I suppose it's possible it has nothing to do with Cox."

"Very possible. But whatever it is, it involves leaving Washington."

"She's not happy with the arrangements at the German Embassy?"

"No. She was given a tiny cell in the garret. And the countess so mistrusts her she confides nothing."

"She was expecting to be taken into her confidence?"

"Oh, yes. She wanted to write her biography."

"Honestly? I heard that was your plan."

"Apparently we were thinking along similar lines. But how did you know? Have you been seeing the countess?"

"Well, our paths crossed this afternoon."

"Did they?"

"Yes. At Mrs. Spinks' literary salon."

"What was the topic of conversation today?"

"Tolstoy."

"What are your thoughts on Tolstoy, Harry?"

"No complaints. Did I mention that the countess invited us to the embassy tomorrow evening? To a fancy-dress ball."

"I wonder why she didn't mention it to me?"

"Can't say. She's sending costumes. And she told me something else."

"What was that?"

"She was being a little cryptic, but she seemed to imply that you had gotten the better of her in some way. Any idea what she meant?"

"Not the slightest. Is that all there was to it?"

"I believe she may be cooking up some sort of rematch."

"What does that mean?"

"It means you had better be on your toes, Emmie."

"Oh, I'm always on my toes. And you had better heed your own advice, Harry."

"Why do you say that?"

"You told that man last evening that you had money to give to Richard Cole. Now we're going to a rendezvous with a man neither of us have met in a city we don't know, and it's been arranged by a man we have no reason to trust. A man who thinks we have some sum of money to dispense and has had a full day to arrange something untoward."

"You paint a grim picture, Emmie."

"Yes, I've even frightened myself. Still, it's better than spending the evening in a hotel room."

We arrived at the watchman's shed just after seven. It was a warmish winter evening and misting.

"There you are." He leaned out the door and whistled.

"Yes, here we are. Did you find him?"

"I found him. But he wasn't sure he wanted to meet you."

Just then a colored boy of about ten showed up.

"The boy will take you to Cole."

"All right. Is he nearby?"

"Not before I get the five dollars."

"Why should I pay until I see Cole?"

"How do I know you'd come back to pay me?"

I paid him the five dollars and the boy led us a couple blocks west to a car stop. We got in a car going north to Tenallytown and within a mile the landscape became almost rural. A little while after that, we got off and he led us to the west a block or two. Then we wove back and forth through a dimly lit neighborhood, skirting the university, and finally arrived at a long set of steep stairs. We followed him down these to M Street. By my reckoning, we were about four blocks from where we caught the car a half hour before. There was a car barn nearby, and quite a few saloons. He picked the meanest-looking one, which bore no sign at all, and led us inside.

I'd taken Emmie in some rough barrooms before—a wharf-side tavern in Newport, a Canal Street concert saloon in Buffalo, and a couple Raines Law hotels in Williamsburg—so we had some idea what to expect. Still, it's always a little disconcerting when you enter a room and the conversations all end abruptly. Particularly when you're as over-dressed for the occasion as we were. It was a shadowy place, with only a couple gas jets providing illumination—a wise choice on the part of the management, since what could be seen of the room didn't invite further inspection. There were a few other women there, but I deduced from their comments that they weren't feeling very comradely toward Emmie. The crowd numbered less than a dozen, so I took the easy way of defusing the situation. I stood a round for the house. From then on, the gibes aimed our way were whispered. In the meantime, the boy had left us. I was beginning to feel the fool when several minutes later a colored fellow of about thirty-five came in and approached me.

"Are you the man looking for Richard Cole?"

"Yes."

"I'm Cole."

We took a little booth that was curtained off from the rest of the room.

"My name's Reese," I told him. "I'm looking into some burglaries. Including the one at General Sachs' home."

He smiled, but just nodded. "Did you bring my money?"

"Yes, how much are you owed?"

"Oh, quite a lot, I'd say."

"By whom? I mean, are we talking about the same transaction?"

"What transaction are you talking about?"

"Well, of course you were told you'd be taken care of."

"No, no one ever promised me that."

"But didn't you come here expecting that someone was delivering money owed to you?"

"Owed to me by who?"

"Let me put it this way, you feel you are owed something. Is that correct?"

"Most definitely. Don't you? And the lady?"

"He's right, Harry."

"He's right about what?"

"Well, don't we all feel there are debts owed us that will never be repaid?"

"Are we having a philosophical discussion here?" I addressed this to the two of them, but neither answered.

"Mr. Cole," Emmie said. "My husband was trying to be clever. He suspects that there was no burglary at the Sachses' home. That a claim was made on an insurance policy simply to raise money for some other purpose. Perhaps to invest in real estate."

"What business is it of his?"

"If the money is returned to the insurance company, he will receive a fee."

"Why did he tell the man he had money for me?"

"He thought perhaps you'd been offered money to make yourself inaccessible, and by pretending to be delivering the money, he could induce you to meet with him."

"If no one had promised you money, why did you come this evening?" I asked.

"What did it matter if *I* thought someone owed me money? What mattered was what *you* thought. You see, if *you* thought you owed me money, I was willing to take your word for it."

"So no one offered you money in exchange for staying out of sight?"

"No, but I was told to look out. That that police sergeant was looking to blame me."

"Do you think there was a burglary?" Emmie asked.

"If there was, they sure were quiet about it. But what's it matter to me?"

"If you could have your job back at the Sachses', would you want it?" I asked.

"Of course I would. I've been doing drudge work."

"Suppose I make a deal with them. They give back the money to the insurance company and give you your job back."

"If?"

"If I can prove there was no burglary."

"If I help you, they ain't likely to give me my job back."

"They don't need to know. I'll have plenty besides anything you tell me."

"All right," he agreed. "The old man was talking to some people about buying land."

"Did Kalorama come up?" I asked.

"Yes, it was up that way."

"Do you know what piece of land exactly?"

"No. But I heard Mr. Easterly... you know him?"

"Yes, what did he say?"

"He wanted to buy some land but needed more money. So he asked if the general would like to come in with him. He said he would. In that case, Mr. Easterly said, the general would need to raise $10,000."

"That's a lot of money," I said.

"Yes, more than the general had."

"Did he tell Easterly that?"

"No, but I knew it."

"What else did Easterly say? Did he mention why they were buying the land?"

"Not while I was there. The only thing else I heard was something about a widow's mite, like in the Bible," Cole said.

"The parable?" Emmie asked.

"That's right. The rich man gave a purse of gold to the poor, but the widow gave all she had."

"And do you know if they bought the land?"

"No, it was just that one evening I heard them talk about it."

"When was that?"

"Five, six weeks before I had to go."

"Who told you to go?" I asked.

"The general. He said he knew I didn't do nothing wrong, but I should leave just the same. He said that policeman would make it seem like I did it. He was right about that, they even had me in a cell for a night. The general said to wait a few weeks, then I could come back. But when I did, he said they didn't need me no more."

"The general told you that?"

"Yes. You think you can make him change his mind?"

"People have a way of becoming agreeable when they've been caught at something," I told him.

It was then that I saw a rat run up the wall just behind Emmie. I checked my impulse to shout a warning. I'm not altogether sure what her reaction would have been, but mine would have involved hysterical panic. She noticed my troubled look and gave me one back. I touched my head, which she interpreted as I hoped, adjusting her hat. Then I turned back to our guest.

"Do you think Chappelle had anything to do with buying the land?" I asked.

"No reason to think so, but he don't confide in me."

"He told me about how you helped him."

"Did he? Then you don't need to ask me about it."

"No," I agreed. "Seems like a smart man, Chappelle."

"Sharp as a steel trap and sly as the fox what keeps out of it."

"Should I believe what he tells me?"

"He never lied to me, but then he couldn't have gained by it if he did."

He asked the time and then said he needed to go. We said good-bye and headed back to the hotel.

"What would the widow's mite have to do with buying property?" Emmie asked.

"I don't think it's a biblical reference. It's also a term used in common law. Say an old fellow with a big estate dies. His wife was a bit of a Xanthippe, but he had a very amiable horse. So, in his will he leaves everything to the horse."

"So the widow in this tale winds up with nothing? Sounds like less than a mite."

"Well, that was the old fellow's intent, but it seems the other burghers weren't too keen on having Xanthippe move into the poorhouse and live at their expense. So they came up with the legal doctrine that a wife can't be disinherited completely. She can elect to have her share no matter what the will says. So the horse has to split it with her. Luckily, his needs are modest, so he doesn't mind. Now, if the old heathen had a very large estate, the widow's mite might not be particularly mite-like."

"The widow's mite might not be particularly mite-like? Were you saving that up?"

"No, it just came to me. But it makes the point nicely."

"I see. And how do you expect to persuade the general to hire Richard Cole back? As soon as you bring up the subject, it will be obvious he helped you in some way."

"That's something I'll have to figure out later. After I've proof of the fraud."

"Sounds distinctly like blackmail."

"Does it?"

16

The next morning, Saturday, I went down to the lobby to buy a newspaper. The desk clerk called me over and gave me a hand-delivered note from Alice Sachs. She asked if I would stop by that morning as she had something to show me. When Emmie came down, I omitted any mention of Miss Sachs' missive. I wasn't keen on bringing her along. What charms the young denizen of a mythical kingdom has quite the opposite effect on the comfortably ensconced snob. When she asked what I'd be doing that morning, I told her I would be taking a walk up to the area the countess had described as the fabled Kalorama.

"How will you find it, Harry?"

"She gave me the general direction. I think I can find my way."

"What do you hope to see?"

"Well, maybe why it's valuable enough to be worth all the risks."

"Are you wearing scent, Harry?"

"Scent? No, of course not." She was smelling Miss Sachs' stationery. "Must be someone else."

"I suppose it must be." She sniffed the air like a cat, but then turned back to me. "I should go with you. So you don't get lost."

"It's raining out, Emmie."

"I'll wear my riding outfit."

And she did, complete with the little bowler. We caught a Connecticut Avenue car and as soon as we boarded a fellow stopped her and asked in mock-solicitude if she had misplaced her horse. There were chuckles all around. Even Emmie smiled. At Dupont Circle we got off and walked up Massachusetts Avenue to the second traffic circle. There wasn't any traffic, but there were some men doing street work who paused as we passed.

"E'scuse me, lady," one fellow said. "D'you know you lost your horse?"

His workmates laughed approvingly, but this time Emmie didn't smile. Her expression was similar to that of a dog just before he gets to the teeth-baring stage. And she was making that same sort of proto-growl. I feared a repeat of the episode with the fellow at the canal, but the foreman told his men to get back to work and we continued on our way.

From that point on, the streets were mostly unpaved, some not even graded. The houses, though few and far between, reminded me of what you'd see up Riverside Drive in New York. We circled north and east, heading uphill and through the old orchard I'd seen from Mrs. Spinks' place. Then we headed straight west until we came back to Massachusetts Avenue. There were no houses on this stretch and just below us was woods. Emmie pointed out a bridle path and we followed it down until we came upon Rock Creek. It was then that a shot rang out. And a little later, a second. I could see the shooter far ahead of us, an older colored fellow. He'd now shouldered his gun and was headed in the opposite direction.

"We should follow him, Harry."

"Why?"

"To find out why he was shooting at us."

"I think it's pretty unlikely he was shooting at us, Emmie. And if he was, that seems an excellent reason to avoid the man."

She proceeded as if I hadn't spoken. Even picking up the pace. We approached an old mill and could now see the fellow clearly as he crossed a small foot bridge over the creek. He was accompanied by a dog and, slung over the shoulder without the gun, a dead rabbit. I said nothing.

As we climbed back up to Massachusetts Avenue, Emmie slipped in the mud and tobogganed down to the bottom of the embankment. I went back and helped her up, but now she was so thoroughly covered in mud, she had difficulty keeping her footing. She slipped twice more before we reached the top and there's no denying that when we did, Emmie was not looking her best. A gentleman out for a ride came upon us and asked—with genuine concern in his voice—if Emmie had lost her horse. If he hadn't been a kindly-looking, older fellow, I think she might have set upon him then and there. As it was, she responded politely. Or nearly so. She insisted we hire a cab back to the hotel at the earliest opportunity and I hailed one as soon as we reached Connecticut Avenue. The cabman looked over Emmie and demanded an additional dollar.

"I don't see how we learned anything from that, Harry."

"We learned you don't need a spiteful horse to come home covered in mud."

"I meant anything relevant."

"I just wanted to get some idea what the rush was about."

"What do you mean by rush?"

"No doubt that whole area is going to be filled with expensive houses over the next ten or twenty years. But it isn't going to happen next week. These fellows needed money quickly. And a lot of it. I think it was in anticipation of some big transaction, something that requires the resources of several well-to-do people. And it's going to take place soon."

"Won't that be too transparent?"

"My guess is they see the claims as temporary loans. Most likely, they intend to give back the money after 'finding' the missing jewels. It may still be a little obvious, but the insurers will probably go along."

"What if they pay it back before you catch them at it?" she asked.

"That's an unpleasant thought."

The Normandie's doorman helped Emmie down and inquired if she'd been thrown from her horse again. Luckily, she'd left her riding crop up in the room.

As soon as Emmie had gotten into a hot bath, I slipped out to visit Alice Sachs. She let me in herself and, unlike at our first meeting, she was pleasantly cordial. However, the dog beside her was anything but. This was a younger version of the ghost-chaser we'd met previously. And his manner was even less restrained than Emmie's. His teeth were conspicuously bared and there was nothing incipient about his growl. After taking me to the parlor, she led the dog down to the basement. His now somewhat muffled bark continued after Miss Sachs returned.

"We thought we needed a good watch-dog."

"He seems sufficiently menacing."

She offered me a chair and then made her limited confession.

"There's something I think we should have mentioned on your first visit."

"About the burglary?"

"No, not directly. About my brooch."

"It wasn't taken after all?"

"Oh, it was. Of course. But afterwards, father saw how upset I was and tried to have a duplicate made."

"How do mean, 'tried'?"

"It's a very poor replica. I've worn it once or twice, just to make him feel better about it. But it's rather embarrassing. Anyone knowing enough to appreciate a Boucheron would see at once it was a clumsy attempt at mimicry."

"May I see it?"

"Yes, of course." It was just beside her on a table, in its own little case. She opened this and handed me the brooch. It was about four inches wide and two high. It looked like a large housefly, but I suspected this wasn't the intent. The head and abdomen were covered in what looked like diamonds and the wings dotted with blue stones. I supposed the craftsmanship wasn't as impressive as what the countess had shown us, but I didn't feel confident that I could tell the real from a fake. On the back was the name Boucheron, the only hallmark the firm used.

"These stones are all imitation?" I asked.

"Yes, isn't that obvious?"

"Oh, yes," I said. "Where did your father have it made?"

"At a jeweler's in New York."

"Do you have the name?"

"No, I'm sorry. And father is out just now."

"Might there be a name in the case?"

"Oh, I suppose there may be." She opened it, then handed it to me.

There was a card pasted to the inside: M. Pomerleau, with an address on 37th Street. I copied it down.

"How was M. Pomerleau able to make a copy, even a crude one, without the original?"

"I'm sorry?" She had been distracted by something, or pretended to be. "Oh, father wrote out a description. And there was a photo."

"I didn't realize that. May I see it?"

"I'm afraid M. Pomerleau didn't return it."

"Is there anything else you'd like to tell me?"

"I don't know what you mean. I just thought the replica may have caused some confusion, since I've worn it out once or twice."

"And you thought perhaps someone saw you wearing a brooch that was supposed to be missing?"

"Yes."

"I see. Well, if there's nothing else, I should be going."

She led me out and on the way back to the hotel I puzzled over her revelation. Something about it didn't make sense. If there had been no burglary—and I was sure there hadn't been—then why bother making a copy? Before going up to the room, I stopped at the desk and sent off a wire to M. Pomerleau. Upstairs I found Emmie tearing open a package. It contained our costumes along with a note from the countess:

> *My Dears,*
>
> *Please humor me by wearing these tonight. Harry, you will be the policeman, and you, dear Emmie, his prey.*
>
> *Until this evening...*

A stick of charcoal rolled out as Emmie was removing the dark shirt and trousers meant for her.

"What do you think that's for?" she asked.

"I think you're meant to play a brigand of the night. You need to smudge that about your face so I can't see you as you dart in and out of alleys. How are you at darting?"

"Oh, I can dart well enough," she said. "There's that scent again. Where were you just now, Harry?"

"If you must know, I had a tryst with Alice Sachs. It was her stationery you nosed this morning."

I told her all about the copy of the Boucheron brooch.

"So it *was* Alice Sachs the countess had seen wearing the faux Boucheron."

"Yes, and she saw her wearing the brooch again the night before last. Only this time, the countess insists it was the real Boucheron."

We went down for lunch and it was obvious Emmie was as perplexed by the faux brooch as I was. When we had finished I told her of my intent to telephone my old friend at the *Syracuse Herald*.

"Does he know anything about jewelry?"

"Not likely. I'm hoping maybe he, or one of his cronies, might know something about real-estate transactions."

The *Syracuse Herald* told me he couldn't help me, but suggested I stop by and he would round up someone who could. Emmie, having done some short, inventive pieces for placement in British newspapers, saw this as an opportunity to hobnob with her fellow scribes. But I cautioned her.

"Emmie, if you come along, you need to appreciate the perils involved."

"What are you talking about, Harry?"

I described my previous two encounters with the boys of the press and the consequences for my wallet. She thought I was exaggerating. But I made her pledge that under no circumstances would we allow ourselves to be dragged into any saloons, restaurants, cafés, or anywhere else where drink might be served. She agreed, and then she took out her scrapbook of clippings to bring along.

Newspaper Row was centered on 14th Street and Pennsylvania Avenue, and the *Syracuse Herald* had a little office in a building full of journalists. All the office doors were open, and a few of the boys could be heard typing up something to wire back home. But most were chatting out in the hall, or passing the time playing cards. The *Syracuse Herald* laid down his hand when he saw us.

"You're in luck, Harry. As soon as I hung up I remembered a fellow at the local *Star* who follows that sort of thing. They told me he was over at the Ebbitt having lunch. I sent a fellow to make sure he doesn't leave before we get there."

"How about we send another fellow and ask him to meet us here?"

"I can't be asking people to run errands for nothing, Harry. These fellows have their work to do."

I glanced about.

"It looks slow now," he said. "But you should see it when some little news comes in."

Yes, like there's a sucker buying drinks over at the Ebbitt.

"Harry, why are you being obtuse?" Emmie chimed in. "There's a man who can help us and you're standing here quibbling over the cost of a round of drinks."

Just the sort of thing you want your wife to announce to a roomful of jaded men. Well, the die was cast. The three of us went off to the Ebbitt and into its dining room. The man from the *Washington Star* wasn't anywhere to be found.

"Maybe you could just give me his name?" I suggested.

"Oh, he'll be here, Harry."

"I thought the idea was he was already here?"

"I was misinformed. Let's take a table."

Eventually, the man from the *Star* did show up. But by then, so had the *Newark News*, the *Seattle Post-Intelligencer*, and the *Omaha Daily Bee*. While Emmie was showing her scrapbook to the others, I took the man from the *Star* aside and told him what I was looking for.

"How did you hear about it?" he asked. "I just found out this morning."

"Hear about what?"

He took a copy of an early afternoon edition from his hip pocket and handed it to me. It was folded to a particular page. He pointed to a story with the headline "French Government's Purchase of Property Recorded."

> *The French Republic this morning acquired title to valuable real estate between Decatur and S Streets, comprising a tract of nearly an acre and a half. The purchase price is approximately $100,000. It is understood the property was purchased for the purpose of erecting a building suitable for the accommodation of that country's diplomatic representatives.*

It then went on to describe the lots involved, identifying them as in Kalorama Heights and as originally part of the Widow's Mite. The name of the seller was given as Charles Davidson.

"Who's Charles Davidson?"

"He's a real-estate speculator."

"Do you know if he's held this property for long?"

"Maybe, why?"

"Well, I think some people have been raising money for a big deal of some kind, something exactly like this. Only there's no Davidson among them."

"Maybe he fronted for them."

"His name appears, but they take the risk and the profits?"

"Something like that. But you can be sure he'll get his share of the profits. And there will be some big profits. Prices are high up that way, but not usually that high."

"What's this Widow's Mite?"

"It was a huge tract, left to some widow long ago."

"That used to be Kalorama?"

"Kalorama was part of it."

I thanked him and we rejoined the others.

The boys were exhibiting their customary alacrity at draining bottles, closely followed by their customary trips to the john—each announced with a colorful euphemism. There was the familiar "see a man about a dog," the then-novel "give a Chinaman a music lesson," and the always-odd "visit the Widow Jones." None of that would be worthy of note, except that when the time came for Emmie, she wasn't going to slip away quietly. She rose to her feet, placed her hat on her breast, and solemnly proclaimed, "Gentlemen, I take my leave. I must deliver a message to Señor Garcia!"

The fellows loved this, and there's no denying it was truly inspired. But since the reference might be obscure for anyone who wasn't residing in the U.S. at that particular moment, I'll elucidate. You see, there was a fellow named Elbert Hubbard who peddled a sort of philosophical quackery from his citadel somewhere outside of Buffalo. Well, right about the time the country was feeling all noble about freeing the Cubans from the Spanish yoke—and before it started feeling sorry about having to put the Filipinos in ours—he wrote a little tract about an American officer who was ordered to take a message to Garcia, the leader of the Cuban rebels. In spite of innumerable trials, tribulations, etc., the American succeeded and lived to tell the tale on the lecture circuit.

Hubbard's hackneyed depiction of the event brought tears to the eyes of simpletons the length and breadth of the country and it wasn't long before the phrase "take a message to Garcia" came to be a cliché. It was chiefly used to goad some poor fellow who had sense enough not to take on an unpleasant task with the promise he'd be ennobled if he did. Any profits from the endeavor, naturally, accruing to the man doing the goading.

Well, as I said, the ink slingers were impressed. I took a vicarious pride in Emmie's triumph. And I would have been happy to stick around and bask in her glow. But I had learned something during my previous outings with the gentlemen of the press. So, while Emmie was indisposed, I crept out of the room. I knew the boys would never suspect I'd abandon my wife like that, and I felt kind of ruthless doing it. But a lesson had to be taught and I didn't care much who learned it, as long as it wasn't me.

17

I walked up to the Normandie and at the desk asked for a city directory. Charles Davidson, the fellow recorded as the seller of the Widow's Mite tract, had an ad under real-estate agents. I phoned him from the lobby and his girl put me through. Davidson was pleasant enough, but when I brought up the land purchase he went mum. The only thing he admitted was that there were others involved. I went up to the room and an hour later Emmie came in. She didn't have the look of someone who'd just suffered a financial setback.

"Why did you sneak off like that, Harry?"

"Discretion is the better part of valor," I said. "How'd you avoid getting stuck with the check?"

"I didn't."

"It must have been staggering."

"It was rather sizable, yes. In fact, it cleaned me out. Could you advance me a few dollars?"

"A few. I've been going through it pretty quickly myself."

I wasn't surprised Emmie had been carrying an ample purse. She prided herself on having independent sources of income. Some of which I knew about, and some of which I didn't—and was probably the better off for it.

"You're taking the loss well, Emmie. Comrades of the quill?"

"Oh, I consider it a loan."

"If you think those pikers will be ponying up, you're

in for a disappointment. They've made cadging drinks into a fine art."

"I didn't say *they* considered it a loan. But that's not important. The man from the *Star* told me about the land purchase you were interested in," she said.

I handed her the paper with the story circled.

"How can you be certain this involves the same men? None of their names are mentioned."

"I can't be certain. But when I described the outline of what I was looking for, that fellow from the *Star* identified it immediately, so it must be unusually large. And he seemed to think the buyer paid too much."

"Meaning what?"

"Say you hear that the French Republic, or any government, is looking at a piece of property. And you also happen to find out who will represent it in the transaction. People spending money that isn't their own can get pretty careless about doing proper appraisals. Especially if they're confident they'll be remembered later."

"But why the insurance claims?"

"Suppose Easterly found out the French were interested in buying that tract well before it became generally known. Sesbania mentioned there was a Frenchman at the house—maybe he's with their embassy and had the job of arranging the purchase. Easterly et al. want to buy up the land from the unsuspecting owners so they can sell it to the French for much more. But they can't come up with the full amount necessary. No bank will lend for a scheme like this, so they raise the money by faking the burglaries. Their claims are settled and then they buy up the land for, say, fifty thousand dollars. Which might be double what the owners paid even a few years ago. Then they hire Charles Davidson to front for them. They pay him a few thousand, and the Frenchman a few thousand, and they've made a profit of over eighty percent in the matter of a few months."

"It seems amazing they could organize it all so quickly."

"Oh, you can be sure they've had plenty of practice."

"But now they have their money, Harry. Won't they pay back the insurers right away?"

"Well, I doubt they have the money in hand. It needs to move from bank to bank and that could take days. But you're right, time is running out."

There was a knock at the door. It was a messenger with a response from M. Pomerleau, the New York jeweler who made the duplicate brooch for General Sachs. He told me he had been hired for the job during the last week of September—more than a month before the alleged burglary—and had finished it in October. He added that he would send a letter with more details. Emmie was reading over my shoulder.

"Now you have some proof, Harry."

"Proof of what?"

"That the Sachses are lying. And, if the countess saw it the other night, the real brooch is probably at their house right now."

"I think that's fairly likely. And probably the same is true at Easterly's and Senator Merrill's. But that doesn't help me unless they allow me in to make a search."

"Can't Sergeant Lacy get a warrant?"

"Sergeant Lacy is perfectly happy to let the whole matter drop. He realizes it's a case of fraud now. But he's not interested in making a move against anyone who might hurt his career."

We went down for dinner and were back up putting

on our costumes by seven. The police outfit the countess had provided was a little roomy, but a couple pillows filled it out nicely. Included was one of those absurd walrus mustaches cops used to wear. No gun was supplied, but the club looked fully functional—and so it would prove later that night.

Emmie took a great deal of care with her transformation into a marauder of the night. She piled her hair up under the cloth cap, and the jacket and trousers were loose-fitting enough to obscure whatever shapes were in the wrong place. She also had a mustache, but a more modest one. The application of the charcoal was done with painstaking thoroughness, and we didn't leave for the embassy until sometime after eight.

A footman in an elaborate costume greeted us and we joined the line of arrivals in the hall. Most of the costumes were far more elaborate than ours and, frankly, more flattering. The women all seemed to be dressed as Marie Antoinette or one of her chums at court. The men gravitated towards musketeer regalia—big hats and sabers and what-not—though there were a good number of Abe Lincolns, and a Swedish-speaking Robert E. Lee. At the entrance to the ballroom, we were each greeted in turn by the ambassador and his wife. I don't know what it pays to be an ambassador, but right about then I felt sure he'd agree it was hardly enough.

We saw General Sachs in the guise of his idol Sherman, no doubt planning to pillage the midnight buffet. The only Marie Antoinette I recognized was Mrs. Merrill. But she vanished into a sea of Antoinettes before I could point her out to Emmie.

I sensed that Emmie was becoming self-conscious about the contrast between herself and the other women.

Her anxiety was lessened when Elizabeth arrived dressed in an outfit that resembled her own, but looking a good deal more ungainly. The costume simply didn't work on her. Her bundle of hair was about three times too large for the cap, which sat precariously on top. And no clothing, no matter how loose-fitting, would obscure her sex. Whereas Emmie appeared unadorned, Elizabeth looked ridiculous. And it was soon obvious she'd come to the same conclusion. Whatever good feelings had come over her at our last meeting had vanished. She was now her usual caustic self, and the first bit of venom was directed at the countess.

"She's had us all dress like clowns. I can't wait to be rid of this place," she added.

"Are you planning a journey?" I asked.

"I most certainly am. And it can't happen soon enough."

The countess arrived just in time to hear the last of Elizabeth's wishes for her.

"There, everyone is just as I planned," she said. She herself was dressed as, well, herself. She wore a green velvet jacket with a fur collar over a white gown and had on the tiara we'd seen before. But she wore her hair casually, loose and streaming down the sides of her face.

"Isn't the Abraham Lincoln who just entered Mr. Easterly?" the Gräfin asked.

"Yes, with his wife as Mrs. Lincoln."

As I mentioned, there was no shortage of fellows playing the old rail-splitter that night, but Mrs. Easterly seemed the first of their consorts willing to take the part of Mary Todd. She had the general look for the part, but her manner was all wrong. Mrs. Easterly found nearly everything amusing, and Mrs. Lincoln, at least from what

I've heard, absolutely nothing. The countess insisted I fetch them. When I introduced her, Mrs. Easterly made a deep curtsey. I don't know if she realized this was a real countess, but her daughter had probably muddled her distinction between the real and the imagined enough that it didn't matter. The women somehow got into a discussion about the Oz book and Easterly suggested we look for a billiard room. As I took leave of Emmie, I noticed Elizabeth giving me a pathetic look. Its meaning was clear enough: her interest in children's literature was slight. I took pity on her.

"Perhaps we could find a game of cards?" I suggested. "Then Miss Strout might be persuaded to join us."

Elizabeth actually whispered something resembling gratitude. I was struck dumb for a moment. At least until she became impatient and jabbed me in the ribs. As we made our way out of the ballroom, I saw Alice Sachs as a shepherdess out on the floor. She wasn't wearing either the real or the fake Boucheron brooch. And she was dancing with a wolf. What her little lambs thought of the alliance can only be guessed. Eventually, we came upon a small room where a few men sat about chatting and smoking.

"Is this all right, Miss Strout?" Easterly asked.

"Oh, quite all right."

Senator Merrill was one of the gents in the room and he was looking surprisingly wakeful. We invited him to join us and Easterly instructed a footman to bring in a table and a deck of cards.

I can't imagine ordering someone else's footman about, but Easterly made it seem simple enough. Elizabeth and I played the two others and it was an agreeably casual game. We had finished our first hand of bridge when the senator told us he was unfamiliar with the game. He thought we were playing whist. Then two more hands were played before we realized no one had been keeping score. We all laughed. This is how cards were meant to be played. Emmie drained the fun out of it completely, my every error recorded and used for my future edification.

The conversation was as desultory as the game, but eventually I brought up the large purchase of land by the French Republic. Elizabeth was impressed by the sum involved, but neither Easterly nor the senator was made uneasy by the topic. I expected as much from Easterly. He was the type who'd happily board a doomed ship, confident he'd survive unscathed and knowing the wreck would make a good anecdote. With the senator, I had the feeling it was genuine lack of interest. Then I asked Easterly if Mrs. Spinks would be coming.

"No, she takes her own entertainment in the evening. A very private person."

I found that a little difficult to reconcile with the former stage performer who ran a gambling parlor in her dining room and conducted tours of her bedchamber. But I suppose he knew her better than I did. About then, Mrs. Easterly arrived.

"Why don't you take my seat?" I offered. "I'd like to stretch my legs some."

"That's very kind of you, isn't it, George?"

"Yes, very gallant," her husband replied. "Just remember, dear, our evenings away from home are evenings away from Oz."

"It was the countess who brought it up. She has a wonderful plan," she giggled. "But I must not tell."

"I don't suppose you know where my wife is?" I asked her.

"She was speaking to the countess about something. Not far from here."

I ventured into the ballroom looking for Emmie, but saw no sign of her. It was a warm evening, for December, and a number of people were taking air on the terrace, so I went out to see if she was among them. She wasn't, but I did see Mrs. Merrill in an intimate conversation with a wolf.

I went back in and made a complete tour of the public rooms, then inquired if the countess was in her apartment. She was not. After spending most of an hour in the futile search, I found myself back where I'd started. The game seemed to be breaking up.

"You just missed your wife, Mr. Reese," Easterly told me. "She went off with Miss Strout."

Then he and his wife went off to the dance floor. A moment later, Amanda Merrill and the wolf arrived and agreed to join the senator and myself for cards. The wolf was forced by necessity to remove his head. It was Dr. Gillette.

The conversation wasn't as undirected this time. Mrs. Merrill went through the guest list, making biting remarks about each of the attendees. She was sometimes witty, but invariably vicious. The senator merely issued grunts now and then. Some seemed to signify amusement, some censure, and a few indigestion. I found it difficult to participate at all. And Dr. Gillette was looking more uncomfortable than usual. What he'd been doing with Amanda Merrill I couldn't imagine.

I brought up real estate again, but the transition was an awkward one and they didn't warm to the subject. So it was even more awkward when I mentioned the French purchase. But I did hit a nerve, with both the doctor and the senator's good woman. The doctor had already been perspiring, and now the pores really let loose, making his handkerchief about as effective as a mop at Niagara. Meanwhile, Amanda Merrill gave me the same hard look she always had, only now there seemed to be some warm loathing about the mouth backing up the cold contempt of her eyes. Unfortunately, because of my clumsiness in introducing the topic, I had revealed my hand. They knew I knew, and they probably also knew I knew that they knew.... Well, as I said, I had revealed my hand.

We'd played for more than an hour when the countess arrived.

"Harry, may I speak to you a moment?"

She drew me into a corner.

"Harry, Emmie wasn't feeling well. I had Elizabeth take her back to the hotel."

"Really? She seemed fine earlier."

"Oh, it's nothing. There's no reason for you to go back there." She glanced at the card table. "How did you arrange this, Harry?"

"Arrange what?"

"Isn't that Senator Merrill's wife with you?"

"Yes, though you wouldn't know it. Not a match made in heaven." Belatedly, I realized my words might be taken personally by the countess, who was likewise a good deal younger than her husband, but she just smiled.

"Don't be judgmental, Harry," she said. Then she changed the subject. "Don't you appreciate the possibilities here?"

"Which possibilities?"

"Well, here the Merrills are, and back at their home, no doubt, is the jewelry they say was stolen. And you in a policeman's uniform."

"I see where you're heading, but it's a little out of my line."

"One must play one's part, Harry. Everyone else is cooperating." Then, when I didn't acquiesce quickly enough, she added, "I command it."

"You command it? By what authority?"

"Oh, quit being an ass and get on your way. I'll invite them to a private supper. Americans love a title and they'll do my bidding. You'll have at least two hours. Now go."

She went over and extended her invitation. Just as she predicted, they accepted. I made to leave, but realized I was missing my helmet. I remembered placing it against a wall, but it was nowhere to be found. Who, I wondered, would snatch a policeman's helmet?

18

I took a cab to the Merrills' neighborhood, just northeast of the Capitol, and had the driver drop me about a block away from the house. It was nearly midnight when I arrived, but this being a Saturday night, a fair number of people were still wandering about. I strolled down Maryland Avenue, greeting the passers-by with little nods and twirling my stick until coming upon my destination. Except for a light in the front hall, the house was dark. Then I had my first surprise. A cop was rounding the corner up ahead. At the last moment, he turned on his heels and walked back the way he came. When he had walked thirty feet or so in that direction, he turned around again. He'd taken station beside the Merrill house, pacing back and forth, but never looked my way. All his attention was focused on a house across the street. Probably having a dalliance with the cook, I imagined. I waited as long as I could stand, but there seemed to be no deviation in his routine. It was clear action on my part was required.

I meandered my way a block in one direction and two more in another. Then I positioned myself at the mouth of a wide alley and began pounding my club on the pavement. This is a well-known signal policemen use to alert their brethren that they're in need of assistance. At least it's well-known to the readers of dime novels. Whether policemen themselves are aware of it, I'm not altogether sure. I did a nice steady beat, but added a little flourish every fourth measure. It wasn't long before the street's inhabitants began to make their feelings known. About the time the first thrown object whizzed past my head—an apple, I believe, but perhaps some other fruit—my man rounded the corner. I immediately made my escape to the other end of the alley.

Unfortunately, I was now thoroughly disoriented. The combination of the unfamiliar geography and the German ambassador's generosity with his cellar had rendered my normally sound compass inoperable. There were some people about, and I considered asking one of them for directions, but I just couldn't work out the proper phrasing. There seemed no getting around the fact that a policeman who becomes lost while walking his beat is likely to arouse suspicion. It was then that things took a rather unexpected turn. Not that the events of the previous thirty minutes had been in any way anticipated. But they became a good deal stranger. I was standing on a corner, surveying the street signs, when a hysterical young woman ran up to me.

"He's killing her!"

"Is he?"

She seemed unsatisfied with my response and became even more hysterical.

"For God's sake! Hurry!"

She seemed bent on attracting attention, so I agreed to go with her just to quiet her down. She led me to a small tenement and then up to the second floor. We waded through a crowd of women and children, eventually coming on a couple who seemed to be involved in a dispute. The fellow, a big man, had apparently run out of ready cash during his Saturday evening revelry at the local saloon and come home to squeeze the house money from his wife. The wife, whose face already bore a bruise, objected to his plan and was wielding an iron pan in order to make her position clear.

I tapped the fellow on the shoulder and suggested he sit down. Typical of his breed, he had little respect for the law. He shoved me onto the floor.

"Club him!" the crowd yelled.

I thought I'd give the fellow another chance, but this time he dispatched me to the floor before I'd uttered a word.

"Club him!" the crowd yelled.

And I'd come to agree with them. I wasn't normally fond of the decision-making skills of a mob, but when the mob is right, it's right. I clubbed him. At first, not nearly hard enough. He turned and I could tell immediately that my efforts hadn't improved his mood. The second time I spared nothing. He went down, and the crowd cheered.

"You'd better call the wagon," someone advised.

"The wagon?"

"To take him away."

I wasn't looking forward to meeting up with my comrades on the force and thought another course might be preferable.

"Why don't we just tie him up?" I suggested. "If I call for the wagon, he'll just get a night in jail and come back all the meaner tomorrow. But if we tie him up in the basement, you can read him temperance tracts until he takes the pledge."

The mob's response was a cool one.

"What good's reading to him going to do?" a woman asked.

"What if we don't feed him?" another suggested.

"And give him one to the head, every now and then...."

The crowd laughed with approval. I could see sentiment was moving in my direction.

"You can torment him in whatever way you think proper," I acceded.

Eventually, the doubters came around and we began dragging him downstairs. Throughout the process, however, women were continually piping up with novel methods of torturing the fellow. I was beginning to wonder if my original concerns about the soundness of the mob's judgment were not well founded. It was then, as we were passing a first-floor doorway, that I caught a glimpse of a fellow wearing prison stripes.

"He saw Jimmy!" an old woman cried. "Please don't turn him in."

"All right," I said, and returned to the dragging.

"He'll have to turn him in," some fool bent on complicating matters said.

"No, I won't," I corrected.

"He's just saying that."

"Look, as far as I know, the fellow just came from a costume party."

"He didn't do it!" the old woman pleaded.

"Well then, what would be the point of turning him in?" I asked rhetorically. But the crowd had lost the cooperative spirit.

"What if we pay you?"

"Pay me?"

"Pay you not to turn Jimmy in."

"It's on the house—your thanks is graft enough."

They were unconvinced, and so began taking up a collection. Evidently Jimmy ranked high in their esteem. It was at that moment that inspiration struck.

"Look. I've an idea. Jimmy, I take it, is a good boy

who's just been dealt a bad hand. Given another chance, he'll redeem himself. Am I right?"

They seemed to agree, though a few skeptics were snickering in the distance.

"And this fellow," I said, pointing to my victim, "is a thoroughly unpleasant miscreant. Correct?"

"Completely worthless," his wife confirmed. "He lost his job today."

"Well, the solution seems simple enough. These two fellows look something alike. What if they just trade places? We put Jimmy's state-supplied garments on... what's this fellow's name?"

"O'Conner."

"We put the prison garb on O'Conner. And have Jimmy hide upstairs in O'Conner's apartment. Then you can send round to the precinct house and tell them you've caught an escaped prisoner."

Generally speaking, they took to the idea. They began the switching of dress.

"Are you a real cop?" a boy asked.

"I clubbed him, didn't I?"

"Where's your gun? And your helmet?"

"I misplaced them."

"Want one?"

"One what?"

"A helmet. What size?" He surveyed my head and left us.

"Mister," a little girl was tugging at my sleeve. "You lost this."

She handed me a small bit of fur. I looked at it, puzzled.

"It's your mustache," her mother announced. She went and got some paste and proceeded to reattach it.

Then the boy showed up with the helmet. It fit perfectly.

"One dollar."

I paid him.

"Five dollars for a gun."

"No, no. I'm sure mine will turn up."

The women had completed the costuming of O'Conner, but they seemed unsure whether he was convincing in his new role. They were right: Jimmy was ten years younger and a good deal better-looking than O'Conner. Which was undoubtedly the reason Mrs. O'Conner, also younger and handsomer, had warmed to the scheme so readily.

"The men from the precinct know Jimmy."

"It will just take some finesse," I said. "Give O'Conner here a shave and a couple black eyes. Then when they come around for him, Jimmy's mom can put on the keening act, in spades. Plead with them, cry on their boots. They'll just want to get out of here and get rid of him. And the fellows at the penitentiary won't care, just so the head count comes out right at morning roll call. Then on Monday, Jimmy can apply for O'Conner's job."

I suggested they send the house gun dealer off to the precinct to inform on "Jimmy's" whereabouts. They seemed genuinely appreciative of my Solomon-esque wisdom. But with my work done, I bade them adieu.

"How do we explain the dent on his head?"

"Just tell them Jimmy was chased here by an officer, but he eluded him after the bash to the head."

"What officer?"

I took off the helmet and read the name scribbled inside: "McDonald."

"McDonald? That's no proper name for a cop."

"Ah, what would you suggest?"

"Callaghan."

"Sounds a bit hackneyed, doesn't it?" But Callaghan it was.

While they were taking turns blackening O'Conner's orbs, I asked for directions then slid out and sauntered over to the Merrills'. The delay had brought one advantage, the streets were now a good deal more deserted. I made my way to the house and found the hall light still on. Meaning, I hoped, that the senator and his missus hadn't returned. I debated some about methodology. On the one hand, the bedroom in question was in the front of the house and the fewer rooms I had to enter the better. On the other hand, entry at the rear of the house would offer a certain amount of cover. What decided the issue was the fact that I couldn't imagine how to get up to the second floor of either side without breaking my neck. Another manner of entry was called for. Then I hit upon it. Isn't one of a policeman's duties to test that doors are locked at night? I started a few houses up from the Merrills' and was startled to learn that the first two doors I checked were unlocked. What was a policeman's duty in that event? If I were to lock them, someone coming home late might be forced to sleep on the street. I'd never appreciated how full a cop's life was with dilemmas.

Sadly, the Merrills were not among the naïve. The door was locked. And the key was not under the mat. It was, however, under a prominently placed rock in the flower bed. I let myself in and removed my boots, the better to creep. Then I crept upstairs. No one was stirring and I was able to reach the chamber with no more than three or four stray creaks of the floorboards. I closed the door behind me and turned on a light. My first order of business was to determine where Mrs. Merrill stowed her lingerie. From my limited experience, women always hide things among their lingerie in the belief men feel inhibited from going through these unmentionables. But they are under a misapprehension. And none more so than Mrs. Merrill. She had some very arresting attire. I wondered if the senator, who slept in a separate room, was ever made privy to any of it. In the midst of her unmentionables, I found a stack of letters. Love letters, it seemed. They had nothing to do with the case, but they did make interesting reading. Not wanting to take the time for a careful study, I stuffed them in my pocket. Then I came upon a little velvet bag. I'd found the jewelry—three items of early Tiffany.

I wasted no time celebrating but turned off the light and crept back downstairs. Just in time to see the Merrills coming up the front steps. I crept toward the back of the house, unlocked the rear door, and made a flawless escape. Or nearly flawless. The only fly in the ointment became immediately apparent when my stocking feet hit the cool flagstones outside. My boots were in the front hall and the Merrills were probably tripping over them at that very moment—no doubt imagining a member of the force in bed with the maid upstairs.

As I mentioned previously, it was a warmish night so I wasn't sorely discomfited by the lack of footwear. Until it started raining. The euphoria I'd felt earlier, both in the finding of the jewelry and in the solving of the O'Conner-Jimmy affair, was waning. And when I realized a roundsman was calling out to me, it vanished completely.

"Where are your boots, man?"

"Stolen, sir."

"Stolen? While you were wearing them?"

"They came off when I was chasing that escaped prisoner."

"You? What's your name?"

"Callaghan."

"So it *was* you. We just put him in the wagon. What's your precinct?"

"Next over but one."

"Next over but one? What the hell does that mean?"

"Third?"

"Are you asking or telling?"

"Telling, tentatively."

"You chased him all the way from the West End?"

"Yes, sir."

"Christ! You lost your gun as well? They'll hang you for that."

Then he started shaking his head in a worrying manner. But as luck would have it, inspiration was springing forth that evening with a helpful abandon.

"You see, sir, I'd just arrived home after my shift, and I was taking off my things and I see this fellow in stripes run down the back of the house. I didn't have time to grab my gun, just the club. And the boots came off because I didn't stop to tie them back up. I caught up to the fellow somewhere around the theatre district, and landed a good one on his head, which you perhaps noted if you saw the fellow."

"I saw that. But how'd he manage to get up again?"

"That sound prison diet. He took off like a flash."

"A flash?"

"Rabbit?"

"And what happened to his face? You might hear some about that. What a mess."

"Can't say. I chased him all the way up here and lost him again. I thought he went into a tenement, but they said they hadn't seen him."

"And you believed them?"

"They had honest faces."

"Honest faces?" He started the worrying head shaking again, but then his mood became more charitable. "Well, I guess you did a job tonight. You go on home. And better soak those feet."

Then he found me cab and commandeered it. The cabman wasn't keen on the idea until I assured him I'd be only too glad to pay. When we arrived at the hotel, I had the fellow drop me off at a side entrance, but still had to slosh across the empty and otherwise silent lobby in wet socks. The night clerk looked concerned.

"Costume ball," I explained.

He nodded, but his expression didn't change.

19

As I opened the door of our room, the light from the hall illuminated Emmie's costume on a chair. I undressed in the dark and got into bed. Something immediately struck me as odd. Emmie's heart was beating so strongly and her breathing was so rapid I could hear both distinctly. It was obvious she'd had an invigorating workout shortly before I arrived. And yet I'd been told she returned to the room hours before.

Normally, when a man comes home and finds his wife breathless in bed, his first instinct is to check the closet for visitors. However, I knew Emmie had been escorted home by a fellow Smith College alumna. So there was nothing to worry about on that score. Then a stray remark of the countess's came to mind. When she was admonishing me for my reluctance to burgle the Merrills'. "Everyone else is cooperating," she'd said. The scales fell from my eyes.

"Emmie, I'll show you mine, if you show me yours."

She sat up and turned on a light.

"Where were you, Harry?"

"Mrs. Merrill's bedchamber—sans Mrs. Merrill."

I got up and poured out my loot on the bed beside her.

"Where were you?" I asked.

"The Sachses'." She got up and fetched her own swag. She had two, seemingly identical, Boucheron brooches, along with several other items the general had claimed.

"So the countess had planned this all along?" I asked.

"Yes, that became obvious early in the evening. Do you remember how she brought up Oz when we were speaking with Mrs. Easterly?"

"I remember making every effort to flee the scene."

"Well, as soon as she mentioned it, Mrs. Easterly told her how like Glinda she looked. Then the countess steered the conversation in such a way that she was soon agreeing to go visit Sesbania that very evening, as a surprise. Mrs. Easterly thought this would be a wonderful present for her little girl and even wrote a note to the governess. Then the countess took me aside and gave me my instructions."

"Gave you your instructions? How come I've never been able to give you instructions?"

"You must reason that out for yourself, Harry. Anyway, she told me to wait one hour and then to feign illness and ask Elizabeth to accompany me back to the hotel. When we got outside, I was to convince Elizabeth to help me burgle the Sachses'."

"How difficult was it to persuade Elizabeth to join you?"

"It wasn't at all difficult to persuade her to leave, but she wasn't too eager to help commit a felony."

"It would have required an altruistic spirit foreign to Elizabeth."

"Yes, but of course the countess had thought of that. She told me that if Elizabeth proved at all reluctant, I was to tell her that the countess knew all about her plans and was prepared to foil them."

"What are Elizabeth's plans?"

"She didn't divulge that, only that she knew."

"What a cunning woman."

"I knew you were soft on her."

"Am I?"

"Don't tell me you haven't been spending afternoons with her. That episode in Baltimore, and the tickets to the matinee—she just wanted to get me out of the way."

"Emmie, you're always doing things behind my back."

"Not *that*."

"Well, this wasn't that either. I merely took her to Mrs. Spinks' salons. It was the salons I wanted to keep from you."

"Honestly?"

"Yes, honestly."

"Then what is it that goes on at these salons?"

"You remember the Frauenverein back in Williamsburg?"

"Gambling?"

"On the out-of-town horse races. And at reasonable odds."

"I told you I was done with that, Harry."

"Yes, but I couldn't see much point in testing your resolve," I told her. "I suppose we can assume the countess's visit to the Easterlys' involved her own burglary."

"Oh, I doubt she needed to do that. Mrs. Easterly may not be aware of her husband's machinations, but you can't for a moment think there's anything hidden in that house that Sesbania doesn't know all about."

"So Glinda would just need to say the magic words."

"Something like that. I suspect none of Madame B_____'s thefts involved anything as crude as an actual burglary."

"Not when there are people like us about."

"I don't see what you have to complain about. These

were for your benefit, Harry. Now we have these people in a bind. They can't very well report a second theft of the same jewelry. And frankly, I enjoyed it. How did it go for you?"

"Eventful." I gave her the details of my adventures. All except those involving Mrs. Merrill's missives. I thought they'd make a nice Christmas present.

"Is any of that true?"

"It's all true, Emmie." I handed her the soaking socks as verification. Then showed her the dent O'Conner's head put in my nightstick.

"Ours was dull in comparison."

"Did you encounter the new dog? He looked a good deal more alert than the one we met earlier."

"He seemed to find Elizabeth comforting and quieted almost immediately."

"Odd. And you found the jewelry without incident?"

"It took some searching, but that part went fine."

"Which part didn't go fine?"

"The get-away. It almost seemed as if a policeman had been lying in wait for us."

"But you outran him?"

"Yes. Well, *I* did anyway."

"But not Elizabeth?"

"There's some reason to believe she may be in custody. The last I heard from her, she was screaming curses at me."

"This sort of thing has undermined friendships before. The question is, would she rat on you?"

"Oh, willingly. But I'm hoping she interprets the countess's threat broadly enough to encompass me."

"Well, I suppose we'll know when a cop comes knocking at the door."

Then we turned out the light and attempted to go to sleep. Unfortunately, my ill-chosen last words kept Emmie restless. And she did what she could to make sure I shared in her discomfort. At about eight o'clock the next morning, there was a loud rap at the door. Emmie bolted up.

"Who is it?" I called.

"Detective Sergeant Lacy. There's been a new development, Mr. Reese."

"Just give us a moment."

"What will we do, Harry?" Emmie whispered.

"Come clean, Emmie."

"You don't mean that?"

"Just a thought. I'll take him downstairs. He probably just wants to tell me about the Sachses' break-in."

"Do you think they reported it?"

"Or the cop saw it." I got dressed and answered the door. "Perhaps I can give you breakfast downstairs, Sergeant."

"If you like, Mr. Reese." He was peering around me, watching Emmie as she tried to squirm out of view. "A little late-night dictation?" he added when I'd closed the door.

I winked and we went to the dining room.

"There's been another burglary at General Sachs' house."

"Really? What was taken?"

"Not much, some little things. One was a brooch. A copy of the one stolen last go-round."

"Miss Sachs showed me that copy just yesterday morning."

"Did she? But that isn't all. The general was home at the time."

"And he confronted the thief?"

"That isn't clear. You see, he's dead."

"Killed?"

"No, heart failure, the doctor thinks. He treated the general for heart trouble. But he suggested the excitement of the burglary may have brought on the attack."

"Was Miss Sachs home as well?"

"No. They both had been to a ball at the German Embassy."

"Yes, I was there too."

"You were?"

"Yes, a friend of my wife, er, Miss McGinnis, is employed there. I suppose this means you're back on the case."

"Oh, yes. And it means your theory about insurance fraud is probably in error. I mean, if this valuable brooch hadn't been stolen, why bother making a copy?"

"That's a good question. So what's your theory?"

"I've men out looking for Richard Cole."

"You think he came back?"

"Yes, but with an accomplice. Who I have in custody."

"Has this accomplice talked?"

"No, she insists she had nothing to do with it. But she was caught in dark overalls with her face all blackened. Says she was at a costume party. The same costume party, in fact. And that she's employed by the Germans."

"You begin to interest me, Sergeant."

"Good. I thought that you might want to accompany me back to the Sachses'. I asked the doctor to meet me there."

"He wasn't there earlier?"

"He'd come and gone by the time I'd gotten there."

We finished eating and I went back upstairs for my hat and coat.

"What did he say, Harry?"

"The general's dead."

"Dead?"

"Yes, heart failure, or something like that. Did you see him?"

"Don't you think I'd have mentioned it if we had? We didn't see anyone. Just the dog."

"And the cop."

"We were well outside of the house then."

"Did he see you leaving it?"

"I wouldn't have thought so, but perhaps."

"Where's your loot, Emmie?"

"I hid it." She went to a bureau and retrieved her bundle. "Did they report it?"

"Just the fake. Which one is it?"

"You can't tell from the stones?" she asked. "Well, the real one weighs more. Are you giving them back?"

I stuck the faux Boucheron in my pocket.

"Just this one. I plan on finding it there. Maybe I can convince Miss Sachs there was no burglary. Then we can see about getting Elizabeth released."

"So she hasn't mentioned me?"

"Apparently not, but we'd better get her out before her mood sours."

"Should I contact the countess?"

"Yes, let her know what's happened, but both of you stay away from Elizabeth. No sense provoking her."

"All right, Harry."

Lacy and I took a cab over to the Sachses' house.

"How exactly did your people apprehend the culprit?"

"Interestingly, the precinct house received a telephone message alerting them to some suspicious characters in the neighborhood. When our man arrives on the scene, he sees two men dressed in black. When he calls to them, they run. He catches the one and he turns out to be a woman. Just then, he hears a lady yelling for the police. It was Miss Sachs. She'd just come home and discovered the burglary."

"How had they gotten in?"

"The parlor window was open, but it must have been unlocked. It hadn't been forced."

A maid let us in and led us to Alice Sachs in the parlor. We could hear the dog barking off in the distance.

"I was sorry to hear of your loss, Miss Sachs."

"Thank you, Mr. Reese."

"Did you see anything of the burglars last night?"

"No, but the window down here was open when I came in."

"How did you know it was a burglary?"

"After seeing the open window, I went upstairs to see if anything had been taken and saw that the brooch was missing."

"The copy you showed me yesterday?"

"Yes. And two or three other things of little value."

"Where was your father found?" I asked.

"In his room, beside his bed."

"So there was nothing to indicate he'd confronted the thieves?"

"No, the things were taken from my room."

"He left the ball before you did?"

"Yes, long before. He suffers from pyrosis. Sometime around ten o'clock, he said it was bothering him and he'd go on home alone."

"Might we go up to the room and look around?"

She took us up to her bedroom and showed us

where the items had been—in a lingerie drawer. I walked around the room, looking at window sills, under furniture. And there, under a couch, I found the missing brooch.

"Here it is."

I held it up and she leaped across the room and grabbed it from my hand—clearly disappointed when she saw it was the fake.

"I wonder, Miss Sachs, is it possible there was no burglary? Perhaps one of the servants had been airing out the parlor and just neglected to close the window."

"I don't think that's likely."

"By the way, did I mention I'd exchanged wires with M. Pomerleau yesterday?"

She turned a kind of magenta color. Then, gradually, she recovered.

"Perhaps, Mr. Reese is right, Sergeant. I may have just jumped to the wrong conclusion. Having been broken into once has given me a sense of vulnerability."

It was pretty easy to get Lacy to come around to this conclusion as well. The waters had been muddied again and if there was a chance the mighty would be inconvenienced, he wanted to play it safe. A moment later, Dr. Gillette joined us and muddied the waters still further.

"Good morning, Doctor," I said.

He just gave me a little nod and then turned to Lacy.

"Sergeant, I've found a wound on the head."

"A wound?"

"Yes, I believe the general was struck, and it was then he suffered heart failure."

"Could he have struck his head as a result of the heart failure?" I asked.

"He was found face down, and the wound is on the

crown. But an autopsy would make that clearer."

"May we go see the body?"

"Why, yes." He led us to another room, where the general had been placed on his bed. Then he gently turned the head. The wound wasn't obvious, except that the hair on the back of the head was matted. I touched it, and felt the stickiness of semi-congealed blood. There was a small stain on the pillow.

"Was it you who attended him last evening?"

"Yes, but when I arrived, he'd been moved to the bed."

"By whom?"

"By myself and the police officer," Miss Sachs volunteered. "At first, I thought he was just ill. It wasn't until we'd put him on the bed that the officer said he was sure he was dead."

"He was face down when you found him?" I asked.

"Yes, but I didn't notice he'd been hit."

"The thieves must have come in here, found the general unexpectedly and knocked him unconscious," the doctor interjected. "Probably not realizing they induced his death."

"Yes, a reasonable explanation," I agreed. "But for the fact we just determined there was no burglary."

He looked over at Miss Sachs.

"Yes, that seems to be the case, Doctor," she told him.

"Well, then perhaps I was mistaken," he said. He was starting to sweat again. "Somehow he must have hit his head falling, and then rolled over."

"If you gentlemen don't mind," Miss Sachs said, "I'd like to go lie down. The doctor can show you out."

"Of course, Miss," Lacy told her.

Then he and I looked for blood stains, trying to see what might have caused the general's wound. We saw nothing.

"Perhaps the maid wiped it off something?" the doctor said.

"The maid? What would she be doing in here?" Lacy asked.

"It was just a thought."

Then we looked about the room for anything that the general might have been hit with. Again nothing. The three of us went downstairs.

"I'll have the house searched. And outside," Lacy said. "The van from the morgue is already on its way, Doctor. If you could show them where the body is?"

"The morgue?"

"Yes, they'll want to do an autopsy in the morning."

"I suppose I could have the body taken to my practice and perform an autopsy this afternoon."

"No, that won't do, Doctor. Not in a capital case. Let the coroner earn his pay."

"Capital? You mean murder?"

"Yes. You see, if there was no burglary, we must find another explanation for the open window, and the general being hit on the head. And I have a theory. Richard Cole came here with the sole purpose of killing his former employer."

"I see."

"Here they are now."

While the doctor took the men from the morgue upstairs, Lacy and I went out.

"What do you think of this theory, Mr. Reese?"

"I think this Richard Cole certainly is a malleable suspect. But I imagine someone must have hit him on the head. When do you think they'll perform the autopsy?"

"I've already put in a call. I hope first thing in the morning. Shall I keep you informed?"

"Yes, please. But in the meantime, would it be possible to talk to the woman apprehended here last night?"

"Yes, I suppose so."

20

We took a car down to police headquarters and Lacy led me to the women's area of the jail. It being a Sunday morning, the holding cell was crowded with the previous night's haul. When Elizabeth spotted me, she jumped up and came to us.

"Get me out of here, Harry."

"You know her?" Lacy asked.

"Yes. Do you remember I mentioned Miss McGinnis had a friend at the German Embassy?"

"She's employed at the German Embassy?"

"Yes, by the Countess von Schnurrenberger und Kesselheim," Elizabeth elaborated. "Just as I told you."

"'Schnurrenberger und Kesselheim'? Sounds like a vaudeville act. I assumed that was all nonsense."

"You will find out what sort of nonsense it is, you yap. Wait until the count hears of this."

"The count?" Lacy looked at me.

"Yes," I said. "Apparently a man with a temper, and an expert swordsman besides. How are you at sword play, Sergeant Lacy?"

The sergeant apologized for the error, but it wasn't enough to improve Elizabeth's mood. The ride to the embassy was a long one.

"Where's Emmie?"

"Lying low," I said.

"She was going to leave me there?"

"I think she was afraid she might have to join you. General Sachs died last night."

"Who is General Sachs?"

"The owner of the establishment you were ransacking."

"I didn't do any ransacking. I waited downstairs. What did this general die of?"

"Heart failure, possibly induced by a blow to the head."

"Emmie hit the man on the head?"

"She insists she never saw him."

"Yes, I'm sure she does."

"Was it the cop on the beat who spotted you?"

"I saw him rounding the corner and alerted Emmie. We both got out of the house and ran in the opposite direction. That was a mistake. If we hadn't been running so wildly, I wouldn't have hit that lamppost, and I don't think he would have seen us. I stood there dazed for a moment, and Emmie, the little...."

"Didn't you tell him who you were?"

"Of course. But dressed as I was he was naturally suspicious. Although he might have let me go then and there if some fool hadn't started yelling for the police."

"Victims of crimes often become unreasonable in that way. What happened then?"

"He used his handcuffs to attach me to the lamppost." She stopped to sneeze. "It was raining then, did I mention that?"

"No, but I had direct knowledge of it."

"Well, he went off and didn't return for some time. By then there were dozens of cops about. They took me to their precinct."

"Which precinct?"

"Third, I think."

"You didn't happen to catch that first cop's name?"

"Yes, it was McDonald."

"You're kidding. Was he wearing a helmet?"

"What? Of course he was wearing a helmet." Then she heated up again. "It was that damned countess behind this, you know."

"Yes, but to her credit, I think she was intending to aid my investigation."

"To her credit? She blackmails me into helping your bedlamite wife burglarize a man's home—at the risk of my life—and you say, *to her credit*?"

"I only meant it's a mitigating factor. But there's no denying her methodology was somewhat ruthless."

"Oh, she's completely ruthless. And quite as insane as your Emmie."

"I find that difficult to imagine."

"Yes, so did I. At first. Do you know what she said to me the other day? I was complaining that the count's flirtations were becoming increasingly lubricious. But instead of addressing the issue, she asked if I thought it would be at all suspicious if he were to die choking on a chicken bone."

"I suppose you would find it so now."

"Yes, but only if I were fool enough to remain here to witness it. I'm leaving Tuesday for a new position."

"So I've heard, but none of the details."

"That suits me fine. I'm sorry, Harry, but as long as you're mixed up with those two, you can't be trusted."

"The countess says she already knows."

"She says she does, but I suspect it's a bluff."

When we arrived at the embassy we were told that the countess was in her apartment. Elizabeth went in for an audience, and I followed. We found the Gräfin lounging on a couch and reading out loud, apparently to Emmie. But the latter, sitting with her legs folded beneath her on a large armchair, seemed to be engrossed in a book she was reading. She hid it in the cushions when she saw us.

The picture of relaxed comfort they provided contrasted rather starkly with Elizabeth's current state and she seemed not unaware of the fact.

"You two were going to leave me to die in prison!"

"Harry thought it best if he handled it," Emmie told her.

"And you see, here you are," the countess added.

"Yes, in spite of you."

"You are far too excitable, Miss Strout. I don't think I'll require your services any longer."

"You are dismissing me?"

"Yes, as of tomorrow. But you may remain in your quarters until the end of the week."

Elizabeth then lost what little composure she had left. When her verbal fusillade finally concluded—from simple exhaustion rather than any lack of ammunition—Emmie helped her to her room.

"What a silly girl," the countess said.

"I think she felt she was being used."

"What purpose did she have for entering my service but to use me? If she wishes to play the game, she must learn to do it with poise. What upsets her is that I have continually gotten the better of her. But now she is in love, and will retire from the field."

"Retire to where?"

"I have no idea. I merely made a guess that there is some reason she wishes for it to be a secret. And I was right," she smiled. "Honestly, a week or two in jail would have done her some good."

"And Emmie, too?"

"Yes, Miss Slyboots, too."

"So it was you who alerted the police after sending them to the Sachses'?"

"You figured that out, Harry," she smiled. "I think Emmie has as well, but she has a little more finesse than her friend."

"Was this to get even for Emmie's outwitting you on that trip to Baltimore?"

"Don't use that word. It may be true, but it pains me to hear it. Yes, I did want my revenge on Emmie. But I've decided to forgive her. I was even considering making her my acolyte."

"Oh, I wouldn't go to all that trouble. Maybe you shouldn't forgive her...."

"Perhaps you're right. But she can be quite amusing."

"So people tell me."

I had sat down in the chair Emmie had been in previously and was discreetly probing the cushions.

"Find it?" the countess asked. "It's the book I was telling you about. You may borrow it, but I insist it be returned before you leave town. And quit blushing, for God's sake."

I made no reply, but tucked the book away in my jacket.

"You should be satisfied, Harry. Emmie showed me the jewelry you both brought home. And I suppose you know where I was last evening?"

"Playing your role as Glinda?"

"Yes, and I must say, my performance was very well received." She pointed toward a small table. "In that drawer."

I opened it and found three bundles. The first two

were mine and Emmie's, and the third contained the jewelry Easterly had claimed. I put all three in my pocket.

"How did you persuade Sesbania to tell you where the jewelry was? She clung pretty firmly to the winged monkey story when I asked her about it."

"We went on a treasure hunt."

"I hadn't thought of that," I said. "Why did you do this for me?"

"I could tell you it was because you were friendly to me. Escorting me to Mrs. Spinks', and so on."

"Yes, you could tell me that."

"But you wouldn't believe it? Let's say it was simply for the joy of the game."

That seemed a little closer to the truth, but I had a feeling it was something a little more mercenary. Emmie rejoined us and announced that Elizabeth was taking a bath.

"She seems much calmer. Were you serious about dismissing her?"

"Yes, I won't need her after tomorrow. Besides, I wanted to dismiss her before she had the effrontery to resign her post."

Emmie and I exchanged looks, and the countess laughed. Then she picked up a stack of papers. "Have you read these, Harry?"

"Read what?"

"These letters. Emmie found them in your uniform from last night."

"Mrs. Merrill's correspondence," I said. "She seems to have multiple admirers. I glanced through them. They reminded me of *The Dolly Dialogues*, only with more feeling. I was thinking of giving them to Emmie for Christmas."

"You'll have to buy her something, I'm afraid. But you might be glad I took the time to read them."

She paged through the stack and handed me one. It was on Alice Sachs' stationery and dated October 21st.

> *My Dear,*
>
> *I suppose you might know what the brute has done now, but if you don't, I will tell you.*
>
> *The Boucheron brooch, the one treasure of my mother's I have remaining, has been sent to a jeweler in New York named Pomerleau. It is to be sold and I've been given a cheap copy in its stead. He honestly seemed fool enough to think I wouldn't notice the switch.*
>
> *He's bent on ruining us. Always a new scheme to make up for the losses from the last venture. And always some new sacrifice from me to finance it. But this is just too much. I thoroughly despise him.*
>
> *I'm determined to get my legacy returned to me, whatever the cost, but I may need your assistance. Can I depend on you?*
>
> *Yours, Alice*

When I finished, I folded it up and put it in my pocket.

"What do you think of it, Harry?" the countess asked.

"Well, we know the general needed to raise money for a real-estate deal."

"Yes, Emmie told me about this French purchase."

"I also knew he had hired a jeweler in New York,

Pomerleau, to make a replica. Ever hear of him?"

"No, I don't think so."

"I assume the general wanted the replica so he could sell the original. But apparently Alice intended to go to New York to get it back."

"But why would Alice Sachs be asking for Mrs. Merrill's help?" Emmie asked.

"She wasn't," the countess said. "Nor were any of these love letters sent to her. If you had listened closely, you'd have noted that all the others we've read begin with some generic endearment."

"What are you getting at?" I asked.

"Mrs. Merrill is agreeable-looking, and no doubt an able seductress, but I don't think this is a collection of her personal correspondence. All the letters go far enough to compromise the sender. These aren't mere flirtations."

"You think she was blackmailing the authors of the letters?" Emmie asked.

"*And* the recipients, no doubt."

"But the letter from Alice Sachs wouldn't be useful as blackmail," Emmie said. "I'm sure her father was well aware she disliked him."

"It may not have been the subject of the letter, but who it was written to," the countess pointed out. She flipped through the stack of letters as she spoke. "And here's a companion to that one."

She handed me a letter written on the stationery of M. Pomerleau & Son and dated November 12th.

> *Doctor,*
>
> *In spite of recent developments, I am still awaiting payment for my work for General*

Sachs. As he will not respond to my requests for a resolution, I must insist you yourself make payment. I remind you that I am still in possession of the promissory note you signed and will make use of it if the payment of $500 is not soon forthcoming.

Georges Pomerleau

I handed it to Emmie to read. When she handed it back, I put it in my pocket with the other.

"Who's the doctor?" she asked.

"There's a Dr. Gillette, the general's physician. He was at the house this morning. An odd character."

"In what way?" the countess asked.

"Nervous. He may have some other connection to the affair as well. I've seen him at Mrs. Spinks' place a couple times. You met him on your first visit—he was talking to Easterly and myself."

"Yes, I remember now. I believe he was also the man I saw escorting Alice Sachs the evening she was wearing the genuine Boucheron."

"How would Amanda Merrill have acquired all these letters?" Emmie asked.

"Servants, usually," the countess told her. "They are underpaid and underappreciated."

"Did I see her last night?" Emmie asked the countess.

"Let me think." She leaned her head back and gazed at the ceiling for a moment or two. "Yes, remember when you and I had our conference on the terrace? General Sachs came out and handed a drink to a Marie Antoinette. That was Mrs. Merrill."

"The lady who dropped her handkerchief."

"If she had this other source of income, I wonder why they bothered with the insurance claim?" I asked. Emmie and the countess both laughed.

"You don't suppose she shares the fruit of her labor with her husband, do you?" the countess asked. Then, as was her way, she hinted that our audience was over. Emmie had had our costumes cleaned and they were stacked on a chair near the door, with two policeman's helmets on the floor beside it.

"The other helmet turned up?" I asked.

"Yes. How did you come to have two?"

"It's a long story. But I need to return one."

I determined which was Officer McDonald's and put it under my arm. Then we went off to the hotel for lunch.

"Did you pick up the rest of the letters, Harry?"

"No, the countess secreted them away when she thought she was unobserved."

"Oh. That's probably just as well."

"I doubt those who sent them would agree with that sentiment."

"You think she'll take to blackmailing them?"

"I know I'd prefer she didn't hold any of my compromising correspondence. Just how graphic did they get? Can you give me a taste?"

"Oh, some were quite graphic. I don't remember the details...."

She was blushing uncontrollably. I came to her rescue by changing the subject to that of the morning's events at the Sachses'. Including the doctor's discovery of the head wound.

"So the general may have been killed?"

"Lacy thinks so. He's arranging for an autopsy. He thinks Richard Cole came by to seek revenge for losing his position."

"He didn't seem the type to do that, did he?"

"No. Lacy just seems to enjoy hounding the poor fellow."

"But someone else may have done in the general just the same."

"Yes, I suppose so."

"What will you be doing this afternoon?" she asked.

"Going to see a man about a helmet. And you?"

"I was thinking of attending mass somewhere."

That she could maintain a serious mien while uttering these words frightened me. Emmie hadn't been to mass since her mother visited us the previous Easter. But there was no use pursuing the subject further. We left the hotel together and I went off to the third precinct, over on K Street, and asked for McDonald.

"Off."

"Know where he lives?"

"Sure. Why do you want to see him?"

"To return his helmet." I held up Exhibit A.

"He's on 25th Street."

He gave me the house number and I went off. A child came to the door and informed me that Officer McDonald was enjoying Sunday dinner with his family. When his father arrived, his eyes fixed on the helmet.

"I've come to return your helmet." I handed it to him.

He looked inside and saw his name. "How'd you get it?"

"It's a long, sordid story and someday I'll come by and share it with you. I just wanted to make amends."

"I don't see how you've done that."

"By returning it."

"I already had to buy a new one."

"Well, I was just trying to be helpful."

"Then give me the eight dollars. That would be helpful. Where'd you find it?"

"I purchased it from a lad."

"That's receiving stolen goods!"

His interpretation of the law had the ring of truth to it. I gave him eight dollars. He softened a little and so I proceeded to the primary reason for my visit.

"Coincidentally, I'm investigating the burglary at General Sachs' last night."

"For who?"

"The insurance company. There seems to be some question about the position of the general's body. The doctor didn't notice the wound on his head until this morning."

"What wound on his head?"

"Right up on the back of the head." I illustrated.

"I didn't see any wound."

"But you found him face down?"

"I didn't find him. His daughter did. I was looking about the scene of the burglary, and she calls me from across the hall. She was trying to turn the old man over, to see if he was all right. When I came in, she asked me to put him in bed. I laid him on the bed and could tell right away he was dead. She could tell too, by then. Then I asked her to send for the doctor."

"Did you see any blood at all?"

"No. Doctor said it was heart failure."

"Did you get any blood on your sleeve when you were lifting him up?"

He went and got his uniform jacket and we both examined the sleeves.

"Nothing. It was raining last night, but I don't think that'd wash off blood," he said.

I agreed that was unlikely and left him to finish his dinner.

21

When I returned to the hotel there was a message from Lacy. He'd apprehended Richard Cole and had him at headquarters. I took a car and found the sergeant in his office just finishing a phone call.

"The autopsy will be tomorrow morning at nine," he said.

"All right, where do I go?"

"The morgue, across from the B&O depot."

"Any luck finding a weapon at the Sachses'?" I asked.

"No, nothing. Not a trace of blood anywhere. Cole must have taken it away with him."

"What's he told you?"

"He's being shrewd. Wants to see his lawyer. He's on his way."

"There's something I didn't mention yesterday. I exchanged wires with the man who made that replica brooch. A jeweler in New York. He said it was finished in October. Before the original was stolen."

"What does that mean?"

"I'm not sure, but I thought I should tell you."

"Puzzling."

A uniformed man came in and told Lacy that Patterson, Cole's lawyer, had arrived.

"Where is he?"

"In with the prisoner."

"In with the prisoner?" Lacy leaped up and charged out.

I followed him down a hall to a small room. There was a fellow on guard outside and inside Patterson and Cole were speaking quickly, obviously trying to finish some conversation before we'd hear.

"You were called to be present during questioning, not to be given the opportunity to instruct your client how to obfuscate matters."

"My apologies, Sergeant." Patterson had risen and put out his hand. Lacy ignored it.

"Sit down. Where were you last night, Cole?"

"Cabin John."

"What if I were to tell you I have witnesses seeing you leave the Sachses' home just after midnight?"

"I'd say they're wrong. I was at Cabin John, until the last car."

"And who'd you see there?"

Cole carefully recited a list of three names.

"Saturday night, and you only saw three people up there?"

"I saw a lot of people, only three I know."

Lacy turned to Patterson. "You mucked things up for me again. Well, I'll get to the bottom of this."

He marched out and the officer took Cole back to his cell. Patterson was picking up his things.

"What's Cabin John?"

"A little village up the river, in Maryland. A street car runs out there, and there's a saloon that offers various entertainments. A busy place."

"So, easy to find a witness he was there?"

"Easy enough," he smiled.

We walked out of the building together.

"Look," I said. "It's obvious Cole had nothing to do with it. Why go through the subterfuge?"

"It's obvious to *you* Cole had nothing to do with it."

"Doesn't he have a real alibi?"

"Oh, yes. He was in bed with another man's wife."

"And he doesn't want to stain her honor?"

"Nothing that noble. To a man like Lacy, an alibi provided by a colored jezebel is tantamount to an admission of guilt."

"And the three gentlemen he named are pillars of the community?"

"No, hardly. But two of them are white."

"How could you come up with them so quickly?"

"That I can't divulge."

I took a car back to the hotel and a half hour later Emmie showed up.

"Long mass?"

She smiled.

"I had to get back the money I spent yesterday at the Ebbitt."

"From the scribblers?"

"Yes, they were most forthcoming."

"Cards?"

"Poker."

"I thought you'd sworn off games of chance, Emmie."

"Oh, chance didn't enter into it."

She held up her lucky deck.

"It's a curious philosophy that considers cheating morally superior to gambling, Emmie."

"But surely it's the gambler who has morally compromised himself. You might say I'm merely teaching him the error of his ways."

"Very admirable. How much did you win?"

"More than enough. Mrs. *Post-Intelligencer* is likely

to be rather upset when she asks for her allowance this week."

"If you turned such a large profit, you can reimburse me for the checks I paid."

"I can't imagine why I'd do that. But I'll pay back what I borrowed."

A while later, we went down to the dining room for dinner.

"The autopsy is tomorrow morning, if you'd like to come along."

"I've never attended one. How bad is it?"

"Pretty bad. The trick is to stare at the wall."

"Then what's the point in going?"

"To listen, ask questions—and maintain the illusion you're one of the fraternity."

"Hmm. Do you think Alice might have killed her father?"

"I have the feeling she wouldn't have found the thought outlandish."

"And so she took advantage of the burglary to dispatch him?"

"It would have taken a cool head, what with the cop just across the hall. And what did she use to dispatch him?"

"She could have tossed whatever it was under the bed," she said. "Then removed it later, before the doctor discovered the head wound."

"But how could she be sure he wouldn't find it during his first examination?"

"That's a good question."

We were having our coffee when I noticed a tall, blond fellow coming towards us. It was Detective Sergeant Tibbitts, of the New York Police Department. I had worked with him on a case the previous spring. Emmie—who'd met him just once—greeted him as an old friend and invited him to sit down.

"Are you in town on business, Sergeant?" Emmie asked.

"Yeah. In a way, your husband called me down here."

"In what way?" I asked.

"Your wire to the jeweler, Pomerleau."

"You're investigating counterfeit jewelry?"

"Nope, still homicide. He was murdered."

"Yesterday?"

"A month ago."

"Then who answered my wire?"

"His son. After talking to me."

"What's the connection with this brooch?"

"Pomerleau was hired to copy a Boucheron brooch back in late September. There's no written record, only the son's account. The father did a lot of this duplicating of jewelry, but never told his son the details. He had the original Boucheron to work from, and spent two or three weeks on the job. When he was done, he sent the copy to the buyer. Then, a week or two after that, when the father was out, a man showed up and asked for the return of the Boucheron brooch. The son didn't even realize his father still had the original. Apparently he was supposed to sell it, but the owner now wanted it back. When his father returned to the shop, he got into an argument with this man. Seems Pomerleau hadn't been paid for making the copy. He was supposed to take it out of what was received for the original. So if the sale was off, he wanted the cash. Eventually, the old man let the visitor have the original after signing some receipt and assuring him he would be paid the five hundred dollars owed him.

"Then a week or so later, the old man reads something in the paper that makes him mad enough to burst a valve. He mentions the amount five hundred dollars again, so the son assumes there's some connection to the Boucheron brooch. About two weeks later—this is Saturday, November 16th—the old man tells his son a client is coming by and the son should go off for the afternoon. This happened fairly frequently. When he came back, his father was dead. As soon as the police doctor sees the body, he says Pomerleau was poisoned. The coroner identified it as aconite. There were still traces of it in a coffee cup."

"What did that first visitor look like?"

"About thirty, maybe older. Oily dark hair and eyeglasses."

"Did anyone see the second person who came by?"

"Oh, sure. There were five witnesses who saw someone go into or come out of the shop. Three saw a woman go in, but the descriptions didn't match each other. One saw a fat man enter, one saw a thin man leave."

"Then how did you link the murder to the Boucheron brooch?"

"The old man kept a little ledger book for the discreet work. I have it. The son and I went through it and found one page had been torn out. He saw notations about all the recent work he'd seen his father doing, but nothing on the Boucheron brooch. I checked the others, and nothing panned out. Most of them were women who needed some ready money. They want to sell the family gems, but keep it from the husband. So they have a copy made and the husband never notices. Nothing illegal, but you can see why they want it done quietly.

"Then your wire comes asking about the Boucheron brooch. The son calls me and asks what to do."

"I don't suppose you've gone by Sachs' home yet?"

"No, I just got into town. I figured I'd let you give me the lay of the land."

"General Sachs died last night."

"Of what?"

"Probably heart failure. But there was a wound to the head. There'll be an autopsy in the morning."

"Did he have these brooches?"

"Yes, or at least his daughter had them."

"Had them?"

"Well, right now, I have the original and she has the copy."

"How is it you have the original?"

Answering that question took most of an hour, and that was with leaving out the countess, Mrs. Spinks, and the outings to Oz. I did, however, include the portion where Elizabeth was nabbed by the police. Not because it had any real bearing on the matter, but I knew it would be of personal interest to Sergeant Tibbitts. He had twice encountered Elizabeth during his investigations and had exploited her compromised position by using her as his pigeon. It was her work as police informer that first brought her to my attention, and it was only later that I learned she'd been to school with Emmie. It's astounding what a small world it really is.

Then I gave him the two letters from Mrs. Merrill's collection, the one from Alice Sachs asking an unknown friend for help in getting back her brooch, and the other from Pomerleau to an unnamed doctor, asking for payment of five hundred dollars. I didn't conjecture about who the doctor was. I figured Tibbitts would be meeting

Gillette soon enough and could come to his own conclusions.

Once we had each other informed, Sergeant Tibbitts seemed anxious to visit Miss Sachs. It was after ten, on a Sunday evening, and most people would think it an inappropriate time to make house calls. But policemen have strange ideas about etiquette.

The three of us walked up to 19th Street. We agreed to let him ask the questions, and he agreed not to mention the burglaries. It took some pounding on the door to elicit a response, but eventually it was answered. By Dr. Gillette, in shirtsleeves. He started out acting pretty abrupt and not at all friendly. But once he learned who Tibbitts was, he became amenable. He led us to the parlor and said he'd call Miss Sachs. Tibbitts gave me a look that made it obvious he recognized the doctor as the first visitor to Pomerleau's shop. When he returned, Tibbitts asked him what he knew about the brooch. I didn't expect him to say much, but I was wrong.

"The general got it into his head he could replace the brooch with a copy without his daughter, Alice—Miss Sachs—noticing the change. He then planned to sell the original."

"To raise money to speculate on a tract of land?" I asked.

"Yes. But Alice noticed immediately. She was very upset and confided in me. I confronted the general on the matter and he told me he had sent the brooch to New York to be copied and then sold. He agreed it was a mistake. I was going to New York a few days later, so I offered to return the copy and get back the original. He produced the case the jeweler, a M. Pomerleau, had sent the copy in and I took it and the copy."

Just then, Alice came in and handed Gillette his jacket. I introduced Tibbitts and we all sat down again.

"Go on, Doctor," Tibbitts said.

"I took a train to New York, visited the jeweler in his shop, and asked him to make the trade. He refused. He pointed out the copy had no value to him, as he couldn't very well go out and market a copy of another man's work. It had taken him three weeks, he said, and he expected five hundred dollars as payment before he would release the original. I pointed out he was in a difficult position, but agreed he was due the payment. He had me sign a receipt and a promissory note before he would hand over the original. But he refused to accept the return of the copy.

"When I returned to Washington, I gave Miss Sachs the brooch."

"Both brooches?" I asked.

"Yes. But then the original was stolen, as you know."

"Yes," I agreed. "I know all about that."

"Did you hear from Pomerleau after that?" Tibbitts asked him.

"No. But as it happens, Sergeant," the doctor continued, "the investment the general had made has paid off. And M. Pomerleau will receive his money shortly."

"His estate will receive it," Tibbitts corrected.

"What do you mean? Has he passed away?"

"He was poisoned."

The doctor and Alice exchanged looks. He was startled by the news, but she held steady.

"Poisoned?" the doctor asked. "When?"

"About three weeks after you saw him."

"But what does that have to do with Miss Sachs?"

Tibbitts pulled the book out. It was maybe seven

inches tall, with a black leather cover. "Did you see this book, Doctor?"

"Yes, I believe so. He had me sign twice, once that I had received the original, and once that he would receive payment."

"Both on the same page?"

"Yes, they were just brief notations."

"That page is missing now."

"I can't explain that."

Tibbitts then asked them where they both were on November 16th, the day Pomerleau was poisoned. After some thought, they told us they had spent the day together, going for a drive.

"We had dinner at old Hancock's, on Pennsylvania Avenue," Alice added.

Tibbitts asked to see the room where the general had died. The doctor led us upstairs without much enthusiasm. Then he and I explained to Tibbitts how the general had been found and what had happened subsequently. As we were coming back downstairs, Emmie suddenly appeared, and the three of us left the house.

"Do you think they were telling the truth, Sergeant?" Emmie asked.

"Sometimes it's not even worth guessing," he said. "There're good liars and then there're bad liars."

"Which were they?"

"Both bad. He's the nervous type, and she's the stone. He sweats even when he's mostly telling the truth. And she's so careful not to let on she's hiding something that it's obvious she *is* hiding something. But it might not have anything to do with Pomerleau. Maybe she's just embarrassed by what was going on upstairs before we came."

"Why didn't you mention that letter from Pomerleau? Doesn't it seem likely he was the doctor it was addressed to?"

"Sure he was," he told her. "But I didn't see any point in showing my cards."

"What about the day of the murder?" Emmie asked. "I think they were telling the truth about that."

"Maybe. But it would be easy enough to catch an early train, visit Pomerleau, and be back in time for a late supper. And did you notice what the doctor asked, when I said Pomerleau had been poisoned?"

"He asked when," Emmie said. "What's odd about that?"

"He's a doctor. I expected him to ask what poison was used. What difference did it make when?"

When we reached the Normandie, I asked Tibbitts where he was staying.

"A place called the Fredonia. What kind of name is that?"

"It has a familiar ring to it," I said. "What's it like?"

"Cheap. They always put us in dives so we'll hurry home."

We agreed to meet in the morning and then he went off.

22

I was in bed reading the countess's book when Emmie finished her ablutions. It was by a fellow named Vatsyayana, and just seeing it made her blush. She said nothing, but got in beside me. We read intently, and silently, until sometime after four, both falling asleep with the light on.

I woke up exhausted. Then Emmie nearly ruined breakfast by bringing the conversation around to poisons.

"How would the police in New York know there was aconite in the coffee cup?" she asked.

"There must be some test a chemist can do. They have tests for anything you can think of."

"What sort of chemist?"

"I imagine any chemist would either know the tests or have a manual of some sort. Why, are you planning on poisoning someone?"

"Me? I can't imagine what reason I'd have to poison anyone. How's the coffee taste to you?"

"Bitter."

I left her at the table and went off to the Fredonia to pick up Tibbitts. It wasn't a dive, but certainly a couple pegs down from the Normandie. We boarded the Fourteenth Street car and took it all the way to the B&O depot.

"I should prepare you for Sergeant Lacy," I said.

"How so?"

"He's the detective here who was investigating the

burglaries, and now the death of the general. He thinks he's Sherlock Holmes."

"Oh, one of those. Well, if he gets the job done."

"From what I can tell, Sergeant Lacy's preferred method of getting the job done is to find the nearest suspect without the pull to make trouble for him—preferably a colored man—and lock him up."

Then I told him about Richard Cole, and how Lacy suspected he had killed the general in revenge.

"Let's see what the old man died of before we worry about who killed him," Tibbitts said.

We found the morgue just across from the depot and I introduced the two detectives.

"Sergeant Tibbitts is investigating the death of a jeweler in New York. The man who made the copy of the Boucheron brooch."

"And you think there's a link to the general's death?"

"Who knows?" Tibbitts shrugged.

"I hardly think it's possible," Lacy smiled.

We went in and Lacy introduced us to Assistant Coroner Glazebrook. A stenographer and an orderly were there as well, and a moment later Dr. Gillette joined us. I half suspected he would. But it was Glazebrook who ran the show. First he examined the head wound. The skull had a slight facture. He noted the quantity and consistency of the blood gathered at the site, but sounded unsure about something. Next, he scanned the body for other wounds and found nothing. Then he opened him up. I'd seen a man eviscerated once, and didn't feel in need of a reprise. Hearing was quite enough. I found a spider crawling along a wall and focused on him.

Dr. Gillette stood around like a fellow waiting for his wife to give birth. He folded his arms one way, then a few seconds later he folded them the other way. I preferred watching my spider. He had a pretty ambitious web going on. At first I thought he'd made an error in stringing one of his guy wires, but then I could see he was right after all. I suppose for a spider civil engineering is just part of the standard curriculum. After half an hour, the web looked pretty complete. I'd say his one mistake was in making it too conspicuous. When the charwoman came in that evening, she was sure to take a broom to it. In the meantime, Glazebrook announced that the general appeared to have died of myocardial infarction, otherwise known as heart failure.

"But brought on by the blow to the head," Lacy said.

"Yes, perhaps," Glazebrook told him.

"What about poison?" Tibbitts asked.

"Poison?"

"As a possibility," Tibbitts said.

"Yes, certainly. It's possible. There would likely be some evidence in the digestive system," Glazebrook said. Then he went looking.

"There's an inflammation to the lower esophagus, and the stomach wall," he narrated for the stenographer.

"Pyrosis," Dr. Gillette said. "I treated him for that also."

"Yes, it could just be that," Glazebrook said. "Was there any vomited matter?"

"A small amount," Gillette said. "Consistent with myocardial infarction."

"Was it saved?"

"No, I'm afraid I didn't think it significant. At the time, there seemed nothing suspicious about the death."

Glazebrook turned to Tibbitts. "Was there a particular toxin you had in mind?"

"Aconite, but I'll take whatever you're selling."

"Was his heart condition treated with aconite, Doctor?" Glazebrook asked.

"Aconite? Yes. A very small dosage," Gillette told him. He had his watch out. "I'm sorry, gentlemen, but I have an appointment. If there's anything else, I'll be at my office this afternoon."

He left us and Glazebrook looked over at Lacy.

"Did anyone see the man during the hours before death?"

"He was attending an embassy ball, but left early complaining of pyrosis," the sergeant told him. "He was found dead about three hours after that."

"I would say poisoning is a possibility," Glazebrook said. "But it would take me some time to run the tests. I should have an answer by noon."

Lacy said he would see us then and hurried off.

"Where are you off to now, Sergeant?" I asked Tibbitts.

"Back to the Sachses', doing what I should have done last night."

"What's that?"

"Looking for aconite. Gillette said he'd prescribed it for Sachs, so there must be some about the place. Care to come along?"

"I'm headed in that direction, but I have to attend to my own business."

"I thought you had the missing jewelry?"

"Yes—now I need to arrange for selling it back."

We caught a car heading west.

"What do you think was making Gillette so nervous?" I asked.

"Who knows? It could just be he recognized the old

boy was poisoned and is worried he'll be blamed for giving him the wrong dose."

We got off the car and went our separate ways. Mine led me to Julius Chappelle. I was shown into his office, where he was putting some books into a crate.

"I didn't realize you were leaving so soon," I said.

"Nor did I, but my plans have been accelerated by events."

"Any events I know about?"

"Which events do you know about?"

"General Sachs' death, for one."

"No, that's of little concern to me. Likewise the other events of Saturday evening. I take it you've solved your insurance case?"

"Well, in a sense. That's one of the things I wanted to talk to you about. You've spoken with the people we mentioned earlier?"

"I did. And I'm sure they would now be amenable to entering into negotiations with you."

"You mean, now that the French government's purchase has gone through?"

"Very good, Mr. Reese. And you've only been in town a week. Yes, I mean precisely that."

"One thing that puzzles me is: why couldn't these reputable people come up with a more legitimate way of raising money?"

"Because they'd bled those vessels dry. People like that are often short of ready cash, even as they accumulate more wealth. That's why they're so badly burned when the crash comes."

"Is there a crash coming?"

"There's always a crash coming."

"Yes, I suppose that's true. Where are you heading?"

"France. Have you been there?"

"We spent a few days there this summer. Didn't see much, though. You're planning an extended stay?"

"Yes, perhaps for the duration," he smiled.

"Parlez-vous français?"

"Pas très bien. But we expect to be among other expatriates."

"We?"

"An indiscretion, please ignore it."

"When does the new owner move in?"

"Soon. You know him—my brother, Samuel."

"Do you think he'll run the business in the same way?"

"You mean, will he subvert my network to further his more disreputable business interests?"

"Yes, I guess that is what I mean."

"I don't think so. I imagine he's at an age where he'll welcome a quieter life. But he's his own man."

"It seems to me if one had an inclination toward extortion, a network like yours could prove very profitable."

"Certainly. *If* one were inclined that way."

"That brings up the second reason for my visit. You know Amanda Merrill, the senator's wife?"

"Yes."

"Well, I happen to have come into possession of certain correspondence."

"Yes, I know all about that."

"The correspondence, or my coming into possession of it?"

"Both. But you don't believe I had any connection with her collection?"

"No, it seemed a little crude. But I thought you

might be able to tell me something about it. For instance, how did she acquire the letters?"

"Bought them. Mostly from servants, sometimes from the victims' friends."

"Friends?"

"This is a town where one must be very careful in choosing one's friends. But I suppose that's true everywhere. It's a sad truth that most of us are focused on our own corrupt interests."

"Speaking of my own, do you think you could set up a meeting with Easterly and the others?"

"Mrs. Spinks is planning a celebration of sorts during this afternoon's salon. If you can attend, I think you will find all the interested parties assembled there."

"Will you be there as well?"

"You may see me."

I left him and took a car back to the morgue. Lacy was there and a little later Tibbitts arrived. Just after noon, Dr. Glazebrook let us into his laboratory. He was watching a mouse in a cage. The mouse was not looking his best.

"I isolated a substance from the victim's stomach contents. The mouse has been injected with it. Gentlemen, I would say this man died of heart failure brought on by poisoning," Glazebrook announced.

"And definitely aconite?" I asked.

"The definitive test for that is rather crude. But I suppose…."

He then took a small part of something he'd concocted and put it on his tongue. He spit it out and flushed his mouth.

"Yes, aconite."

I'm no pathologist, but it seems to me any test that

involves possibly poisoning yourself leaves something to be desired.

"I imagine this puts Richard Cole out of the running," I said to Lacy.

"Yes, perhaps," he said. "But what about the head wound?"

"I was just going to bring that up," Glazebrook said. "That was done after death."

"He fell after his heart failed?" Tibbitts asked.

"No, nothing so simple. The wound was made some time after death. Probably a number of hours later."

"How can you tell that?" Lacy asked.

"There was no bruising. At least, no legitimate bruising. You see, the blood gathered at the site wasn't human. I believe it came from a cow."

"A cow?" Lacy said.

"Or possibly a horse," Glazebrook said. "Look at these slides." He led us to a table where there were two microscopes side by side. "The slide on the right contains human corpuscles, the one on the left is a sample from the head wound."

They did look different.

"But how did you know to look?" I asked.

"It didn't seem right. The blood should have congealed more. You must remember, I see a lot of bodies."

"How was the blood put there?" Lacy asked.

"It was injected. I shaved the scalp and found a needle mark."

"Very ingenious," Lacy pronounced. It was obvious the Holmesian complexity of it appealed to him.

"How so?" Tibbitts asked him.

"Clearly, the culprit wanted to obscure the cause of death."

"He didn't do a very good job of it," Tibbitts pointed out.

"Nonetheless, the intention was clear. And who but Dr. Gillette had the opportunity and the means?"

"To fake the wound, or poison the general?" I asked.

"I suspect the same person did both. Don't you agree, Sergeant Tibbitts?"

"It isn't my case. I don't have to suspect anything. But the odds say the person who poisoned the general was the same person who killed my jeweler."

"Of course, the doctor has some powerful friends," I said. "The same people you feared before, Sergeant Lacy."

"Oh, I don't fear them, Mr. Reese. But I respect their power to do me harm. As I would a flame, or a mad dog. No, I won't proceed until I have a warrant for his arrest. I'll keep it all nice and proper."

Then he left us to find a judge willing to perform the task.

"How long before death would the poison have to have been administered?" I asked Glazebrook.

"That would depend on how large the dose was, but from the quantity I've seen, I would guess two to four hours."

"And there's no way he just took too much, by accident?" Tibbitts asked.

"Normally it's given to a patient so diluted it would require taking an extraordinary amount. No, I think it must have been deliberate."

"Assuming it was undiluted, how hard would it be to mask it?"

"In its purest form, a grain can be fatal. A druggist works with a mixture that's already diluted, but even that would require less than a teaspoon to be fatal."

"But the taste?"

"The taste isn't distinct, but it causes a tingling feeling on the tongue."

We thanked him and on our way out I invited Tibbitts back to the Normandie to dine with Emmie and me.

"How long will it take Lacy to get a warrant?" I asked.

"It's lunch time. He probably won't be able to find a judge until two. But then it should just take a few minutes. Unless he makes the mistake of picking a judge who's friendly with the doctor."

23

We found Emmie waiting for us in the dining room. I can always tell when she's feeling particularly pleased with herself. She had some surprise to reveal and was just waiting for the moment that would provide the maximum dramatic effect.

When I told her about the coroner determining that the general had been poisoned with aconite, she seemed a little surprised. And then Sergeant Tibbitts made his own revelation. He placed a small bottle on the table. It was the type druggists give out. I picked it up, read the label and passed it to Emmie. It was a prescription of aconite. The printed label was that of a local pharmacy, with the dosage and Dr. Gillette's name written on it in script.

"I found it at the general's this morning, while we were waiting for the coroner to finish up."

"You should have asked him to test it."

"I didn't need to. I went by the drug store, and the fellow said he filled it just yesterday morning. The doctor called on him at home, said it was an emergency. He mixed the standard dosage and handed it over."

"Miss Sachs didn't object to you searching for it?" I asked.

"No, she didn't seem to care a hoot. But I wasn't too surprised about that."

"Where did you find it?" Emmie asked.

"In the old man's bedroom. Tucked in the drawer, but not hidden."

"That's curious," she said. Then she place her own

bottle on the table. It was identical to the other, but the information on the label was typed and included the general's name.

"Where'd you find that?" I asked.

"Remember when we were there last evening? I excused myself to use the bathroom. It was in the cabinet. It's the same dosage as the other. I took it by a chemist's this morning and he verified it."

"Someone's being too clever," Tibbitts said.

"What do you mean, Sergeant?" Emmie asked.

"Do you want to tell her about the last bit at the autopsy?" he asked me.

"Remember that head wound, Emmie? It seems the doctor created it himself."

"But why?"

"That remains to be found out. But I imagine it's the same reason the spare bottle of aconite showed up."

"I don't understand," she said. "Doesn't it seem obvious whoever killed Pomerleau in New York also killed the general?"

"Not definite, but very likely," Tibbitts said.

"Well, I checked their story, about that day when Pomerleau was poisoned. They were definitely here. The manager at Hancock's remembered them."

"Does he know them?"

"Yes, apparently they go there often."

"Then maybe he remembers the day before, or the week before," Tibbitts said.

"He showed me the reservation book. They came in for an early dinner," Emmie told him. She had a pretty satisfied look. "Now that we know it wasn't the doctor or Miss Sachs who killed these men, who is your chief suspect, Sergeant?"

"Oh, I'm not so sure what I know. Who do you have in mind?"

"I'd rather not say for the moment, but I have my suspicions."

"Elizabeth? The countess? The Wizard himself?" I asked.

"Go ahead, play horse with me, Harry. You'll see."

Emmie's never been one to harbor much self-doubt, but that day she'd lost the sensation entirely. Pride goes before a fall, I thought. Of course, often when I have those thoughts, things have a way of getting turned around.

"Where will you be later this afternoon, Harry?"

"I've been invited to a soirée at Mrs. Spinks'. I'm sure you both will be welcome, too. And all the others are likely to be there."

"Mr. and Mrs. Easterly, and the senator and his wife?" Emmie asked.

"Yes, and the countess, and perhaps Elizabeth, too."

"Oh, yeah?" Tibbitts asked.

"Are you hoping to renew your acquaintance, Sergeant?"

"I might have some questions for her."

"Ask them quickly—my understanding is she's planning to leave Washington."

"To go where?" Emmie asked.

"She declined to say. It seems she didn't trust that I wouldn't divulge it to you," I told her. "This may come as a surprise to you, Emmie, but I think recent events have left your friendship with Elizabeth in a precarious state."

"Yes, I sensed she was feeling some bitterness toward me when she threatened to drown me in her bath," she replied. "Now I must be going. There are one or two things I need to establish."

I gave Emmie directions to Mrs. Spinks' and she was off.

"There's something else I should share with you, Sergeant. Concerning how I came by those letters I gave you."

"By breaking into people's houses?"

"Yes, but it's a little more involved than that. I found those amongst Mrs. Merrill's lingerie. She's the senator's wife. There was a whole stack of correspondence. From a number of different authors and apparently to various recipients. It seems Amanda Merrill has a line in extortion."

"You think she's been bleeding the doctor?"

"I've no idea. I just thought I should tell you."

"All right, you told me. Now let's go find Gillette."

We went by his office and were told he was in with a patient. Ten minutes later, we were shown in. He was trying to be affable, but sweating too much to make it convincing.

"What can I do for you, gentlemen?"

"You missed the finale over at the morgue," Tibbitts said. "Lose interest?"

"What did Dr. Glazebrook determine?"

"Death by aconite poisoning."

"Was it? I wonder if the general overdosed himself. People often panic when they're in acute pain."

"Do they?" Tibbitts smiled.

"Very often, yes."

"Do they also hit themselves on the head after they've been dead a good while?"

"Whatever do you mean?"

"Dr. Glazebrook found the puncture mark and identified the blood as an animal's," I told him.

"I suppose I should talk to my lawyer."

"Why are you trying so hard to complicate things?" Tibbitts asked him.

"That's certainly not my intention."

"This morning, my wife verified your alibi for the day the jeweler in New York was murdered," I told him.

"Did she?"

"Yes," I said. "So you know Miss Sachs didn't kill him. But you suspect she killed her father?"

"That's absurd."

"Then are you trying to protect someone else?" Tibbitts asked.

"No, certainly not."

"Do you remember receiving this?" He handed him Pomerleau's letter.

"How did you get this?"

"What's that matter? What matters is you lied to me last night."

"I simply forgot about this letter. Nothing came of it."

"You're wasting our time, Doctor," Tibbitts told him.

"What is it you suspect me of?"

"Just misreading things," I said to him. "Miss Sachs told you herself she despised her father. Saturday night, she telephoned you with the news that her father was dead and her house had been burglarized. When you arrived, you realized—or at least strongly suspected—he'd been poisoned. You couldn't think of anyone else who would have killed him, so you suspected her. Maybe she even said something about being glad he was dead."

"No, she never said anything like that."

"Nonetheless, you suspected her. She's the type who offends easily and you couldn't bring yourself to ask her point-blank. You hoped that since the general had a chronic heart condition, no one would bother questioning your diagnosis of heart failure.

"Then Sergeant Lacy showed up. He linked the general's death to the burglary. That meant there would probably be an autopsy. That night, you came up with the scheme of faking a head wound, giving the coroner something to find that would explain the heart failure and at the same time providing the link to burglars that Lacy was looking for. You knew if you just fractured the skull, there wouldn't be any bruising, so you drew blood from a horse, probably your own. Then, Sunday morning, you went back to the general's house. When you were alone, you gave him the head wound and injected the horse's blood."

"That's pretty good," Tibbitts said to me. "When'd you work all that out?"

"Oh, not long ago."

"Look, Doctor," Tibbitts said. "No one is accusing your lady friend. But you're just drawing attention to her. What's the point now? We know what you did. And Sergeant Lacy's swearing out a warrant right this minute."

Gillette looked over at me.

"Yes, that's what he told us."

"I see." It was difficult to imagine anything could have unsettled him more than he already was, but this news did the trick.

"I found that bottle of aconite you got from the druggist yesterday," Tibbitts added.

"I seem to have just made things worse."

"Yeah, so far," Tibbitts agreed. "There was something else that made you suspect Miss Sachs, wasn't there?"

"What do you mean?"

"You found a bottle of aconite, but one mixed strong enough to poison a person. Maybe just as the druggists get it. You thought maybe Miss Sachs had switched bottles on the general. You took that bottle away, then replaced it with one having the right dosage. But what you didn't realize was that his bottle was still in the house."

Gillette looked surprised at this news.

"My wife found it in the bathroom last night," I told him.

"So if Miss Sachs had poisoned him, all she had to do was hide that full-dose bottle. She could have tossed it anywhere. Do you really think she was cool enough to get the poison and use it on the old man, but too thick-headed to get rid of it afterwards?"

"So you don't suspect her?"

"The only thing that draws suspicion to her is your trying so hard to make us look somewhere else."

"I did find the bottle, just as you say. It had the wrong label—I could tell at once it wasn't what I'd prescribed. I took it away with me that night. At home I tasted it. Just a tiny amount. But I could tell it was far stronger than is normal. I took an emetic immediately."

"Do you have the bottle?"

"I have the bottle, but I disposed of the contents."

He went to a shelf of medicines and returned with a clean, empty bottle. It had a handwritten label with nothing identifying the source. It had the general's name and the same dosage listed as the others.

"Any idea where it came from?"

"None. I can't believe any druggist would give it to someone."

"From a supply house?"

"Perhaps, but they're required to check on their buyers."

Tibbitts put the bottle in his pocket. "Let's go see Miss Sachs."

"Why?" Gillette asked.

"She might be able to clear things up."

He agreed reluctantly and the three of us went off in a cab. We found Alice upstairs in the library, packing.

"Are you planning a move, Miss Sachs?" I asked.

"What? Oh, no. I was just putting away some things of my father's."

It seemed a safe bet that every trace of the old fellow would be gone in a week. We all sat down at the big table.

"We've been talking with the doctor here," Tibbitts told her.

"Yes?"

"Yes. You see, your father was poisoned, Miss Sachs."

"Poisoned?"

"Yes. An overdose of aconite. But it wasn't an accident. The doctor found this in your father's room."

He handed her the bottle.

"It was filled with aconite so strong a regular dose would kill a man."

"What? Why would he have that?"

"You think it was your father's?"

"It's his handwriting."

"Yeah, I thought maybe it was," Tibbitts said.

"He intentionally killed himself?" She looked at each of us in turn.

"That I don't know," Tibbitts told her.

"But why would he have this in the first place?"

"Well, you might not want to hear that," Tibbitts said.

"Why not?"

"I think the sergeant is reluctant to malign your father in your presence," I said.

"He was a greedy war profiteer. Nothing you say could lower my opinion of the man."

"Okay, since you asked. I think he got hold of this to kill that jeweler in New York, M. Pomerleau."

"Yes, I was afraid that might be the case," she said.

"You have reason to think your father killed Pomerleau?" Tibbitts asked her.

"If you'll wait here a moment, I have something to show you."

She went off and returned a few moments later. She placed a letter on the table before Tibbitts, and the doctor and I stood over him to read it. It was written on the stationery of M. Pomerleau & Son and dated November 6th.

> *General Sachs,*
>
> *I happened to have been in Washington last week and read about the robbery at your home. You have my condolences. I also read the loss will be covered by your insurance. How very fortunate.*
>
> *I will not be so crude as to suggest that your insurer might be interested in the details of my recent work on your behalf. But let me remind you, I am still awaiting payment of the $500 owed me.*
>
> *Georges Pomerleau*

"Well, he gets his meaning across, all right," Tibbitts said. "But why didn't your father just pay him the five hundred dollars?"

"He didn't have it. At least, not then."

"Where'd you find this letter?" I asked her.

"It was in his hand when I found him," she said. "Then he must have killed himself. I suppose even he had some conscience."

"You think he took it deliberately?" Tibbitts asked.

"What else?"

"Maybe he mixed up the bottles. Maybe it was just an accident."

"Yes, you're probably right. The old fool." Alice seemed kind of happy at the thought. Then she jumped up. "What time is it?"

"Just before two," I told her.

"I must hurry and dress. I'm sure you gentlemen can find your own way out. And thank you for coming by."

She flew out of the room. Tibbitts looked over at me, and then at the doctor. But he seemed as puzzled as we were.

The sergeant put the letter in his pocket and we all went downstairs and out of the house.

"That was easy," Tibbitts said.

"Are you heading back to New York now?" I asked him. "It would mean missing Elizabeth. And I think Emmie has something planned as well."

"I suppose I can catch a late train."

"Gentlemen," the doctor interjected, "I'm glad you're satisfied with things as they are. But what about Sergeant Lacy?"

"Oh, yeah. I'll go with you and we can explain it to him."

"Then you can bring Sergeant Tibbitts along to Mrs. Spinks' house, Doctor."

"Yes. Gladly. If I'm available."

24

Back at the hotel, I took out the three bundles of jewelry and put them in my pocket. Then I took a cab up to Mrs. Spinks'. In spite of Chappelle's assurances, I suspected my negotiations with the conspirators might prove contentious. I needed to make them believe I was willing to reveal their fraud. But it wouldn't be easy. The only proof I had was in the three bundles, and I could only use it by exposing Emmie and myself to charges of breaking and entering. Of course, they couldn't very well accuse us without admitting that the first burglaries were fictitious.

I assumed Easterly would be amenable to a deal. That was his nature. Mrs. Merrill, on the other hand, would pose a problem. I'd set back her business by taking that packet of letters and I imagined she might be a little cross about it. That left Alice Sachs. I had a feeling she wouldn't be too concerned with the arithmetic of the deal. Perhaps a little divide and conquer was in order. When I arrived at the door, I asked the butler if Miss Sachs had arrived. She hadn't, so I decided to wait outside. There was a constant stream of carriages and cabs dropping off guests. One brought Emmie.

"Hello, Harry. Waiting for me?"

"I pine for you every moment we're apart, Emmie. But in this instance I'm waiting for Alice Sachs."

"Has Mrs. Merrill arrived?"

"I can't say, but I expect she'll be here."

She went in and a few minutes later a carriage arrived with Dr. Gillette and Alice Sachs.

"Everything go all right with Lacy?" I asked.

"Yes, thank you," he told me. "Sergeant Tibbitts was most helpful."

"I'm glad to hear it," I said. "What happened to the sergeant?"

"He went to change hotels. But he'll be along."

Then I turned to his companion and held out her bundle. "Miss Sachs, I thought I'd return these. My business sometimes requires methods which are...."

"Distasteful?" she supplied.

"Yes, exactly. But I have to play the hand I'm dealt."

"I understand. And you are hoping for my support when terms are arranged?"

"Frankly, yes."

"Rest assured, Mr. Reese, the two of us want nothing more than to put this behind us."

"There's one other thing. I told Richard Cole I'd try to get him reinstated."

"That's already been taken care of."

They went inside and I followed. As soon as I entered the hall, I heard a familiar voice upstairs, then another. Sesbania, Easterly's little girl, was up there with the countess. I went up and found Emmie and Mrs. Easterly watching as the countess—in her guise as Glinda—and Sesbania—wearing the golden hat I'd seen at Chappelle's office—went from room to room, making up stories to go with each of them. Emmie drew me aside.

"The countess is giving a tour of her new palace," she whispered.

"*Her* palace?"

"Yes. The most curious thing has happened, Harry. The countess and Mrs. Spinks have made an exchange of some sort and the countess has taken over this house."

That explained the catalogue of furnishings the two of them had been making the previous Friday. But not the timing.

"Where's that leave the count?" I asked.

"Sadly, the count passed away last evening. Apparently, he choked to death on a chicken bone."

"That sounds somehow familiar."

"What do you mean?"

"Nothing. But in the future, let's send our regrets to any meals hosted by the countess."

"What a silly suggestion, Harry. Besides, I don't think we'll be in town long enough to receive any more invitations."

"Have you cracked the case, Emmie?"

"If you mean the two murders, yes, I have. But you'll have to wait."

She and I went downstairs to the room where the races were posted. We were handed our wager sheets and learned there would be three racing events that afternoon. The first coming from Charleston, then one from New Orleans, and finally one from Oakland. They were half-way through the Charleston card. Emmie perused the sheet and then handed it back.

"You aren't tempted, Emmie?"

"Not in the least," she said. "Look, there's Elizabeth."

We went over to the corner where she was standing by herself.

"You've come in time to see Emmie's triumph," I said.

"I came to say good-bye. What triumph is he talking about, Emmie?"

"The two murders. I've identified the killer."

"What two murders?"

Emmie gave her a brief synopsis of recent events. Only one point seemed to impress her.

"Tibbitts is here in Washington?"

"Yes," I said. "And he should be arriving momentarily."

"Then I shall be going. Good-bye, Harry. Good-bye, Emmie. I may never see either of you again."

"Why the drama?" Emmie asked. "Where are you off to?"

"Bangkok. I've taken a position with the family of the new Siamese ambassador here. He wants an American governess to teach the children he left behind."

"So you *are* chasing after this Cox fellow?" I asked.

"I'm not chasing after anybody."

"Good. I didn't like the fellow at all."

"I never had the impression you cared for me much either, Harry."

"I take a certain proprietary interest. As I would in a sister." That didn't sound very believable, so I thought I'd elaborate. "Say an older sister. One who tormented me throughout our childhood. I remember one summer when I was six...."

"Does he ever make any sense?" she asked Emmie.

"Occasionally. Not often."

Just then, the Merrills entered the hall behind us. Then they disappeared upstairs. Emmie became impatient. She didn't relax until Tibbitts arrived about five minutes later.

"Thank goodness you're here, Sergeant," Emmie told him.

Tibbitts greeted us, but his attention seemed fixed on Elizabeth. He found the encounter amusing, and the more uncomfortable he made her, the more he seemed to enjoy it. Never having had the ability to make Elizabeth uncomfortable, I took a vicarious satisfaction from it. They were both tall, blond, and handsome and seeing them together you might mistake them for a couple. But not if you'd heard them speak of each other as I had. Before I met her, Tibbitts had described Elizabeth in the most unflattering terms. None of it was untrue, but a friend might have allowed some of the details to remain unsaid.

For her part, Elizabeth had made Tibbitts out to be a cop of the worst type, who abused misunderstood souls like herself to achieve his diabolical and selfish ends. That was a bit of an exaggeration. As cops go, Tibbitts was about as honest as any I'd come across. That wasn't saying much, of course. For instance, I had little doubt he'd received some sort of remuneration from Dr. Gillette for disentangling him from Lacy's clutches. But he probably couldn't have been bought off if he thought Gillette was guilty. At least, I think not.

Emmie pulled me away from the little reunion.

"Harry, we need to persuade Sergeant Tibbitts to help us."

"Help us what?"

"Arrest the culprit, of course."

"Oh, yes. I forgot about that."

We went back over just in time to hear Elizabeth announce she needed to go catch her train. We walked her out to the hall.

"How long a voyage is it?" I asked.

"Quite long. Weeks. I need to catch a boat in San Francisco which takes me to Hong Kong, then another boat, and I can't remember what else."

"Make sure you write us," Emmie said.

"Oh, I will."

We exchanged the perfunctory hugs. All except Tibbitts, of course. Then she went off. When I turned, I saw Julius Chappelle approaching.

"Good afternoon, Mr. Reese."

"Good afternoon. Has the syndicate arrived?"

"Yes, they're assembled upstairs, finalizing various details. But the parties in question should be free to discuss matters with you shortly."

He led me upstairs. Emmie followed, pushing Tibbitts before her. Off in one of the bedrooms, we could hear Sesbania still at it with the countess. After I introduced Emmie and Tibbitts to Chappelle, the four of us stood outside the study making small talk.

"Where exactly are you going in France?" I asked.

"A town called Étaples. Have you heard of it?"

"No, I don't think so."

"Nor had I. It's a sort of artists' colony. A number of Americans reside there."

"I've read about it," Emmie said. "I'd love to live someplace like that."

"You must come and visit us. My fiancée has taken possession of a hostelry."

Very suddenly, Alice Sachs came out of the room, followed by Dr. Gillette. She charged downstairs, but I managed to stop him.

"What happened?" I asked.

"Everything went as planned," he said. "But Mrs. Merrill had some sort of contract the general had given her the night of his death. Turning his profits over to her."

"So Alice got nothing?" Emmie asked.

"No, no. It turned out all right. Mrs. Spinks objected. And then Mr. Easterly said it would be legally unenforceable. He suggested that Mrs. Merrill destroy it. Eventually, she conceded, and a match was put to it."

"What?" Emmie shouted. "That was evidence."

"Evidence?" the doctor inquired.

Mrs. Spinks came out with two fellows I hadn't seen before. But I guessed one was the Frenchman and the other Davidson, the real-estate agent who had been listed as the seller of the property. The two men went downstairs and Mrs. Spinks put her arm in Chappelle's and gave him a peck.

"Everything's done," she told him. "Hello, Mr. Reese. I believe the others are ready for you now."

Then they left us.

"I hope Miss Sachs hasn't left, Doctor. There's still the resolution of the matter of the insurance claims."

"If you don't mind, I will represent her."

"Oh, that's fine with me," I told him. "You'll need to wait out here, Emmie."

"All right, Harry. You finish what you have to, but then the Sergeant and I will see to our business."

"Our business?" Tibbitts asked her.

The doctor and I went in and found Easterly and Mrs. Merrill seated at a table. The senator himself was asleep in an easy chair off in a corner. Easterly rose and shook my hand warmly.

"Glad to see you, Reese. Sit down, please."

I did and then he continued.

"You know Mrs. Merrill, of course."

"Yes," I said. "I feel on intimate terms with her."

I suppose alluding to the fact I'd recently pawed through her lingerie wasn't the best approach with someone like Amanda Merrill. But that sort of reasoning is always easier in hindsight.

"Well, let's get down to brass tacks, shall we?" Easterly suggested. "I understand you have a proposition for us."

"Yes, I think we can straighten the whole thing out quite equitably."

"Myself as well. What do you suggest?"

"I'll tell the insurers the jewelry has been found and that the claim payments will be returned."

"Will that satisfy them?"

"I think I can make it believable, with the right story. But for me to receive my compensation, I'd need to show that I had brought about the resolution. Which would have the unfortunate consequences of exposing you all to charges of fraud."

"And you to charges of burglary," Mrs. Merrill helpfully pointed out.

"Yes, there's that, too."

"So it would make things more comfortable for all of us if you could receive your compensation in some other way," Easterly said.

"Yes. Suppose you all return the claim money, leaving the explanation to me. Then I return the jewelry in return for a payment of, say, ten percent of the claim amounts."

"I was thinking of a figure closer to five percent."

"That would be impossible for me to accept. I've incurred a large number of expenses while here."

"Yes, I'm sure that's true," he agreed. "Well, let's split the difference and make it seven and a half."

"Eight."

"Done," he said. "Assuming that's agreeable?"

"That sounds perfectly reasonable," Gillette said.

"You'll return all that you took?" Mrs. Merrill asked.

"Are you missing something other than jewelry?" I asked.

"You know exactly what I'm speaking of."

"Mrs. Merrill, do you really think you are in a position to make a demand like that? Perhaps we should consult the senator?"

Ultimately, she agreed and the senator remained undisturbed—until it was necessary for him to write me out a check. Dr. Gillette wrote another, on behalf of Alice Sachs. And then Easterly handed me one he'd already filled out. The amount had been calculated to exactly eight percent of his claim. While I was handing Easterly and Mrs. Merrill their jewelry, the doctor left the room and the countess entered. She was accompanied by her man, Thomas, who closed the door behind them. The countess stood before Mrs. Merrill and addressed her.

"I suggest you leave down the back stairs and through the rear entrance, my dear. Thomas will show you the way."

"Why would I do that?"

"There is a New York detective out in the hall with some questions about the death of a jeweler."

"I had nothing to do with that."

"But you knew about it?" I asked.

"What crime is that? I was in New York, and it was in the newspapers."

"Unfortunately, Mrs. Reese is of the opinion you are guilty of murder," the countess explained. "Regardless of the outcome, the confrontation would spoil my party and I simply won't have that."

"Your party?"

"This is my home now, my dear, and I must insist

you do as I request. If you use the door on the right, you can leave unseen."

Mrs. Merrill rose and tried to wake her husband.

"I'll see that the senator is sent home. But you must go now."

Mrs. Merrill cast one of her contemptuous looks at the countess. But the countess just laughed.

"My dear, do not even think of ever crossing me."

Thomas led Mrs. Merrill out the second door.

"I think we have a very prosperous future ahead of us, Frau Gräfin," Easterly announced.

"Yes, Mr. Easterly, I think you're right. But please use 'My Lady.'"

"Aren't you at all worried Mrs. Merrill will begin spreading rumors about your past, My Lady?" I asked.

"Oh, we're counting on that," Easterly explained. "You see, if you want to impress a congressman from Kansas, a countess is more than sufficient. But for the cynic from Philadelphia, you need something more. What better than a mysterious past?"

"What about the other items I took from Mrs. Merrill?"

"The letters? Mr. Easterly suggested if we discreetly return them to their authors, out of the goodness of our hearts, it will be worth more than Mrs. Merrill could have hoped to get through blackmail."

"Good will—it's worth much more than mere money," Easterly added.

"Mr. Chappelle told me you'd given Mrs. Spinks a French inn."

"As part of our trade. It's a wreck, really. But near the sea, and in a place where they'll be free from the torment they'd receive here."

"Yes, I'm afraid they'd find it pretty tough," Easterly said.

"Love seems to be in the air. Elizabeth is heading to Bangkok to take a position as a governess. She's following that British fellow, Cox."

"Oh, good. She deserves to have her heart broken."

"You think the omens are bad?"

"I would bet one thousand dollars—and give odds—that this young man requested the move to Bangkok just to get away from her."

"That hadn't occurred to me. But he did seem the type. Makes a habit of enforcing petty rules at the billiard table. Perhaps we should warn her?"

"And spoil the fun?"

In the meantime, Easterly had reached for a decanter and poured out four sherries. He handed one to both of us and set the last beside the senator.

"To the future!" he said.

We all toasted, even the senator, stirring long enough to quaff his portion.

"Now I suppose we must face your Emmie," the countess said. She opened the door and Emmie charged in, followed by Tibbitts.

"Where is she?" Emmie asked.

"Who, dear?" the countess answered.

"Mrs. Merrill."

"Left, I'm afraid. Through the other door."

"You had it wrong, Emmie," I told her. "It was the general who bought the poison. He visited Pomerleau and poisoned him. Didn't the sergeant tell you?"

"I told her, but she didn't like it enough to believe me."

"She was up to something, Harry. I found out she

was in New York that same day. And the other night, at the ball, I saw her with the general. They were each holding a glass of champagne. Then Mrs. Merrill dropped her handkerchief and the general gave her his glass to hold while he picked up the handkerchief for her. But then she handed back the other glass."

"Did you see her put anything in it?"

"No, but we can assume she did. And champagne would be the perfect drink, it tingles just like aconite."

"Do you have the letter from Pomerleau threatening the general?" I asked Tibbitts.

He handed it to Emmie and she and the countess read it together.

"Where'd you find this?" Emmie asked.

"Alice Sachs found it in her father's hand. She hid it before calling the policeman. Presumably, Mrs. Merrill had this letter. Then when she was in New York, she read about Pomerleau being poisoned. She either learned the general was in New York at the time, or perhaps she just guessed. And then she threatened to expose him."

"Unless he turned over his profits from the deal," Emmie added.

"I imagine so. Do you remember I told you I'd seen her leaving the Sachses' that first day we arrived?"

"Yes."

"The subject of the interview must have been blackmail. The general decided it was worth ten thousand dollars not to be hanged and, the night of the ball, he signed her contract. Then in return, she gave him the letter. So what reason would she have to kill him?"

"What about her switching drinks at the ball?" Emmie asked.

"I wonder if Mrs. Merrill isn't more clever than I

thought," the countess said. "Here is the general, plagued by a blackmailer, and with a bottle of poison nearby. He offers to get her a glass of champagne. But he has also underestimated her. His solicitude makes her suspicious—perhaps she saw him put something in her glass. So she contrives the switch. I'll need to be careful with her."

"Well, then he killed himself just the same," Tibbitts concluded.

"Yes, I suppose you're right," Emmie agreed.

"Poor Emmie. Come along and I'll make it up to you," the countess told her. "Harry, your wife will meet you at your hotel later. You and the sergeant may go."

The two of them went off.

"You and the sergeant may go?" Tibbitts asked.

"She likes to remind people she's a countess. Come on, let's go get a drink."

25

We'd been inside only a few hours, but what had been a cool afternoon had already turned into a very cold evening.

"Where should we go?" I asked Tibbitts.

"My hotel. The Shoreham. Nice place."

"You moved to the Shoreham?"

"The doctor insisted. He's having the bill sent to him," he said. "Might as well get my money's worth."

"His money's worth, you mean."

"You don't mind drinking on his dime, do you?"

"No, no. I'm broad-minded about these things."

We took a car down to the hotel and while we were crossing the lobby, Tibbitts stopped me.

"Hey, I was thinking of giving the papers the story. That way I can get my name in it. You see, if I wait until I get to New York, my captain will make sure he gets all the credit. Do you think I can get any of the New York boys to come by?"

"Let them know the drinks are free at the Shoreham and you won't be able to beat them away with a stick. I'll make some phone calls."

The *Syracuse Herald* was out, but a goodly sampling of New York papers—the *Journal*, *World*, *Tribune*, and *Sun*—all expressed interest in attending.

"All set," I told Tibbitts. "You better have a story ready."

"I've already got it worked out in my head."

"Any truth in it?"

"Sure, the general killed Pomerleau. But the rest is too complicated. I'll just say he took a dose from the wrong bottle and killed himself."

When we entered the barroom, just a minute or two later, the *Sun* was already waiting for us. And before the first round was served, most of the others I'd called had arrived to join the party. By the second, so had the *Louisville Times*, *St. Louis Post-Dispatch*, *Cincinnati Enquirer*, and *Buffalo Evening News*.

Tibbitts' account left out most of the characters—including myself. Not to mention the burglaries, the land purchase, and Mrs. Merrill's extortion. It was the kind of succinct, easy-to-follow story that readers of dime novels prefer, told in the undemanding language they can understand—with Tibbitts in the role of Nick Carter. But I didn't begrudge him taking all the credit. It would have complicated my arrangement with the syndicate if he hadn't. I suppose the only person who could have a legitimate complaint about it was the doctor. He'd be footing the bill.

When I finally got back to our room at the Normandie, Emmie was in the bath. I sent down for a late supper and we had our own celebration.

"You don't seem too disappointed about missing the chance to finger the murderer, Emmie."

"That was just a whim. But I did achieve my original objective in coming."

"The countess agreed to let you write her biography?"

"Yes, with certain provisos."

"Such as?"

"Well, I am to write the story of Madame B____, international jewel thief, and only allude to her evolution into the countess."

"And she's willing to share the details of the thefts?"

"No, that was the principal condition."

"Sounds like a rather dull book."

"Oh, there will be plenty of detail. She just insists I use my imagination."

"So yours will be an authorized, fictionalized biography?"

"Yes. But I imagine the only biographies that *are* authorized are those that are fictionalized."

"I see what you mean. What sort of fool would approve of someone telling the truth about him?"

"Yes, and this way I won't be restricted by banal realities."

"I wasn't aware you'd ever allowed yourself to be restricted by banal realities, Emmie."

"The world forces itself on all of us."

"Not the countess, so much. The timing of the count's death seems suspiciously fortuitous. I believe her arrangement to swap abodes with Mrs. Spinks was inked well before the count encountered that chicken bone."

"Oh, it isn't the timing alone that's suspicious. You see, there was no chicken."

"I thought you told me he'd choked to death on a chicken bone?"

"Yes. During dessert."

"What was dessert?"

"A Charlotte Russe."

"How did they explain that?"

"They couldn't. So they fired the embassy's French chef."

"Poor fellow."

"Oh, the countess hired him immediately for her new home."

"It's almost as if it'd been planned out in advance."

"Yes. Very much like that."

"You don't feel any compunction to solve that crime?"

"I prefer to think of it as a miraculous coincidence."

"Quite miraculous. But that's probably the safest attitude to take. I wouldn't want to cross swords with the countess."

"No. And I think she'll prove a valuable ally."

"Ally?"

"Friend, if you prefer."

"You two aren't up to something I should know about, are you?"

"We are not 'up to something' and if we were, I can't imagine what reason there'd be for you to know about it."

I took what little reassurance I could from that.

There was no reading that night and late the next morning we took a cab to the Pennsylvania depot. We were just handing our bags over to a porter when a policeman arrived on the scene. There were three clues that this was not an authentic policeman, and my subtle detective's mind grasped them at once. First, he was wearing the costume I'd worn a few nights before. I recognized a tear on the sleeve I'd received while dragging O'Conner downstairs. Second, he spoke only broken English in a thick German accent. And lastly, he bore a striking resemblance to the countess's driver, Thomas. He informed us that a valuable brooch of the countess's had gone missing and asked to search our luggage. He started with mine, and it wasn't long before he came across the countess's book. He put it in his jacket and shook his finger at me.

"Schämen sie sich," he admonished.

I was feeling pretty sore from the previous night's

studies, so I wasn't overly upset at the loss. How it was that he recognized the book one can only guess. Then he turned to Emmie and asked the blushing belle for the key to her trunk. I was a little surprised how readily she complied.

I could tell Thomas's heart wasn't in his work, but he was doing a pretty thorough job of it anyway. At least, until the second cop showed up. He was suspicious of this unfamiliar colleague and began questioning him. The last we saw of Thomas, he was running up Sixth Street with the genuine cop in close pursuit.

"I hope he makes it," Emmie said.

We packed our things back up and the porter took them away. Once inside the depot, I left Emmie and went off to buy our tickets. When I returned, she had on a decidedly odd expression.

"What's the matter? Leave something behind at the hotel?"

"No, it's just that I would have sworn I just saw Elizabeth leave the station."

"I thought she caught an afternoon train yesterday?"

"Yes, it must have just been someone who looked like her. But even the coat...."

They called our train and once we had boarded, Emmie took off her own coat. She was wearing the brooch.

"It's a good thing Thomas didn't just ask you to open your coat."

"Oh, I didn't think that would be very likely."

"You anticipated his coming?"

"I knew the countess was still upset I'd gotten the better of her. Then last evening she asked if I had a safe place to put the brooch. I told her there was a secret compartment in my trunk. That seemed to please her more than it should have. So I suspected she'd try to get it back, one way or another."

It was a pleasant ride home. It always is when I've been successful. But this time even more so. Usually I need to wait weeks, or even months, to receive my payment from the insurers. This time I was going back with close to two thousand dollars in my pocket. At lunch in the dining car, I brought up Elizabeth again.

"I'm trying to imagine someone turning over their children to your old school chum, Emmie."

"Oh, forging credentials would be the work of a moment for Elizabeth. And the children are twelve and fifteen. I have a feeling girls of that age will take to her."

"You mean, take to being corrupted by her?"

"All children have to be corrupted sooner or later. Better by a sympathetic governess than a selfish lover."

"I suppose that's true," I agreed. "But I never would have guessed Elizabeth would be the type to chase some officious ass half-way around the globe."

"You've certainly developed an animus for this Cox fellow, Harry. Is it really only because he caught you cheating at billiards?"

"It isn't cheating, Emmie. It was a friendly game of billiards. No normal man would stoop to enforcing a trifling rule like that. Suppose you were playing a friendly game of cards and someone misdealt. Would you insist they forfeit the hand?"

"That would depend."

"Depend on what?"

"Well, if we were playing for money, and it was a close match, then yes, I would. But if I was trying to rope in a mark, then no, I would be magnanimous."

"You really don't know the meaning of a friendly game, do you, Emmie?"

"Oh, I'm always friendly about it, Harry."

It started snowing just as we passed into New Jersey. This was only a week or so before Christmas, and Emmie's mother arrived a few days after we got home. She left shortly after New Year's, and a few weeks after that, Emmie received a letter from Bangkok.

All in all, it had been a satisfying, and enriching, case. The only thing troubling me was that Emmie began a regular correspondence with the countess. Her remark about their being allies had left me cold. Emmie is extremely adept at absorbing knowledge from people willing to impart it. I remember one afternoon on the New Haven, coming back from Providence. Emmie went into the parlor car a competent card cheat and came out a master.

Not that I could picture Emmie ever becoming as ruthless as the dowager Countess von Schnurrenberger und Kesselheim. In comparison, Emmie's scheming seemed pretty benign. Still, I never again ate Charlotte Russe without first probing it with a fork.

Made in the USA
Charleston, SC
25 July 2013